A Handful Of Pearls
& Other Stories

A Handful Of Pearls
& Other Stories

Beth Bernobich

Lethe Press
Maple Shade NJ

Published by Lethe Press
118 Heritage Avenue
Maple Shade, NJ 08052

www.lethepressbooks.com | lethepress@aol.com

Cover Image by Vincent Chong

ISBN 1-59021-010-7 | 978-1-59021-010-9

"Air and Angels" first appeared in *Subterranean* April 2008 | "Chrysalide" first appeared in *Polyphony 2* (2003) | "A Handful of Pearls" first appeared in *Interzone* September 2007 | "Jump to Zion" original to this collection | "Marsdog" first appeared in *Coyote Wilde* December 2007 | "Medusa at Morning" first appeared in *Strange Horizons* July 2001 | "Poison" first appeared in *Strange Horizons* January 2003 | "Remembrance" first appeared in *Sex in the System* (2006) | "Watercolors in the Rain" first appeared in *Fictitious Force* September 2005

Table of Contents

Telling Secrets

James Patrick Kelly

You would think, since writers pursue a profession that honors showing and telling, we would despise secrecy. But, in fact, exactly the opposite is the case. Closely held secrets drive our plots—perhaps not always, but much of the time. Our characters withhold past misdeeds and make plans that they tell no one. They keep their thoughts to themselves and hide their true feelings for all sorts of reasons, both wise and foolish.

As do we all.

But there's a secret that no writer wants to keep, one that we yearn for everyone to know. We sell that first story, then another, two more, and are astonished that *nobody seems to notice*. Well, maybe our mom or our boyfriend or our geeky cousin Ellen know what we're about, and yes, the astute editor who pulled our manuscript out of the slush pile will recognize the name on our next submission. But readers' recognition always takes a maddeningly long time. We begin our careers in secret. Then we hope desperately that sooner rather than later the world will take note that we have arrived and are planning to stay, thank you very much. However, it has been a tradition in our little corner of the literary world that established writers take a keen interest in welcoming new members to our tribe. Like many of my colleagues, I'm always on the lookout for someone who can write the glittering sentence, the unforgettable character, the exotic setting, and the subtle plot.

Which brings me to Beth Bernobich. I've known her secret for several years and am happy now to share it with you: a new talent has most definitely arrived in our midst. Beth is a writer to whom attention must be paid.

It is possible that you never heard of Beth until you picked up this book. Although the first of the nine stories collected here was published back in 2001, she is not one of those prolific writers who burst onto the scene by shotgunning stories into print. Rather she has perfected her technique over time, stretching herself and advancing her craft with each new publication.

What kind of writer is she? What are her stories about? Sorry, but what pleases me most about her work is that I can't make general statements about it. Some writers lodge themselves in our memories because of their idiosyncratic voice or obsessive themes. There is no mistaking the novels of Robert A. Heinlein and William Gibson. Do we know a Philip K. Dick story when we see it? Yes, we do. And we love Kelly Link for her unique style. The work of Ursula Le Guin, on the other hand, ranges across many genres and styles. Connie Willis is equally adept at breezy comedy and devastating tragedy. The protean Michael Swanwick and the eclectic Gene Wolfe defy categorization. So too does Beth, and I cite these stories as evidence. Here you will find an odd first contact story that takes place on Mars and alternate history set on a not-quite Haiti. Beth will make you care about the improbable friendship of a six-legged arthropod and a space-faring robot. You will meet a brother and sister (or are they sister and brother?) caught in a web of intrigue on a distant planet, lovers passing technological love letters of astonishing intimacy, and a portrait painter who can literally capture the soul of her subjects. Beth shows a real flair for steampunk and world-building. She brings a variety of characters to life in these pages: the courageous and the reprehensible, the suffering and the redeemed. Oh, and Medusa makes a cameo.

However, because generalizations fail to capture her stories, because her style is mutable and her subject matter various, Beth's burgeoning career has been a secret for too long, it seems to me. Of course, this is the challenge every short story writer must meet. I know, because I struggle with it myself. Every time we curl our fingers over the keyboard, we are trying to create a unique experience for the reader. But when a writer has the restless ambition of a Beth Bernobich, she continually seeks to explore new ground. The risk is that we will leave the fantasy reader behind when we venture to an alien planet. Perhaps the science fiction fan will refuse the invitation to revisit a fairy tale. However, short story writers ought not attempt to satisfy the perceived desire of the reader. Rather we must create the desire in our readers to read whatever we have to write, no matter the subject. I submit that Beth has the skill and the heart to deliver you to places you never thought you'd go.

I do have one observation about the stories which follow: reading them—re-reading some—I was struck by how often they turn on secrets. The brother and sister must hide their true natures from their xenophobic society, the lovers have purloined advanced technology to continue their relationship, the artist must never reveal the truth about her abilities, and the alien boy tries to keep the existence of his new robot friend from his father. But then, as I've already said, the unveiling of secrets is one of the main tasks of the writer: to tell that which no one else knows, to show that which has always been hidden.

And now there is one less secret in the world. I am here to tell you that Beth Bernobich is a writer you need to know. Turn the page and find out why.

A Handful of Pearls
& Other Stories

Chrysalide

High in the palace of Le Songe d'Or, Claudette Theron leaned out her studio window and scanned the gardens below. Somewhere along the dozens of paths, among the mottled greenery, the Duchess of Belfort was walking, oblivious it seemed, that she was late for her first sitting.

A breeze stirred the ornamental trees, carrying with it the thick scent of roses, but Claudette saw no sign of the Duchess. She sighed faintly. On most days, she took pleasure in this glorious view—a masterpiece of crimson lilies and ruby tulips, bleeding heart and rare scarlet orchids. And roses, she added. Roses in every shade of red, from ordinary to exotic. Exquisitely planned, arranged with a painter's eye, the flowers and trees depicted an enormous rose, whose multi-hued petals fluttered with every pulse of wind, like brush strokes rippling across a canvas. In the center, at the heart of the flower, stood King Arnaud's golden palace.

A flurry of movement by the linden trees caught her attention. A throng of liveried servants had just emerged from the arched walkway. Clothed in black, they scattered onto the grassy clearing, like inky blots against the brilliant green. Next a pair of maids appeared. Soon after came the slender figure of a woman, whose gossamer dress billowed around her, much like the train of retainers. In the brilliant sunshine, her hair was like a burnished halo; jewels winked from her wrist and throat.

That would be the Duchess, Claudette guessed. She'd heard all the Court rumors: scarcely seventeen, Anais Mireau had caught Hugh of Belfort's attention last summer. What Hugh desired he would win, so throughout the autumn, he had courted the girl with energy and finesse. In winter they had married.

Now the Duke wanted Claudette to paint his wife's portrait. "Your finest work," he'd said last week. "A masterpiece. Give me that, and you make your fortune." As a token, he had presented her with a ruby ring set in creamy gold—the converse of King Arnaud's palace, which she took for a good omen.

Of the Duchess herself, Claudette had no idea what to expect. Her only contact had been a brief note, describing the dress she planned to wear, and including the unexpected request that they hold the sitting in Claudette's studio—not in the Duchess's apartments. An eccentric, Claudette decided, or simply indulging her curiosity.

Claudette turned away from the sunlit view to her studio where her materials lay ready. On the easel sat a large new canvas, already painted with the background. Jars of paint crowded one table; a second one held a jumble of wooden spatulas, lead sticks, heaps of rags, and flasks of oil and pungent spirits. More important, she had ground the necessary colors the night before and mixed them with oil. The rest would wait until she saw the Duchess in person.

A glance toward the gardens showed that the Duchess's entourage had gathered by the fountain. The party moved slowly, and Claudette calculated another half-hour at least before the Duchess arrived. She retreated from the window and paced the room, pausing now and then to straighten her brushes, or to flick dust from a worktable. Her impatient gaze landed on her son's latest letter, lying open on her crowded desk. She took it up and scanned its lines again.

Chère maman, began the letter. A number of pretty phrases came next. Claudette skimmed over them until she came to the letter's main point. The spring floods in Alouette-sûr-Rive had risen higher than usual this year, and the rivers had crested over the banks, smothering the newly sown fields with mud. Too late and too much, Jean-René wrote. He'd salvaged half his crops, but if she could spare a small sum….

Claudette thrust the letter into her pocket. If all went well, the Duke's commission would answer Jean-Rene's needs—and more. If not… She could ask the Marquis de Goncourt for a loan, but that was risky. Philippe would indulge her, no doubt, but the servants already suspected their dalliance, and it might prove difficult to disguise so large a transaction. She didn't want the gluttonous hounds of gossip to scent a weakness in Arnaud's favorite artist.

The idea made her throat dry. No one must know of their affair, especially not the king. Arnaud might acquit the Marquis de Goncourt of his indiscretion, but Claudette's penalty would be her situation.

Arnaud might as well order me to forfeit my life.

Nervously, she poured and drank a glass of water. No matter how many gifts from the king, or from his courtiers, she never felt secure. Court expenses drained her savings, and now this latest difficulty with Jean-René. Her thoughts drifted away, toward the town where she'd lived, and where her son now tried, sometimes erratically, to establish his farm. The cramped streets, littered with dung and garbage, the shrill girls and their thick-set husbands—Alouette-sûr-Rive might lie in another kingdom from Arnaud's exquisite palace, for all they shared a common tongue.

A knock startled her from her thoughts. Claudette set down her glass and hurried to open the door.

A woman stood outside, her face and form shadowed by the corridor's dim light. Claudette could only make out the muted tones of a silk dress and a ghostly cloud of lace. One of the Duchess's ladies, no doubt, with an excuse from her mistress.

But the woman simply nodded and said, "Madame Theron, my apologies for being so late."

The Duchess herself. She must have left her entourage outside. For a moment, Claudette stood in stiff surprise. Then, shaking herself into motion, she sank into a deep curtsey. "Welcome. Come inside, your Grace."

With a murmured acknowledgment, the Duchess stepped into the room, followed by a pair of maids. Her cool gaze took in the cluttered studio, the half-screened bed in one corner, the shelves crammed with jars and rags. One maid wrinkled her nose, either at the disorder or the smell of paints. The Duchess smiled graciously at Claudette and dismissed her followers.

"Where would you like me to sit?" she asked. Her voice was soft, yet assured—a noble's voice.

Claudette gestured toward a cushioned bench set before a backdrop of dark blue satin, where the afternoon's golden light flooded the room. "There, if you please, your Grace."

The Duchess nodded. As she passed, the light fragrance of her perfume trailed after. Without asking for assistance, she removed her shawl, folded its frothy length, and settled herself on the bench.

Claudette stepped behind her easel and studied her subject.

Anais of Belfort wore a summer dress of amber silk trimmed in ivory lace. Her eyes were light brown, her hair dark bronze. Against the shimmering fabric, the girl's fair skin glowed like the first light of dawn.

She is a masterpiece, Claudette thought. *No wonder the Duke desired her.*

Taking a stick of lead, she sketched in the girl's figure. Face at two-thirds mark. Two lines for the slender neck. A sweeping line to suggest her shoulders, more to outline the drapery of her costume. Softer and slower, she traced the delicate face, the slim wrists, and faultless attire. With fainter lines, she drew the body underneath the layers of silk and lace. Anchor points, her father called them.

Claudette set the lead aside and picked up a bristle brush. Along with the description of her dress, the Duchess had sent Claudette a square of its cloth so she could match its colors. She dipped her brush into the prepared paints and blocked in the dress with light strokes. The choice of colors was fortunate. She had rendered the background as a curtain, fluttering in the breeze, and its rich dark blue would make a pleasing contrast to the Duchess's dress and her radiant skin.

She worked without pause, hardly noting when next hour bell struck. The Duchess stirred, and gave a faint sigh. The air was heavy this summer afternoon, and the smell of turpentine overwhelmed the lighter fragrance of the roses and the Duchess's perfume. Claudette was reminded of the hot summer days in her father's studio, glazing rows of canvas and blocking in the backgrounds for his portrait business. Memory skipped ahead, to the year after Michel Theron died, when Claudette, heavy with Jean-René, had labored with her own brushes to support her mother and child. A vivid memory came back: of balancing on her three-legged stool, her belly tugging downward as she bent over a painting.

I was no older than this girl.

Disturbed, she set down her brush and took up a rag to wipe her hands. "Is your Grace fatigued with sitting? If you like, you might walk about my studio. Such as it is."

The Duchess's gaze shifted to Claudette's face. "If you are certain it will not spoil the pose."

Claudette shrugged. "As you will, your Grace. I need to mix new colors, that is all."

While the Duchess made a slow circuit of the narrow room, Claudette busied herself mixing new pigments with oil, cleaning her favorite brushes, staring at the portrait. The lines were strong, and she was pleased with her choice of colors. Nevertheless, the picture lacked the vividness of her best work.

"Ah, the Marquis of Goncourt."

The Duchess had paused by a row of unfinished paintings that Claudette had moved to one side for the day. Some showed children of the court; some were of families gathered in formal poses, with pets and trinkets scattered about. In one corner, half-hidden by a curtain, stood a portrait of the Marquis.

"You captured his look well," the Duchess murmured.

It was one of dozens Claudette had painted of Philippe, and the pretext for their frequent trysts, but the Duchess could not know that. This one showed the Marquis in casual dress, his coat unbuttoned, his shirt loosened and without the usual trimmings of lace and silk. His lips curled, making him appear roguish, Claudette thought. Perhaps the girl knew him by report.

The Duchess studied the portrait a few moments longer, eyes narrowed, before walking on. Claudette watched covertly as she passed a few uninspired landscapes, a grouping of three boys and their dogs, without stopping.

"Ah. These interest me."

The Duchess paused again, this time before a series of Claudette's self-portraits. They were simple—a dozen sketches in charcoal, lead, or crayons. Claudette had used the same attitude for each one: her dark, abundant hair pulled back, her chin resting on her fist, full sunlight on her angular face, the rest lost in shadows.

Study your own features, her father had said. *Portray them accurately, without flinching, and you will discover more than the finest masters can teach you.*

So these portraits. Philippe of Goncourt had called them "uncompromising" when he first saw them. She recalled his

smile that had managed to look both tender and mocking—
quite unlike his usual expression.

As though he understood.

She smiled herself. Perhaps that was the reason he stayed
with her, and she with him, long past her other lovers.

The Duchess had not moved from the series. "I like how
they make a record of your life," she said, her tone thoughtful.
"When did you draw this first one?"

The year before my father died, Claudette thought. He had
been sickening at the time, spitting blood for weeks and months,
because they had no money for a doctor. Odd how the memory
came back so vividly, even now.

It was also, she remembered, the year before she met and
discarded Jean-René's father. After a moment's uncomfortable
silence, she said, "It was very long time ago. Would your Grace
be pleased to resume your pose?"

The Duchess glanced in her direction, but returned to her
seat without comment. Claudette took a deep breath, and when
she felt her hand to be steady once more, continued to paint.

Twice more the hour bell tolled, but absorbed by her task,
Claudette scarcely heeded the passing time. At regular intervals,
she released the Duchess from her pose, while she stared at the
portrait, looking for any flaws. The hair was a vague mass of
coppery brown. The dress too lacked detail, its fold and pleats
merely suggested, but she would add more layers and highlights
to both in the coming days. Besides, these didn't matter in the
end. The focus would be the Duchess's face—more precisely,
her eyes.

The eyes.

Her hands trembled, and she drew back from the painting
before she marred it.

Of course. She would concentrate all her skill on the girl's
eyes alone. The Duke, doubly pleased, would pay her extra.

And Jean-René would receive his money within the month. She would write to him tomorrow.

Still, she didn't move. How many times before someone guessed her methods? The palace knew only that the king had summoned her from the backcountry town of Alouette-sûr-Rive. They'd heard of her string of lovers and Jean-René's unconventional birth, but the details came from Claudette's own romantic fabrication. Just as she would with a flattering portrait, she'd feathered the harsh edges with a brush and picked out the highlights in purest white. Only she knew of the hungry years after her father's death, and before her paintings had become famous. Before she discovered her true talent.

The first time had been an accident. A wealthy merchant had commissioned his daughter's portrait. Claudette had searched the girl's moon-shaped face for some unique feature to illuminate her subject's character, something that would please the merchant father and earn Claudette enough money to satisfy the bill collectors. Her father had lectured her about the artist's vision, how the master could pluck the essential quality of his subject by staring beyond the flesh. So she stared—stared so hard that her vision blurred, and with a jolting shift of perspective, she *had* seen beyond the flesh. The studio's stained walls had vanished, and in their place she had seen the girl's sparkling vitality, soaring like a jeweled butterfly. Unable to resist, Claudette had touched that shimmering creature. A flare of light had arced between them; when it faded, Claudette had seen a spot of darkness against the brilliance—an imperfection that had not been there before. The next moment, her vision had flickered back to the ordinary world. And Claudette had immediately seized her brush and begun to paint.

It was her strongest, truest painting.

The merchant had paid double, calling it a "miraculous likeness." With the money, Claudette fed her mother and child, and she had used the merchant's praise to build her reputation.

She refused to think of his daughter, however. After that sitting the girl had turned strangely apathetic. A few remarked on the change, but other commissions had followed, and finally, King Arnaud had appointed Claudette as Court Artist and had given her this studio.

Use the lightest touch, her father had exhorted. But he had meant the artist's ordinary technique with brush and lines and shades, not this strange contact of souls.

I had no choice, Claudette thought, as though arguing with him over the matter. *You might have done the same.*

In all, she had touched two dozen souls, and produced two dozen portraits of unsurpassed genius. She remembered distinctly the brilliance of an elderly farmer, the wan light of a court advocate, the dark radiance of the king's mistress. But she never painted her son thus. Nor Goncourt. Nor the king. No matter how much restraint she practiced, every touch left a mark on the butterfly's glittering wing. She told herself the changes she wrought were gradual and slow, like a flower withering in the autumn chill—no different than the changes exacted by the passing years.

"What are you painting now?"

The Duchess's soft voice pulled Claudette from her thoughts. "The neckline of your dress, your Grace," she said.

The Duchess's face tinted dark rose, very pretty against the pale gold of her skin. "I hope my description of it was accurate. Did you find the cloth useful?"

Claudette nodded, intent on memorizing the color of that blush.

She worked in silence then, the only sounds those coming from the gardens below. A bird's erratic song. A breeze sighing through the branches. And then, a brittle laugh. Moments later, a medley of voices floated through the window, carried by an errant breeze. Claudette could not discern the words, but the Duchess murmured, "Ah, Lady Clarisse."

Claudette paused in her work. Lady Clarisse had made for herself the reputation with her needle-sharp tongue. Curious, she said, "Does your Grace know her?"

The Duchess nodded. "We met at the king's table, when His Majesty held a welcoming feast for me."

"So you've enjoyed her favor of her conversation."

"I did." The Duchess paused, then added, "Many dislike her, I perceive. I wonder if they have considered how she must dislike herself?"

Her tone was unexceptional and her expression remained smooth, but Claudette bit her lips. "Your Grace makes an excellent point."

Anais colored. "Too pointed at times," she murmured.

Claudette smiled and resumed painting, adding speckles of cream where the sunlight picked out the cloth's subtle patterns. "Tell me about your Grace's family," she said. "Will they visit you often?"

"I do hope so. My brothers promised to come after the harvest."

Ah yes. The Mireau family held fast to its country origins, Claudette recalled. They might not be fashionable, but their name was old, their reputation good. The Duke had gained by the match, certainly. She wondered if the girl had accepted him for the same reasons.

The Duchess's gaze had drifted toward the paintings again. "My Duke tells me you have a son," she said. "Have you a portrait of him?"

Surprised, Claudette set her brush aside and flexed her hands. "By the window," she said briefly.

The painting showed Jean-René in his best coat and breeches, a hat tucked under his arm. The likeness was good, Claudette thought, even using her raw ability alone. Jean-René looked about to raise his hand and brush the hair from his eyes.

The Duchess smiled in delight. "He looks much like you. The hair. The chin."

His father's velvet brown eyes and pliant mouth. Too often her son reminded her of the long-ago man who fathered him. Claudette looked up to see the Duchess watching her closely. She picked up the brush. "Is your Grace fond of children?"

"I am. The Duke as well adores them. We talked about it often, at my father's house."

"The first of many attractions, I'm sure."

She'd made the comment out of politeness. Anais said nothing, but her lowered gaze, her smile, were eloquent. Claudette felt a sting of envy. *Rank and wealth and a great man's affection. She is fortunate.*

She laid aside her brush and took a clean palette. Now she would mix colors for the Duchess's skin. Sienna tempered with umber, saffron and a hint of vermilion. The purest white to lighten the intensity; her darkest blue to create the shadows. Claudette blended colors until she'd matched the tone exactly.

Setting the palette on her worktable, she wiped her hands and selected another brush, her finest sable. "Now you must be absolutely still," she said, smoothing the bristles to a point.

"You begin my face?"

Claudette nodded. Her eyes narrowed, and she stared intently at the Duchess's delicate features. Anais blushed, but held her pose.

Any passable apprentice can paint a face, her father liked to say. *It takes an artist to select and discard, to highlight and cast into shadow. That, however, is not enough. The master... the master must do all this and more. The master must transform.*

Once Claudette had believed she had her father's talent, and she'd stubbornly labored under his tutelage, no matter how he berated her. He died too soon, she thought, to teach her all he knew, so perforce she had learned a different way to fame. She had to.

A slight movement plucked Claudette from her thoughts. Anais had turned her head slightly. Her eyes narrowed, and her lips parted. Claudette followed the direction of Anais's gaze. And turned still.

The Duchess was looking at the first of Claudette's self-portraits. In it, Claudette's young face was unlined, and unlike the later portraits, her mouth had softened into a warm smile. Philippe claimed it was different from the others. Even her father had praised it. Somehow she'd captured—without her gift—a look of expectancy.

She knows, Claudette thought, going cold. Not the particulars, of course—that was impossible. But just as Claudette's touch had ruined other souls, so had the act tainted hers. Anaise of Belfort must have keen eyes to see the difference.

She wanted to thrust away those thoughts. *Finish the painting*, she told herself, but the old questions harried her anew. How would a series of the Duchess appear, from the portrait today to thirty years hence, after Claudette's touch had dimmed her soul? Would her speech be so gentle, her eye so perceptive?

The merchant's daughter, her eyes dull and expression bewildered, came back to mind, and Claudette shivered. *I can't do it. I can't ruin her. She's just a child.*

She was. Despite her rich clothing, her elegant manners, the Duchess was no more than a young girl.

Anais blinked, turned her head slightly, then resumed her pose with a smile.

A heavy weight suddenly pressed against Claudette's chest. She felt as though she'd unexpectedly sighted a monstrous spider, just where she was about to tread barefoot.

I can find money elsewhere, she thought. A dozen schemes came to mind. She could drive herself to work harder. She could paint a dozen lesser portraits. She could borrow from Goncourt and damn the gossips.

But the portrait—this portrait—

She'd promised the Duke her finest effort. If she disappointed Hugh of Belfort, the king would hear of it, and his favor would turn elsewhere. Jean-René would receive no money, and she would exchange her treasured study in the palace for a hovel in Alouette-sûr-Rive.

The Duchess shifted on her seat, wondering perhaps at this new delay. Claudette took a fresh palette from her shelves and mixed a new batch of colors for the Duchess's eyes, glancing from the paint to the Duchess and back. She wanted every shade to match exactly.

For if I succeed, there will be no second sitting.

At last she had the colors she wanted. Claudette selected a new brush, twirled its bristles to a point, dipped it into the paint. She drew a long breath, straightened her back, and stared at the Duchess.

As with her other subjects, she looked into and through the girl's eyes, past them into her soul, to the point where flesh met spirit. Another moment, and her spirit would touch the girl's. One brief contact, and she could transfer Anais's vibrancy to the canvas. So tempting, so easy...

Study your own features, her father had said.

With a painful effort, Claudette turned her gaze inward.

The studio vanished into a dazzling light. A vivid creature, its form like tongues of flame, swerved through the air. Its flight was erratic, she saw, and its wings were pitted by dark specks. *The corrosion of greed,* she thought, *and a talent misused. But it's all I have.* Without allowing herself another thought, she seized the creature.

A savage fire blazed once. A shock of power coursed through her and jarred her vision back to the ordinary world. She found herself clutching her brush, head swimming. No time for weakness, she told herself. She began to paint.

Working at a dangerous speed, she painted the Duchess of Belfort's eyes. The arched brows of umber, the delicate lashes, the rim of pink, the gold irises flecked with brown. *The smallest organ*, Claudette thought. *The most difficult to render truly.* She hurried, wanting to finish before her talent drained away completely, but already the sun was drifting downward—her precious light was fading.

With a blink, the room darkened from luminous gold to gray.

"I believe you're losing the light," Anais said.

Claudette added one last dot of gold to the painted eyes. The Duchess was right—to continue would spoil the painting.

She set down her brush. Tears blurred her vision. For the first time that afternoon, she felt the ache in her wrists and shoulders. *I'm old*, she thought. *My paintings are mediocre. And the portrait isn't done.*

The Duchess was speaking, but Claudette could not bring herself to attend. She heard a faint swish of silk against silk, then felt a light touch on her shoulder. "Lovely," the Duchess said. "Far lovelier than I deserve."

Claudette blinked away the tears and at last saw her work. Saw the deftly rendered background, like a curtain of darkness. Saw the brush strokes transform the amber paint into the Duchess's silken dress, falling in laps and folds. Saw the ivory lace, the rose tinted neck and curved lips, the face. Sections remained unfinished, and she noted a flaw in the hands. But the eyes were perfect.

"You have more than talent," Anais said. "You have genius."

Claudette's heart was thudding painfully. It *was* a masterpiece, however incomplete. She had succeeded. She would never paint so well again.

"I will come back tomorrow," Anais said. "And we can continue the portrait."

Claudette nodded automatically, her gaze still on the painting. The Duchess's perfume filled the air; a warm, sweet breath grazed Claudette's cheek; soft fingertips brushed against her cheek, wiping away the tears. Claudette didn't dare to move, lest she lose her fragile control.

The perfume drifted away. Behind her the door clicked open. Voices murmured. Someone softly closed the door.

Claudette closed her eyes. Again she heard the Duchess's words, *You have genius.*

Not anymore, she thought. *Most likely, I never did.*

Study yourself, her father had said. *The task is painful but necessary, if you are to be a true artist.*

Claudette stared at her left hand, the one she used to paint. She stared past the flesh and spider's web of veins, and inward to the spirit. What would she see, now that she had touched her own soul?

Blackness confronted her. She stared harder. With a shiver, the darkness lifted, and she saw a void—no, a limitless plateau, its gray dust scored by cracks. Desolate. Empty. Lifeless. The vision mocked her. She had ruined herself for eternity, all for a single unfinished portrait. In truth, a just reward.

She was about to turn away, when a spark of light winked and vanished. Claudette went still and breathless. There, she saw it again—a bead of water had welled up from the crack. One drop.

As she watched, the droplet spilled over the cracked earth. Another followed—a second pinpoint of brightness. A faint blur, like the shadow of that fiery creature, fluttered across the void. Nothing more. But she'd felt a pang deep within, and she knew her soul had not entirely died away.

The vision wavered. She'd never sustained it for so long.

Claudette blinked and rubbed her eyes, breathed in the heavy scent of roses. Hours had passed. Shadows had gathered in the studio's corners, a cool breeze skated through the window, and the crimson light of sunset flooded the room, illuminating the unfinished portrait.

Tomorrow, she thought, *the Duchess will return. And I will continue to paint.*

In the darkening room, she touched her face where the Duchess had brushed away the tears.

Poison

Twilight was falling over Bagluar's alleys when I arrived at the south-side wharves, a handful of steps ahead of Yenny. Clouds of pale stars lit the northern skies. In the east, the twin moons were rising, bright and swift. Whenever the *tuhan*—the rich—visited these streets, they came with fast cars, weapons, and guards. I came barefoot, dodging from shadow to shadow.

I paused, breathless. Rows of shacks lined these docks, standing like broken teeth in the mouth of night. Most were in ruins, burnt in the riot fires or left to rot, but a few remained whole. I found the one Eko had described to Yenny, when they thought I wasn't listening, and climbed through a yawning window.

A lizard skimmed over the floor and into a crack. Hide, yes. Quickly I slid behind a wall of broken crates and barrels, taking care to scatter dust over my footprints, so Yenny would not guess at my presence. Then I crouched and waited, counting time by the waves slapping against the pilings.

One, two, three handfuls of moments passed—long enough for doubt to grow—before the door swung open, and a lean dark figure appeared, momentarily lit by dusk's failing light. Yenny.

Yenny glided into the shack and eased the door shut. Floorboards sighed as my brother-sister came further inside. Closer. Closer. The old shack stank of oil and tar and rotting fish—sailing merchants had once stowed their goods here—but above these smells, I detected another scent, a warm and ripe one.

Within a blink, moonlight spilled through a gap in the roof, like a puddle of clean milk rippling over the floor. The twin moons had climbed higher, and by their light, I saw Yenny remained as *doa selmat*, as Yenny-brother. His face was shaped in sudden angles. His eyes were yellow and fringed with short black lashes. When he turned his head, blue-black hair swept over his shoulders. Like me. Not like me.

With a quick glance around, he stripped away his pants and shirt. Moonlight poured over his lean brown body. Like mine, his nipples were flat brown discs upon his chest. But where I had only a stub, Yenny's thick penis curved downward over the night-black hair of his groin. My breath came faster, as I watched. *I want him.*

Yenny-brother stretched his arms toward the ceiling. For a moment, he stood, body arched and tense. The ripe scent grew stronger.

And then it came—and swiftly.

Light brushed Yenny's swelling breasts. His nipples turned full, as though thumbs were pressing outward. My gaze followed the dusky blue shadows as they painted new contours upon his chest, downward over his rounded belly, down further to his penis, already folding into itself. My mouth went dry. My gaze jerked back to his face.

Her face.

Rounded cheeks. Eyes like new gold. Skin a luminous golden brown. I watched as bones and flesh altered themselves as rapidly as moonlight could trace the changes. Yenny made no sound throughout; only near the end did she exhale sharply.

I had asked once, *Does it hurt?*

He had said, *No.* She had said, *Yes, oh yes.*

Tears glittered in her eyes like diamonds in a rich man's mouth, like pearls spilling from a woman's sex. The *tuhan* sometimes paid Yenny lavish gifts to witness this transformation before they used her or him in more conventional ways. Hiding, I had often watched Yenny meet the bolder ones, the ones who came into Bagluar for a dare or a bet.

Yenny brushed a hand over her face. "Daksa," she said softly. "I know you're there."

Reluctantly I emerged from my hiding place. "How did you know?"

She smiled briefly, and her plum-soft mouth was so different from Yenny-brother's thin one that my breath caught. "I heard you breathe."

Ah. Yes. Even now my pulse was beating hard and fast at the sight of her breasts. Forgetting myself, I reached out and ran my fingertips along their fullness.

Yenny allowed the caress a moment before she nudged my hand away. "Not now. He'll come soon, and he wants me fresh. Untouched, he called it."

My breath drew tight inside my chest. "Which one is it tonight? The tattooed man? The one with the hawk-nose and ghost-gray eyes? Or is it the woman who pays double when you cry?"

She shrugged, unflustered by my anger. "A new one. Eko brought me the message this afternoon. The client wanted me for tonight, maybe longer. He promised to pay for extras."

At least he was only an umatu, I told myself. *Not one of our kind.* Then I felt shamed. Sri and Eko were *umatu*; they were also our friends. But my heart gave a painful lurch, knowing there were no more *tikaki* in Keramat or Bagluar or any other district in this huge city. All the others had left the mainland years before, shipped home by our keepers.

I shook away the memories, only to see that Yenny's eyes had gone distant. She was thinking of her rich client, this *tuhan* with his particular demands. Watching her face, I felt my belly tighten. "Tell him everything costs extra," I whispered.

Yenny laughed softly, and her hips swayed, perhaps in unconscious seduction. I shifted uneasily, remembering how we used to couple. We coupled, oh, for half and double handfuls of reasons—for warmth, for easy pleasure, for days when hunger wrapped us in its threadbare blankets. It was just last year we'd stopped, when Yenny first changed from in-between to one-who-ripens. She gave a fingerful of reasons. I argued every one, but in the end, she simply said, "No."

We were both frightened, I think.

Nearby, an electric motor whined. Then a horn bleated—a loud unwelcome sound in Bagluar's not-quite-deserted lanes. Yenny sauntered toward the door.

"Wait," I said. "You forgot…"

Yenny glanced over her shoulder, smiling. "I didn't forget," she said. "It's part of the contract. He'll pay extra, remember? Tell Eko and Sri we can have ice cream tonight."

Still smiling, she walked naked into the night.

I want my sister. I want my brother. I want…

My wants tasted like poison. Muttering to myself, I folded Yenny's clothes and tucked them inside the cleanest barrel, hidden from casual scavengers. For a moment, I considered taking them with me, but the desire was brief. Instead, I flicked my knife open and scratched an *X* on the barrel so that Yenny would know where to look when she returned. Or would she change into Yenny-brother? The idea sent a flicker of desire through my bones and blood, until it occurred to me that Yenny had expected me tonight, and that she always knew when I watched her with the *tuhan*.

She likes it. Likes me watching, not doing.

Anger squeezed my throat shut. Just as quickly I forced it away. Anger gave birth to mistakes, and I could not afford any mistakes, not in this part of Bagluar. *Be cold and hard like the stones, careful like the snake,* I told myself, shoving my blade into its sheath.

I left the shack, sliding like a shadow from its shelter. Overhead, more stars dotted the skies in a silvery mist, and the twin moons chased each other toward the western skies. My bare feet were silent, my nerves alive. I listened with ears and nose and skin and tongue. My hands brushed the mossy bricks of old temples, the knobby wattle of bamboo shanties, the cold slick marble of pillars in abandoned market squares. A few pillars carried the faces of gods old and new, the carvings blunted by rains and hands laid upon them in prayer. *Tuhan* had commissioned artisans to make these statues in Bagluar's richer days, or so Eko told me. He and Sri had lived in this district before the *tuhan* left. Just like Yenny, they had their own stories of forgotten days.

And then I heard it: a breathy sound, like wings beating the air, coming from a doorway to my left.

I spun around and darted back through the alley. At the next crossing, I veered up a flight of steps and into a covered passageway, where my footsteps echoed from brick walls and cobblestones.

Slow, I told myself. *Careful.*

Now silent as leaves falling from the trees, I crossed through the night-filled passageway, into a deserted moonlit courtyard, where I ran once more. Laughter echoed from the rooftops, marking my presence. Monkeys shrieked as they swung up and away, a wild dog yammered, and soon enough, heavy footfalls rang over the stones behind me.

No time to pick a better course. I pelted through another tunnel, into a wide street lined with trash heaps, ashes, and half-chewed bones. The buildings here were dark caverns, their round windows staring down at me. High above, more monkeys hooted in their lairs. Ahead, the street arrowed toward another moonlit plaza.

I skidded to a stop and burrowed into the nearest trash heap. Dust and ashes settled over me, and I willed myself not to sneeze. A tight handful of moments later, two massive shadows lurched past my hiding place. The shadows paused, sniffing the air.

Pemburu, I thought. *Hunters*. My throat squeezed shut. Worse than thieves or addicts or the knife-wielding whoremasters. Hunters might track a quarry for sex or meat or both at once. My heart beat faster, so fast it hurt. All I could think was that Yenny had walked naked and alone to her appointment, without even the deceptive security of a knife.

I swallowed and closed my eyes. *Ears open. Heart beat slow. See how the grass bends and the air stirs. Hear like the stones. Breathe like the wind.* One of Yenny's hunting songs, recalled from our childhood on that faraway island. Yet memory sometimes was true. My skin took on the silvery gray coloring of wood and cloth under moonlight. My fear-scent faded, turning old and musty, like the ashes from a long-dead fire.

Our keepers, the scientists, used complicated words like *metamorphosis* and *hormones* and *camouflage* to explain us. We could turn invisible, they said. We could change from male to female and back. Survival adaptations, they called it, and speculated openly about what other fantastical transformations we could summon. Eyes closed, I wondered if what Yenny did was for our survival.

Gradually my heartbeat slowed. I dared to open my eyes.

The hunters stood motionless. They were tall, half again as tall as any *tikaki*. One crouched, with his knuckles resting on the ground. The other was upright, his long arms held loose and ready. They breathed, a wet rasping sound that drew bile into my throat. *Breathe soft, heart still*, I chanted silently.

Moments and moments, handfuls of them, passed. One *pemburu* turned in my direction. Moonlight made his blunt features into a gray-green mask, much like the moss-covered statues in the temples. His head swiveled around. His chin lifted, and I saw the gleam of his stubby fangs as he appeared to yawn, tasting the air.

Breathe. Soft. Heart. Still.

The hunter scanned both sides of the street; then, with a hollow grunt, he turned and summoned his companion to follow. They shuffled back the way they had come.

More long moments, a mouthful and a bellyful, passed before my muscles relaxed and I dared to breathe deeply. Until scent and sight and quivering nerves told me that yes, the hunters were gone.

I ghosted homeward, still trembling even though no more hunters crossed my path that night. At last, I reached a familiar waterfront neighborhood. Across the harbor, silvery lights from Keramat's thousand lamps stained the night sky, and more lights danced over the harbor's watery swells. Keramat, where the *tuhan* lived in their fabulous houses.

I circled around the vacant warehouse where Yenny and I lived with Sri and Eko. Chains held its doors and hatches closed, and most of the windows were boarded over, but a few shutters had come loose in the winter storms. I climbed through one such window and lowered myself onto the heaps of trash inside, which lay like moldering leaves upon a forest floor. This forest was built of planed wood, riddled with knotholes, and soft from constant damp—a dead forest, and yet it sheltered us.

The scent of fire drifted down from the room above. My skin tightened in apprehension, and my scent altered to that of damp wood. Cautiously I approached the wooden ladder leading to the second story. The trapdoor was propped open, and light spilled through, illuminating the ladder's top rungs. The soft murmur from above sounded like Sri's voice, but others had died of trusting too easily.

I scratched the ladder and drew back. The voice fell silent, then footsteps crossed to the trapdoor, and Sri's head appeared.

"Daksa," she called down. "Come up. Eko has treats for us."

When I had clambered up, Sri dragged me over to Eko, who knelt beside our makeshift grate, poking at the fire with an iron stick. "Look," said Sri.

A pile of kindling burned in the grate. More firewood filled up one corner, and five oilcloth bundles were scattered over the floor. My mouth watered at the scent of rich food. Eko smiled at me, pleased.

"Tea," Sri said. She too was grinning. "Green tea and fresh bread—*fresh*, Daksa—and more sweet potatoes and spiced noodles and pickled eggs than we can eat. A feast."

"You made some good deals," I said.

Eko nodded. "A few."

"Like the one for Yenny."

Eko's black eyes narrowed to slits. "Like Yenny's."

"I made some good deals, too," Sri said.

Sri was brown and wiry, with thick black hair tied up in braids. She was like an autumn storm cloud, lit with eerie moonlight when she smiled. Like other poor *umatu*, she and her brother had learned to forage a different way when the *tuhan* abandoned Bagluar to fire and decay and the hungry *pemburu*. Together, they often crossed into Keramat's richer quarters, either daring the police patrols, or taking to the sewers and tunnels underneath the city. When he was younger, Eko had loitered near the grand *tuhan* hotels, trading mouth and fingers and hands for food. Nowadays, with Sri, he carried messages between the *tuhan* in exchange for iron and copper rupiahs. I asked them once: What kind of messages? Eko had shrugged. "Duels," he'd muttered. "Drugs. Politics. More, I don't want to know."

Eko was taller than Sri, and darker, his scent musky and full and lush. Sometimes I woke to hear Eko murmuring, and Yenny breathing fast and rough, as Eko's fingers brought my brother-sister to climax. Sex for warmth, sex to soothe away our fears—that much had not changed.

We shared out bowlfuls of hot green tea and feasted upon spiced noodles and sweet potatoes and fish cakes. We saved none for Yenny—her clients often fed her, and this one had promised to treat her well, Eko assured me. Indeed, both moons had long vanished before Yenny returned.

My stomach eased when I saw she wore her old shirt and patched trousers. She also carried a new knapsack slung over one shoulder.

"Yenny!" Sri cried out, and flung herself across the room to give Yenny a sticky hug.

Eko stood up, his smile flashing bright against his dusky-dark brown skin. He too had worried, it seemed.

"I brought us presents," Yenny said. She swung the knapsack around and dropped it with a thump onto the floor. "Presents and treats and money."

Like the gods in her tales, she distributed her bounty—mangoes and coconut balls and spiced cakes and sticks of palm sugar. And the ice cream, of course, white creamy squares with chunks of pineapple, packed in layers of straw to keep it cold.

"Those are the treats," Yenny said. "Now for the presents."

From her knapsack, she dug out a new folding knife, which she flourished before handing it to Eko. His gaze met hers, and they both smiled. Next she took out Sri's present—a pair of new boots made from soft brown leather. Sri hummed in delight and pulled the boots over her hard, horny feet.

"And now for you," Yenny said, with a sideways glance at me.

She held out a small wooden box. I picked it up with my fingertips, and turned it over. Carvings of letters and animals and vines decorated its surface. Tiny hinges and a latch, both made from the same ebony wood, held the lid closed.

"Open it," Sri said.

Taking a quick breath, I lifted the lid.

The interior was like a hollowed-out ball, its surface rough like a coconut shell. At the bottom was a small mound of brown dust, caked and damp with an oily substance. I touched it.

A spicy scent filled the air. My nose twitched, and something tugged at my gut. It was a smell from long-ago, from handfuls and armfuls of years ago—the sweet milk-scent of my nursing mothers, the heady tang of my fathers, the grassy scent that recalled a long-forgotten sister who had kissed my cheeks and lips and eyes before our new keepers, the scientists, led me away.

I licked my lips, uncertain whether to weep or laugh. "Thank you."

Yenny smiled. "I found it in the night bazaar, at a shop that sells statues and pipes and spice boxes. The man said he traded with *tikaki*. Not here," she added, seeing the look on my face. "He sends out a ship to all the islands with trade goods from the mainland."

A box from home, carved by our people. I wanted to hear more about this shop, to ask if somehow the owners knew about our family, but Eko's and Sri's stares were like fingers upon my lips. Instead, I hugged Yenny and murmured thanks again. Yenny held me close a moment longer. I smelled flower-scented soap in her hair. I smelled a man's spendings on her breath and skin.

With a shaky laugh, Yenny drew back. "There's more."

More? I thought, but already she was pouring out copper and silver rupiahs from a new money pouch—handfuls upon handfuls—the coins glittering like eyes in the firelight.

"He wants me again, day after tomorrow," she said.

"Again?" I said softly.

She nodded. I saw a look pass between her and Eko, whose face had smoothed into a blank mask. But he could not hide the slight change in his scent. He was unhappy.

"Then tonight we celebrate," Sri said, breaking the silence. "Ice cream first. Then stories."

"Stories," Yenny said quickly. "As many as you like."

While Sri scooped out the ice cream, Yenny began telling tales. I knew them all by word and timbre and cadence. Stories about hunter gods, whose arrows were dipped in magic blood. Songs about treacherous flowers that gleamed like torches, leading lovers along cliffs to their deaths. Tales of islands and peoples so far away, they seemed like dreams to me. When she could eat no more, Sri nestled beside me and laid her head on my chest. A strange scent lingered on my skin, like that from the spice box. It was the scent of almost-change, and my blood rippled in response. But almost was the same as never. I sighed, shifted my position, and idly scratched the blue-black serial number imprinted on my wrist. That, like my memories, was fading with every year.

Subjects in the study of indigenous peoples, our keepers had called us when they gave tours to government inspectors. Just two years ago we lived in clean bright dormitories. Our duties were few and easy enough. Let the doctors poke us with needles, stare into our eyes, and draw blood the next day. Sing. Dance. Tell stories. Ignore them and the cameras when we coupled.

Remembering, I let my thoughts spin and fall and soar in cadence with Yenny's voice, like petals whirling through the dense green jungle light. I might have seen that jungle light once more, had the scientists not lost their funding, had we boarded a different truck, had the drivers not taken the bribes.... Had any number of leaves fallen differently, the forest floor would look different, and trees would grow where others fell. But our truck never met the boat, and the other *tikaki* had died fighting, letting us escape a different captivity. Instead, our paths led us here, to this upper room of a neglected warehouse.

To safety, I thought. To Sri and Eko, our first true friends among the *umatu.*

I'd lost track of Yenny's storytelling, but so had she. Eko lay beside her, stroking her between her legs, and Yenny's soft moans interrupted her tale about a wandering ghost. Their noise woke Sri, who stirred, then pulled my hand over her breast buds. I massaged Sri gently until she drifted back into sleep. Holding her, I wondered if and when the change would come to me.

I woke to the soft pattering of rain against the roof shingles. The air was ripe with the echoes of our feast, with sweat and musk and the sour smell of melted ice cream. A tendril of spice wound through it all. I lifted my head.

Yenny sat perched on a mound of old sacking by the windows overlooking the wharves. She had pushed open one of the shutters, and raindrops spattered through the opening, like a cascade of jewels from the sky.

I eased myself from underneath Sri and padded to my sister's side. "You didn't change."

Her mouth had lifted into a smile at my approach, but now the smile faded. "He insisted," she murmured. "He paid me extra to stay a girl."

"For how long?"

"One, two months."

"Did he say why?"

She shook her head. I waited, hoping she would tell me more—she often did—but Yenny remained silent, gazing over the harbor's blue-gray waters. Though I'd lived and coupled with her for handfuls and armfuls of years, I saw nothing in her face except stillness, heard nothing in her voice but words—no colors or smells or shades of warm and cold. Only her fingers, locked together, betrayed her mood. When Sri rolled over and stretched, Yenny started up like a hunted deer, glided down the ladder, and was away.

Throughout the next weeks, I trailed after my sister when she met her new client. He wasn't truly *tuhan*, I decided. Unlike them, with their expensive cars, he drove a rusted blue van. He wore ordinary canvas trousers, scuffed brown shoes, and ugly shirts with too many colors. His scent was raw and eager and afraid.

Over time, Yenny answered my questions about him. He did not like to linger in Bagluar, she said. After she climbed into the van, he locked the doors and blindfolded her, then drove her to the hotel. "A different one each time," she added.

"Expensive ones?" I asked.

"No. But the rooms are clean. He insists."

"You can hear him, then."

She smiled. "He covers my eyes, Daksa. Not my nose or ears or fingers."

He must be a stupid man, I thought. "What do you smell, then? What do you hear and touch?"

Yenny hesitated. "Perfumes," she said at last. "Soap-washed cotton sheets. More soap on his skin." Another pause, this one longer, before she added, "Clean plastic and new rubber from the sheaths he wears when he fucks me."

My skin prickled with uneasiness. "He keeps you long enough. What else does he do with you?"

Her scent sharpened. "Why do you ask?"

I shrugged. "Curiosity."

She gazed at me, eyes narrowed, but in the end, she told me. He liked a regular pattern, she said. He usually fondled her after he tied the blindfold. Once they reached the hotel, he hustled her through the lobby, and if the elevators were empty, she would suck him. Everything else took place in the room itself. He wore a sheath, she said. One for every time he fucked her, even though *umatu* seed never flowered in *tikaki* wombs. He said he knew it, when she told him, but that he feared catching a sickness.

"How many times a night?" I asked.

Once. Twice, maybe. A long session in bed, with Yenny underneath, while the man groaned and pushed and twisted his body around, rooting for pleasure. Sometimes he fucked her again before driving her to back to Bagluar.

"You spend hours there," I said. "What else do you do?"

Another keen glance before she answered. "I sleep, Daksa."

My skin rippled, the way it did when hunters passed by. No matter how painful the answers, I asked more questions about what the man did, and why, and how Yenny felt afterward. Listening to her answers, my breasts grew tight and full, and my stub shrank inward, revealing the vulva underneath. Then, when she slid off her clothes to demonstrate how the man touched her, my stub thickened and liquid pearls dripped from its opening, like a tiny mouth crying out its desires. Its. Mine. Hers.

I closed my eyes. "Why don't you want me that way?"

"I do want you," she murmured. "But we can't. It's not safe."

Pain gripped my stomach from the poison inside. "None of what you do is safe, Yenny. But you let *him* fuck you. You let everyone fuck you except me."

Yenny stiffened. Her body flickered, almost changing into Yenny-brother, but she regained control and released a long hard breath. "Do not do that again," she said roughly. From her look, she might have spoken to herself, as well as to me. "Daksa, please. He promised me more money—enough that we might buy anything. That we can eat, and be warm, and even—"

Even go home. All the blankness fled from her face, and I could comprehend her scents and moods and yearnings as clearly as I did my own. More clearly.

Yenny took me into her arms and kissed me, as though to make sure I understood. Her body was light and sweet, her smell richer and fuller than I remembered. *Like my spice box,* I thought. *Like the scent of our older brother-sister.* My thoughts leapt and sprang backward to the lab, farther back to the jungle. My mother's face had already faded into twilight, washed away by months and years, but at times her voice still whispered to me. *No more, Daksa. Yes, I know, Yenny. We are all hungry. Eat slowly....*

I strained to hear my other sister-brother's name, but could not.

I breathe in the scent of spices and dream of our island home. I dream of white petals drifting downward in an endless perfumed rain. I yearn for the shimmering green forest, the song of the waterfalls, for the taste and smell of eternal summer. In those dreams my body exudes a strange new scent, and it drives the deer before me into Yenny-brother's nets. In dreams alone, I am complete. I am man and woman, I am sister and brother.

And when I awake, I am neither.

One week stretched itself like a worm into two, and like a caterpillar into three, and like a serpent into four and five. Yenny's client met her every two days. And like a serpent uncoiling toward its prey, each session grew longer until Yenny no longer returned until the ruby-red of sunrise. Each time she brought handfuls of money—never as much as that first time, but soon we had more than Eko or even Sri could count. Every night we burned firewood without care. We ate hot meals, and Sri danced in her new boots.

Six weeks after her first meeting with the strange *umatu*, Yenny disappeared for two days. Fretting, I tagged after Sri and Eko, watching the *tuhan* they watched, running errands they set for me. We were all anxious, even Eko, who spent the second day crouched by our window, his gaze sweeping the lanes and squares and streets in all directions.

"She warned me," he said, when I came to his side. He spoke in a breathless whisper, as though to himself. "She said he wanted longer sessions. Said he would pay more. He promised…"

Eko broke off, his face so filled with misery I dared not ask what this *umatu* had promised my sister.

On the third day, Yenny returned.

Rains had soaked the city throughout the night, but by mid-day, the skies had cleared, and bright sunlight glared from the puddles, turning them into mist. Eko and Sri were away on errands. I had remained behind, sitting in the shade and breathing in the spice-rich scent from my wooden box. When I heard soft footsteps below, I closed my eyes and went still. Hoping and not hoping. More footsteps, careless and quick, then the ladder creaked. Still I refused to look.

"Daksa." Yenny's voice was a whisper, her scent a tangle of strange emotions.

I opened my eyes. Yenny stood a few steps away. She wore new clothes of bright red cotton, and her long black hair was brushed smooth. "You came back," I said.

"Of course I did." Yenny smiled, but tensely. Her cheeks were flushed. Her eyes looked dull, as though she had not rested well.

"Tired?" I asked.

"Hardly." She yawned. "I did nothing but sleep."

"Nothing?" My voice went high and thin.

"Nothing, Daksa. Really. But I do want a nap. It's the weather, I think. All that rain."

She drifted over to her corner and settled onto her blankets, head pillowed on her arm. Within a handful of moments, her breath slowed and she was asleep, so fast, my stomach fluttered. *What happened?* I thought. *What new demand did he place on you, that you cannot share with me?*

Crouching by her side, I touched her cheek. Her face looked plumper, I thought, and beneath the fear-scent, I detected a musky heavy fragrance. When I cupped her breast with my hand, her skin radiated warmth through the cloth. She stirred, and her legs parted, releasing more fragrance into the air.

Mouth going dry, I unbuttoned my sister's shirt and caressed her bare skin. Yenny smiled in her sleep. Bolder now, I pinched her nipples, which hardened at once. My own scent changed, growing salty and rank. Almost male.

I want my sister. I want my brother.

My hands trembled. My blood thrummed loud in my ears. All caution scattering into desire, I lay down beside her and mouthed her breasts and throat. Yenny's eyes flickered open and closed, but when I slid a hand down her trousers and between her legs, she did nothing more than sigh and take my fingers inside her.

Wet. Sticky. So he had not simply watched. Nor had he used a sheath this time. I withdrew my fingers, sniffed. My skin crawled. His sour fear stink was all over her skin. Deep inside was only Yenny's scent, but richer than before. It reminded me of summer rains in the jungles, of sweat-soaked days when the ocean had swallowed all its breezes. Of brother and sister. Of a desire she never showed me. And Yenny—Yenny hardly moved throughout my caresses. She continued to sleep as though she were enchanted, like the heroes in her own tales.

But no heroes lived in Bagluar. No magic flowed through its gutters, unless you counted the magic from pipe smoke, or the spells cast by needles.

Still cautious, I pushed up Yenny's sleeves and examined her arms. There were the old needle marks, from when the scientists drew blood, or injected us with serums. Nothing new. With a light touch, I examined her wrists and neck and ankles—all the places where drug users pricked themselves with needles. Nothing. Nothing.

My breath eased out, until I remembered Eko's words.

They start with the arms, but when those fail, they use the legs, the throat, the wrists, the ankles, and the tongue. Anywhere they can find a vein.

I rolled Yenny onto her back and eased off her trousers. Yes, there behind her knees, I found puckered marks, small red dots where needles had walked. They felt hot to my touch, and hard like pebbles. My hands trembled, and my mouth went dry, but not from desire.

"I took no drugs," Yenny shouted.

"What about those marks?" I shouted back. My fear must have looked like anger because Sri cringed. Yenny trembled, too, and pulled at her tangled hair. Nervous. Only Eko remained calm, his attention on the flute he was carving with his new knife.

"He wanted to watch me sleep," Yenny continued, more quietly.

"With drugs?"

"With drugs," she insisted. "But only sleeping drugs. He said they were safe. He wanted..." She hesitated and glanced toward Eko. "He wanted... to fuck me like I was dead."

Sri shuddered. Eko's face pinched into a frown. "I've heard of that," he said. "He's a sick man—sicker than most. Are you done with him?"

"Yes." Yenny's voice trembled. "Yes, I'm done. Done and rich and now we can eat like *tuhan* ourselves."

She was lying, lies of silence, though I could not guess what secrets she kept. Eko too watched her closely, his hands lightly holding the half-carved flute. He might not be *tikaki,* but he had senses keener than most *umatu,* and I wondered if he could detect her lies as well as I could.

The silence stretched out, thin and raw. Finally Eko breathed out a sigh. "We have enough for forever," he said softly. "You don't need one like him again. Please."

Yenny nodded and turned away. Her eyes were bright with tears.

"No more," she said.

The tightness in my throat eased. We were rich, as Yenny said, but even if we turned as poor as dust, I didn't want her to take another client like that one—a strange frightened man with an appetite like maggots.

As though she heard my thoughts, Yenny opened the box where we kept our savings and fingered the coins. Iron rupiah. Silver ones glinting like raindrops. A few gold ones, as bright as Yenny's eyes. Eko watched her a few moments, then laid aside his flute and stood. "I'm going into the city," he said. "I… I have some deals to make."

Sri stood as well. "I'll come with you."

They climbed down the ladder, one by one. I heard them cross the room and climb through the broken window. It was late afternoon, and breezes carried the strong tang of the retreating tide into our room. A handful of moments passed before either Yenny or I spoke.

"I did it for us," Yenny said.

I touched her fingers. "I know."

She shivered and brushed a hand over her eyes, scattering the tears, which fell like jewels onto her red-dyed shirt. The drops darkened the cloth, making new patterns, then faded into the air.

"Change," I told her. "Be my brother. Be like me. Whatever you wish. Then we'll go running along the docks."

Yenny smiled tentatively. "Like children."

"If you like."

Her smile warmed. "I like."

She rose to her feet, graceful once more, and shucked off her trousers and shirt. She lifted her arms above her head, wrists crossed like a dancer's. Her head tipped backward and she stood, poised between now and yet, a curved and golden ribbon, illuminated by the sunset's burning light. My breath caught. I waited.

Quiet. Stillness. Longer and longer I waited, breathless.

"Yenny?"

Yenny's throat quivered, and her skin gleamed with sweat from an effort I could not see.

"Yenny? What's wrong?"

Another heartbeat of silence, and then, "I can't."

My pulse jumped and ran forward. "Try again."

A stupid suggestion, but Yenny nodded and closed her eyes, as though to concentrate harder on the transformation. I saw her muscles shivering underneath her skin. I smelled a strange new scent—ripe and heavy—overlaid with the sharp edge of desperation.

Yenny's eyes blinked open. Tears glittered in her eyes. I had no need to ask if she felt pain.

Yes, oh yes, my love.

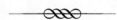

Yenny slept alone that night, tucked into the farthest corner she could find. When Eko and Sri returned, they said nothing, but their clothing reeked of grease and sour smoke, and Eko had new bruises on his face. That night, Sri held me in her arms and stroked my trembling body until I slept.

Dreaming, I imagined myself on the island again. I was darting along a narrow track, a spear gripped in my left hand, hunting. Sunlight dappled the trunks and leaves. A rustling sound marked my quarry's passage. I ran faster, certain the kill was nearby.

Without warning, Yenny's ripe scent rolled through the air. My skin rippled—the forerunner to change—but instead of my body changing, my weapons did. My knife wilted into a handful of leaves. My spear writhed, turning from wood into a sinuous vine that angled around and plunged between my legs.

I woke with a gasp to the hot stinging scent of fire, and the red light of sunrise leaking through the shutters. Eko crouched over the fire grate, his back toward me. Our new iron kettle hissed and clacked on the grate like an unhappy beast.

He woke up early, I told myself. *Wanted tea.*

A whispery moan sounded. Yenny.

I scrambled to her side. Yenny had thrown back her blanket and lay twisted over the bare floor. Her breathing rattled, just like the kettle, and when I touched her cheek, I flinched. Fever. Sun-scorching fever.

"Thirsty," she croaked.

Eko came at once with a mug of cold tea, which he fed to Yenny while I propped up her head. When she had finished, she sank back into my arms, muttering. Eko refilled the cup and set it aside to cool. The kettle was hissing by now. He added tea leaves to a waiting bowl, and poured the boiling water over them. By his looks, he must have been tending Yenny's needs for some time.

"Is it the drugs?" I whispered.

Eko shook his head. "Sleepy drugs aren't like that. I think it's because of the needles. If he didn't bother to use clean ones…"

Silently I cursed Yenny's client. "Will she die?"

His mouth thinned out. "I don't know. But I do know she needs a doctor."

"Then we take her to one," said Sri, who had come to our side without our noticing. She knelt by Yenny and touched her flushed cheeks. After a moment, Sri shook her head, frowning and chewing her lip.

"Clinic?" Eko said.

"No," said Sri. "She needs a *tuhan* doctor."

She spoke as though the choice was obvious, but my pulse beat faster at her words. A *tuhan* doctor meant traveling into Keramat, a place sometimes more dangerous than Bagluar for our kind.

Before I could speak, however, Eko nodded. "You're right," he said. "The clinic would make her wait. And wait. And wait some more." He thought a moment. "I know one who would see us."

"How much does he cost?" Sri said.

"She," said Eko. "And she costs a lot."

I glanced at Yenny, who lay parched and groaning. "Do you trust this doctor?"

He nodded.

"Then we go to her—and now."

We gathered all our coins from their hiding places. Three gold rupiah. A double handful of copper. More handfuls of silver ones than I could count. More than I thought existed in the world.

"Is that enough?" I whispered.

"Has to be."

I shook my head, worried by the doubt in his voice.

Sri stuffed cartons of mango juice into our knapsack, while I filled our canteen from the rain barrel. Eko divided the coins into three heaps, which we hid in our clothes, tied into bundles so they didn't jingle. We ate a quick breakfast, and Sri forced Yenny to drink cupfuls of juice. Yenny seemed to revive, but Eko shook his head and frowned.

"Fever does that," he murmured to me. "Gets better and then worse. Better we go now, while she can still walk."

He led the way through Bagluar's mazes and into a drainage ditch, where we entered the tunnels.

The journey seemed to last for hours. Eko and I helped Yenny when her strength flagged. Sri scouted ahead with our lantern. Every so often, we stopped and coaxed Yenny to drink. At last we reached a ladder nailed to the tunnel walls. Eko climbed up and prised open the metal hatch at the top. He reached down a hand, and with me pushing from behind, we helped Yenny to climb up and out.

A few moments later, we all stood in a dirty courtyard choked with weeds. It was quiet here, but from beyond the courtyard entrance came the whine of electric cars, the blare of their horns, and the shriller clang from bicycles. We had traveled away from the wharves; only a hint of salt-tang carried into these quarters. Instead, I smelled dogs and sweet flowers.

And many many *umatu*.

Yenny crouched among the weeds. Her face had turned pale, and she was sweating again. Sri gently held the juice carton to her lips and made her drink. "Can you still walk?" she asked.

Yenny wiped her hand across her face. "I can try."

With Eko leading us, we threaded our way along Keramat's back streets and half-deserted lanes. Here I saw the light to Bagluar's shadows. Clean whole temples with monks in their sun-golden robes. Farmers carrying baskets of eggs and sweet potatoes to market. Fishermen with carts loaded down with squid and crabs and eels. Scribes at their stalls. Water sellers and vendors with cones of spiced noodles and curried rice. A different world from Bagluar. Different too from the laboratory.

We came down a windswept alley, to a point between a thriving bazaar and a wide avenue, where the traffic hummed past. Eko pointed toward the street. "Around this corner. Twelve steps to the left, and we'll be at the doctor."

Sri gave Yenny another few swallows of juice. We checked over our knives and knapsack. My skin had stretched tight, the way it did whenever I dared Bagluar's darkest streets alone.

A fingerful of steps brought us to the alley's entrance. Another scan in both directions, then we were openly walking down a street choked with cars and bicycles and motorbikes. Tall buildings loomed like mountains above us.

"Here," Eko hissed. "This one. I remember the number." He pointed at a set of stairs leading upward to a moss-covered portico. Ferns and orchids grew from stone pots beside the door, and a brass sign hung from a black rod.

We helped Yenny up the broad curving stairs, and through glass doors the color of old amber. Inside, Eko gestured toward the left-hand corridor. "This way."

He went first, reading more signs, until we came to a plain white door, with a sign beside it. "Here," Eko murmured. He opened the door, and we guided Yenny inside.

We found ourselves in a room lined with benches. Bright weavings covered the walls, except for one entirely covered by gray-white glass. A few *umatu* sat on the benches, hands clasped, waiting. One, an older man, glanced up; the others paid us no attention. I sniffed at the mix of soap and sharp bitter smells. Clean. So very clean.

A window opened in the glass wall, and a stout woman dressed in a pale green smock leaned over the counter. "We don't take charity cases," she said crisply.

Wordlessly, I handed my money sack to Eko. He took out his and gave them both to Sri, who stepped toward the glass window. "We aren't charity," she said. "How much does your doctor charge?"

The woman's mouth twitched. "Routine exam costs fifty rupiah. Pay in advance."

Silver ones, said her voice. Sri counted out the money with a steady hand—a heap of coins so large I had to turn away, even though I would spend twice and thrice that much coin for Yenny. So much, gone so quickly. The woman must have seen my face and what it meant because her throat worked, as though she had words stuck inside, but all she said was, "Put your money away. Let me talk to the doctor."

She vanished from her window. Sri packed away the coins and came back to us. The other *umatu* were now watching us, their eyes curious or bored or suspicious. From the next room, I heard several voices talking in soft tones. A moment later, a different woman beckoned us through another door. We followed her through two short twisting corridors, into an even smaller room, where she left us.

The rich have no colors, I thought, staring at the white walls and white doors, and a high narrow bench covered with crackling white paper. Yenny crumpled onto the floor, groaning. Sri crouched beside her, stroking her hair. Eko paced the room, lightly touching the trays of metal objects, the glass jars, the stacks of white napkins and paper cups. I stood, watching Yenny's sweating face.

A soft rap sounded at the door, and we all started.

A third woman entered the room. She was dark-skinned, brown like Eko and Sri, but square-built, with soft plump hands, and warm brown eyes buried in wrinkles. She wore a vivid green smock over her blue trousers, and she smelled of soap and medicine, just like our keepers.

"I'm Doctor Iskandar," she said.

Her voice was *tuhan*—rich and mellow and slow. And because she seemed to expect an answer, I pointed at Yenny and said, "My sister is sick. She's got a fever."

"So I noticed," Doctor Iksander said. "Well, let's see what's wrong, other than fever."

She stared into Yenny's eyes and ears and mouth. She asked Yenny to cough, breathe, cough again. She laid a hand over Yenny's forehead, then pressed fingertips against Yenny's wrist while she counted to herself, frowning. "Not good," she muttered.

That much I knew. I bit down on my tongue, forcing myself into patience. More touching and staring. Many questions, which Yenny answered in soft slow words. How old are you? Have you been sick before? Have you seen a doctor before? When did you notice the fever? When did you last menstruate? That one caused Yenny to stare silently until the doctor shrugged and went on to the next question.

Finally Doctor Iskandar turned away and opened one of the white cabinets. She took out a plastic cup with a lid. "First you pee inside this," she said. "Let your friend help you into the next room, so you can have some privacy. Seal the cup with this cap and leave it on the counter."

Her words made no sense. Sri and Yenny stared at one another, but then Eko whispered something to Sri, who nodded and took Yenny away to the water closet. Doctor Iskandar washed her hands and pulled on plastic gloves. From another drawer, she took out a needle and plastic tube. When Yenny and Sri returned, she gestured for Yenny to sit on the paper-covered bench. "Now we need some of your blood. Do you understand?" She spoke a bit loudly, as though we might be deaf.

"For testing," Yenny said, with a slight edge. "I understand."

Doctor Iskandar paused in her preparations. "You said you'd never been to a doctor before."

"Not ones like you," Yenny said.

Doctor Iskandar's eyes narrowed. "What were they like, then? Are you talking about the free clinic doctors?"

"Maybe," Yenny said.

She paused, this *tuhan* doctor, and studied us each in turn. "I see. Well." Her mouth tilted into a brief smile that was not a happy one. "Most likely, you have some kind of infection. And while I have my suspicions, we'll draw blood twice, and test twice, just to make sure. Give me your arm. Hold onto your brother. This might hurt."

She drew some blood into the tube. Telling us to wait, she left the room. We waited and waited, until I thought I might have to hunt down the doctor, but at last she returned.

Her eyes were wide and bright. Her mouth was pressed into a pale thin line. "You are not *umatu*," she said.

"No," Yenny said. "You asked me more questions than an ant has children, but you did not ask me that one."

Doctor Iskandar blew out a hard breath. She looked angry. Frightened. No, excited and nervous. Her scent was sharp with those emotions.

"I shall be certain to add that question to my list," she said after a moment. "As for you, let me start with what I do know. You are *tikaki*. You are probably the only *tikaki* in the city, or even the entire province, as far as I know. How you got here, I can guess. Why you are still here, and not shipped home with the others, I do not know. You may tell me if you like, but the important thing for you to know is that you have a rare and nasty infection, the kind that addicts get."

"I'm not—"

Doctor Iskandar held up a hand, and Yenny broke off, lips pressed together.

"I never said you were a drug addict," Doctor Iskandar said mildly. "But you have an infection much like theirs, usually caused by dirty needles, and it threatens your heart. You came soon enough that I can treat the infection with antibiotics and some visits to check its course. There is one problem." She paused and glanced at me. "The tests also show you are pregnant."

Yenny's lips turned pale. Sri's hands fluttered up to her face. Eko's expression did not change, but his breathing quickened. As for me, all I could hear was a thundering in my head. A child? But how?

"Do you know the father?" Doctor Iskandar said.

Yenny nodded, shook her head.

"Is that a yes or a no?"

Yenny met her gaze, but she did not answer.

"Why can't she have the medicine?" I asked.

Doctor Iskandar glanced from me to Yenny and back, as though considering how to choose her words. "Part of it's her physiology. I've read enough articles from the study they made of your people. These antibiotics are dangerous enough for an *umatu* woman who's pregnant. For *tikaki*..." Another pause. "For you, it would mean the child dies."

I didn't need to understand all her words to understand the choice. "Take the child away, then. Can you do that?"

Doctor Iskandar blinked. "Yes, of course. If that is what you wish. We could set you up today and—"

"No!" Yenny pushed off the bench. "I won't kill the child."

I caught her before she could shove past the doctor. "Stop," I said. "Didn't you hear? That *umatu* made a baby on you. He stuck you full of needles."

Yenny tried to wrench away, but could not. "I heard. I know he made sick. But the child can't be his. He's *umatu*."

"What about the others?" I said.

She glared at me. "*Umatu*. All of them. You should know. You watched enough."

I snapped my mouth shut, angry with Yenny and her stubbornness, angry with the doctor because she had no medicine for our kind.

"So you had sex with *umatu* men," Doctor Iskandar said. Her voice carried no hint of her thoughts. "How many times?"

"Handfuls," Yenny said harshly. "Handfuls and handfuls. Why? Their seed is dead to me."

"Then who could be the father? Do you have any idea?"

Silence. Yenny's gaze dropped to her hands. She held them tightly, fingers tangled with fingers. I could almost hear the secrets begging to come out.

Doctor Iskandar studied her a few moments longer. "You're probably right. They tried—with consent, I'm told—to inseminate your females from *umatu* sperm. It never worked, according to the articles, which leaves us a mystery. More important, we still have to deal with your fever. Just to be certain, I'd like to run another blood test, and get some chest X-rays."

"No." Yenny's head jerked up. "I want to go. Home. Now."

Doctor Iskandar frowned. "That's not a good idea. You need treatment."

"You mean poison," Yenny said.

Doctor Iskandar opened her mouth, closed it. "Yes and no. I see your point, but the medicine's not poison to you, just for the fever. Besides, remember that if *you* are sick, your baby will be sick."

Meaning the child would die, no matter what.

Yenny muttered something. When Eko touched her arm, she leaned into his arms, and I glimpsed tears on her cheeks. *We are tikaki*, I thought. *Our keepers thought we could survive anything with our magical bodies. But not this.*

"Listen," said Doctor Iskandar. "Stay a few moments longer. Please. I can give you an injection now, and some pills to take home. They'll help with the cramping and fever without harming the child. Government-tested, you know." Her mouth flickered into a smile, as faint as starlight. "It will give you more time to make your decision."

"I've made it," Yenny whispered, but in the end she agreed.

Doctor Iskandar summoned her nurse. They held a brief conversation, filled with more nonsense words. The nurse left and came back with another needle, and a tube filled with clear liquid.

"Get a week's supply of those new antipyretics," Doctor Iskandar told her, "the ones from Anwar Pharmaceuticals. Plus the three-day course of oral antibiotics. I'll give the injection myself."

She waved the nurse away and turned back to Yenny. "One more shot and we can send you home."

Yenny hardly flinched at the needle. She no longer looked angry, or frightened. *She looks used up,* I thought, touching my sister's warm hand.

We waited another triple handful of moments. Doctor Iskandar checked over Yenny's eyes and mouth again, then touched her wrist, counting. "Better," she murmured. "Not good enough."

"What does that mean?" Sri asked.

"It means your friend will not die of fever today, but she will be quite ill in the days to come. The antipyretics should bring her fever down, but they won't cure her. Truth be told, she'll need IV antibiotics within the week. Ah, here we go."

The nurse had returned and handed the doctor a plastic sack. I heard a rattling sound, like beads in a gourd.

"Pills," Doctor Iskandar said. She took two bottles from the sack and held up one that was colored blue. "These are the antipyretics. They should ease her pain and lower the fever without harming the child. Starting tomorrow, you must give her three every day—one in the morning, one at noon, one at night. Remember, blue for the pain and fever. Three pills a day."

"I can remember," I said sharply.

Her smile reappeared for a heartbeat. "I imagine you can. Now these—" She held up the second bottle, which was colored green. "These are the antibiotics. They can help battle the infection but with some risk to the child. If your sister changes her mind, she takes these at the same time as the blue-bottle pills. One at morning, one at noon, one at night."

"She won't take them," I said.

"Maybe not," Doctor Iskandar said. "Call it selfishness. I want to rest better, knowing I gave her every chance."

She came with us to the building's front door—in case of interference, she said. All the time she talked about caring for children, what to eat, when to see a doctor, what signs meant the child was growing well, and which ones meant it sickened. Eko's attention had already shifted to the streets and planning a route back to the tunnels. Sri hovered over Yenny. I took Yenny's hand in mine. Warm and damp, but no longer scorching. The shot was working.

A touch on my shoulder made me start. Doctor Iskandar bent close, and underneath the soap and medicines, her scent was like summer flowers. "If she gets worse, bring her back to me," she said. "No charge. No matter what she decides about the child. Do you understand?"

"I understand."

It was only later, after we had turned from the busy streets back into the maze of alleys, that I realized she had not asked for payment this time either.

We retraced our path through the *tuhan* city and its tunnels, back into Bagluar and to our shelter. Sri urged Yenny to eat. She did, but I could see she had no appetite. After drinking down the last of our juice, Yenny crawled into her bed-nest and closed her eyes. The rest of us ate a meal of bananas and cold curried rice, the remnants of Yenny's latest bounty. Sri poured tea from the kettleful Eko had prepared that morning.

The rice tasted like ashes, and the tea like stale water to my tongue. Afterward, I knelt by Yenny's side. She breathed like one floating between asleep and not-asleep. Her skin felt cooler to my touch, but sweat matted her hair, and a salty-sour scent overlaid her sweeter one.

Eko and Sri busied themselves around us, but I hardly noticed what they did. I took out the medicine bottles from the plastic bag. Blue for fever. Green for the sickness in her heart. Both were poisons of a kind, I thought. One strong enough to damp Yenny's fever. One strong enough to kill both the sickness and her child.

"We need more juice and things. I'll go for them now," Sri said. She took a few coins from our money sack and slipped away.

Eko lingered a few moments longer, his gaze on Yenny's sleeping form. "I have some friends," he muttered. "People I know. They might tell us more about that *umatu.*"

I nodded. "I'll watch over her."

He paused, as though he wanted to say more, then followed his sister down the ladder.

I spent the next hours by Yenny's side. At times she slept. At times she woke, restless and thirsty. The tide rolled in, and from a distance came the whistling of gulls, the harsh cry of a solitary crane, and the hiss and gurgle of the waves. Yenny's scent called to me even now, while she lay sick and unaware, making my skin tighten. I withdrew from her side, picked up Eko's flute—now complete—and blew into the song-holes, mimicking the night-birds from home.

I have no home.

I laid the flute aside and took up my spice box. From its depths, I breathed in the scents of my homeland. Each breath recalled a different memory—of leaves crushed underfoot, of petals whirling through the emerald-green air, and of the touch of hands upon me as I slept. Memory gave way to dreams, handfuls and armfuls, all drifting downward like leaves from cloud-high jungle trees.

A groaning scattered my dreams like a handful of seeds.

I rolled onto my hands and knees and blinked away the sleep from my eyes. Hours had passed while I dreamed, and sunset was fading into twilight. Another muted creak came from below. A heavy foot stepped on our ladder. I set the spice box on the floor, slid the knife from my belt, and circled around into the shadows.

Soon a hand appeared at the trapdoor. With a groan, a man climbed through the trapdoor. It was him—the *umatu*—his hair tangled and sweaty, his clothes stained with Bagluar's filth. He stumbled to his feet, panting.

Yenny stirred, not quite awake. The man straightened up, suddenly aware of her presence, and his lips drew back in a hungry smile. When he started toward her, I called out, "What do you want?"

He stopped, spun toward me. For a moment, we stared at each other. Then he said, "Who the hell are you?"

"What do you want?" I asked again.

His hand twitched toward his belt. He had a knife, I thought. But then he lowered both hands and smiled. "You must be her brother," he said. "She told me about you. Good things."

He had a wheedling tone. I said nothing.

"Look," the man said, "I know you don't trust me, but we had a deal, me and her. Two months, every other day. Last time, she acted unhappy, and well, we had some words. I got worried, so I tracked her down."

"Liar," I said. "You aren't worried. Not about Yenny."

"That's not nice, kid."

I saw Yenny's eyes flutter open. I hefted my knife, tilted the blade upward so it caught the last rays of sunlight. The man's eyes widened. Then he grinned a false grin. "Nice. I've got one, too. Want to see?"

Before he could reach for his weapon, Yenny rolled into a crouch. The man jumped, then his lips pulled back again. He was sweating. "Hey, you woke up."

"Get out," Yenny said. "We're done."

His grin faded. "What's the matter? Don't you like the money? You liked it before."

"I don't like you."

"Liking's got nothing to do with it," he said. "Look, I'll pay double next time. Triple. Promise. But I don't want to skip any of our nights. That was our bargain. And I can explain everything, but first, I just need a few more times with you. It's important. Trust me, will you?"

He lunged for Yenny. Yenny dodged him, but the man cursed and spun around, much faster than I would have guessed. Swiftly I stood.

And changed.

Fire licked my skin and blood and bones. Within a heartbeat, my nipples shrank to points; a heaviness sank into my belly. Lower. Lower. Bones shifted. My scrotum swelled. My stub unfolded into a penis. Yenny's eyes brightened and her lips parted, as though she could taste my new scent on the salt-heavy air.

"*Doa selmat*," she whispered, smiling. "My brother is born."

Darting in, the man grabbed her wrist. "Enough with the games. You come with me."

Yenny twisted away, but he held her tight. They struggled, both cursing and fighting and kicking. I circled around, knife ready, but could not find an opening. Then Yenny bit down on his hand. He yelped and let go. She darted away.

"Damn it, bitch. All you had to say was *no*."

"I did," Yenny growled. "I did when I found the needles in your suitcase the last time I came to you. Needles and glass tubes. Do you think I would not remember how it was in the laboratory with the doctors? You are one of them."

"What the—? No, I'm not a fucking doctor. I told you. I like to watch you sleep. Can't you understand?"

He was lying. I saw it from his sweating face, his eyes that flickered and twitched like nervous bugs. He wasn't a doctor, but he didn't want just sex, not with his tubes and needles.

I swung my fist around and landed a hard blow in his ribs. His breath whooshed out. Before he could hit back, Yenny snatched up a loose board and swung it toward his head. He ducked one, two blows, before Yenny caught him on the shoulder. He stumbled backward, fumbling for the knife at his belt. I darted in, slashed his hand with my own knife, and caught his when it fell. Swearing, he lashed out with a kick. I fell backward. Before I could regain my footing, he scrambled down the ladder.

Yenny let the board drop and sank to her knees. "Get him," she said. "Before he tells the others."

She looked ill, and I hesitated a moment. Yenny gestured sharply. "Go!"

By the time I swung down the ladder, the man was already out the window and running fast. Two, three bounds got me to the window. I leaped through and pelted after him.

Along the wharves, through a maze of back streets, across an open square with half-burnt buildings looming against the purpling skies. He was faster and more clever than I expected; twice he nearly lost me. We were one and two handfuls of streets away from our home, when he dodged around yet another a corner, with me a double handful of steps behind.

A high-pitched scream stopped me.

Hunters. Their strong scent struck like a fist against my all my senses. I heard a gurgle and a crunching sound. Then the stink of fresh blood rolled through the air. Without another thought, I dove into the nearest doorway and hid among the heaps of broken tiles.

Breathe soft, heart still.

My breath fell silent. My scent changed to dust and salt and the faint ripe odor of decay. Handful by handful, I counted the moments, using the rhythm to keep myself from sobbing out loud. All the while I heard the sounds of their feast—teeth clicking, tongues rasping flesh from bone. Not once did I stir, not even to wipe away the tears. Shadowed dusk changed to moonlight, and still I waited, past first and second moonset, until no trace of *pemburu* scent remained in the air. Only then did I rise and creep back home.

Yenny was there, awake. So were Sri and Eko.

"What happened?" Sri asked.

"Hunters," I whispered. "He... They took him."

Sri stroked my hair, and murmured in comfort. Eko's mouth lifted into a thin smile. "Good. Maybe that will scare the others." He drew a heavy breath and looked from me to Yenny. "And there are more. You see, I went hunting, too. I talked to people. They said others with money had heard about your scientists, and about you. They wanted your blood and tissues to make new drugs, expensive ones for the *tuhan*."

Yenny shivered. "Why? Our blood is poison to *umatu*."

"That's not what the scientists thought," Eko said. "They thought they could make serums, a kind of magic, to help the body change itself, grow new parts, whatever."

Strong magic, I thought. But why the baby? Why give money to Yenny? Then I thought of the dormitories, clean and bright, and how other keepers might breed us like animals, just for their drugs. This *umatu* must have stolen seed from the laboratory, hoping to earn money from those *tuhan* doctors. Seeing Eko's face, I knew he had guessed as well.

"He's gone and it doesn't matter," I said. "Not today. Today Yenny still has the child. And the fever."

Yenny's gaze veered away and she clasped her hands over her elbows. "I won't give up the child," she whispered.

Eko touched her cheek. "You must. There's no other way."

She shivered again, glanced toward me, and away. I sniffed. A flicker of doubt colored her scent. "What is it?" I asked.

"Nothing," she said.

"Liar," I murmured.

Her mouth went tight, and then relaxed into a sad smile. "True. But I have my reasons."

"I don't care about your reasons," I said. "I care about you."

She shook her head. "It's dangerous."

"Tell *us*," Eko said. "And let us share the burden."

Her breath caught, and she glanced at Eko, who stroked her hair, his expression tense and waiting. At last, in a low quick voice, she said, "I know a way. Or I've heard of a way... But it *is* dangerous." Now she turned her bright gaze to me. "Tell me, Daksa-brother, how dearly do you love being my brother and not my sister?"

My stomach quivered. "What do you mean?"

"I mean." She paused. When Eko touched her cheek again, she leaned her face against his palm. "I mean that this way involves both pleasure and a burden."

Understanding, I licked my suddenly dry lips. "I will take that burden, then."

Yenny stepped away from Eko and placed her hands on my shoulders. "*Doa selmat*," she whispered. "Kiss me, my brother."

I took her in my arms and pressed my lips to hers. We exchanged kiss after long kiss, until our lips burned, while other hands brushed over us. Sri caressed Yenny. Eko lightly kissed my arms and neck. When at last I drew back to take a breath, Yenny slid off her shirt and trousers, and I did the same. Already slick with desire, we lay down on the floor. I crouched between her legs, and Yenny took me inside.

"Daksa-brother," she murmured.

"Yenny-sister," I whispered back.

Our bodies moved in ripples, like one wave following its cousin. My hands traveled over Yenny's body, and hers over mine, first light and soft, and then faster and with more urgency as we strained toward our climax. Yenny was babbling, crying, laughing. And I, I was a dancer, a hunter, a lover, a brother.

With a harsh cry, I arched backward. Hot liquid streamed from my body into hers—more and more, like a fountain, like the ocean itself, and then...

And then, like the tide turning, I felt a great rushing and churning inside. The mouth of my penis opened, stretching wider, so much I gasped in pain. Something wriggled inside it, a tiny round object carried by the flow of liquid returning from Yenny into me. Still my body rippled and twisted and reached for new shapes. The pain gripped me so hard, I no longer could see around me. When the pangs at last dissolved, I collapsed onto Yenny, still inside her.

"Your child," Yenny whispered. "Yours and mine together."

Very slowly she withdrew from me, as my penis folded into itself. More changes followed. My bones ached. My breasts swelled, my nipples pushed outward, my skin brightened to the color of new honey. I held my breath for a long handful of moments, and then I exhaled.

Our child, I thought. *Hers and mine*. Ah, no. Not hers but *his*.

Yenny-brother's skin had darkened to a dusky brown. His face had thinned, and his chest was flat and hard with muscles. A warm length pressed against my thigh.

"Does it hurt, my love?" he asked.

"Yes. Oh yes, it does."

Yenny caressed my cheek. The child within me stirred.

Remembrance

March 10th was too early for planting, too early (almost) for anything but raking away the detritus of winter. Kate didn't care. She had promised herself a gardening session this weekend. After a month of long hours in the lab, poring over chip schematics, it would do her good to grub about in the dirt.

Clouds streaked the sky overhead, promising rain within a few hours. Ignoring them, Kate removed the sheets of canvas from the old beds. She scooped the layer of mulch into the wheelbarrow handful by handful, then cleared away the twigs and leaves. The debris would make good compost, along with the deadwood from the peach and pear trees. Good thing she'd invested in the shredder.

A cool breeze fingered her hair. She rubbed her forehead with the back of her wrist, and breathed in the soft ripe scent of spring. If the rain held off, she could finish clearing the beds and cut a new edge. Maybe even replace the old railroad ties with those old bricks she scavenged from the renovation project downtown. After picking through heaps of dark red and brown bricks, Kate had unearthed a jumble of dusky pinks from the old municipal office building, and a handful of aged golden bricks from a long-abandoned bank.

A soft chime sounded—her cell. Kate wiped her hands hastily on her jeans and dug the phone out from her workbasket. The caller ID blinked "Unknown." No visuals either, just a black shiny square with a question mark in the middle.

"Hey, babe."

Jessica. Of course. She was calling from a semi-restricted zone at work, which explained the ID and blank vid screen. "Hey, yourself. What's up?"

"Sorry I'm late. Something got in my way."

Kate suppressed a sigh. Over the past six years, she had learned to expect the holdups and delays and unexpected changes in plans that came with Jessica, but she had never learned to enjoy them. "What now?"

"We need to talk."

A breeze kicked up, making Kate shiver in her flannel shirt. "About what?"

"I got the promotion."

Oh, yes. The promotion. "But that's good—"

She broke off. Not good, clearly. Not when she could almost hear the tension in Jessica's breathing. "What's wrong?" she said carefully.

"Not over the phone," Jessica said. "I'll be there in half an hour."

Before Kate could say anything, even good-bye, her phone chirped to signal the end of call. Kate stared at the blank screen a moment before she returned it to her basket. She glanced at her newly cleared flowers beds, the neat stacks of brush and deadwood, the boxes of bricks waiting for her. She sighed and picked up her tools to wipe them clean.

An hour later, she had showered and changed clothes. Still no sign of Jess, though Thatcher's headquarters were just a few miles away in the city's new corporate complex. Kate made coffee, nibbled on a left-over biscuit, then began to pace. Talk. Jessica liked mysteries, she told herself. She just wanted to tease Kate, push her buttons....

Jessica came through the front door, swinging her brief case. A few raindrops glittered in her dark brown hair, and her cheeks were flushed, as though she'd run the last few blocks. "Hey babe," she said as she dropped the briefcase. She followed up her words with a breezy kiss.

"Hey, yourself." Kate heard the odd combination of excitement and dread in Jessica's voice. Jessica wore her corporate uniform, she noticed—a dark gray suit with just a touch of flare to the skirt and discreet slits at the sleeves. Sexy and sleek and proper. Jessica called the look her Republican disguise. It made a good impression, she said, when she accompanied her superiors to government meetings.

Piecing together all the clues, Kate took a guess and asked, "What's the new assignment?"

Jessica flinched and laughed uneasily. "Smart girl, you. Yeah, I got the promotion, and it comes with a new assignment. Nice bump in pay, too."

Kate noticed that Jessica did not meet her gaze. "What's the catch?"

Another nervous glance, the briefest hesitation, before Jessica answered. "It's an off-site assignment. For the Mars Program. The government wants extra security specialists for their orbital transfer stations, and Thatcher won the main contract. We just got confirmation today. I'll be one of the unit supervisors on Gamma Station."

Kate had heard all about Gamma Station on the news. Alpha for Earth and Beta for the Moon, whose base had doubled in size during the past administration's watch. Now, after numerous delays, came Gamma, the first of the orbital transport stations that would serve as stepping stones toward the planned military base on Mars. Jessica had talked about nothing else these past three months.

"Just what you wanted," she said softly. "What else?"

Jessica smiled unhappily. "All the bad news at once, I see. Well, for one thing, it's a long assignment. Longer than usual."

"How long?"

Jessica smoothed back a wisp of hair that had escaped her braid. "Five years. They want continuity, they said. They're tired of retraining specialists every two years, and they want to cut back on expenses—especially with the draft up for debate." Her glance flicked up to meet Kate's. "But I have scheduled home visits built into the contract—twice a year—and bonuses for every month without any incidents. We could buy that house in New Hampshire."

We could get married, came the unspoken addendum. Even if only six states recognized that ceremony. And Kate did want that marriage, no matter how limited its legality, but Jessica's explanation skimmed over so much. Five years. Home visits were a week, no more. And *incident* was simply a euphemism for casualties. *My lover the mercenary,* she thought, unconsciously rubbing her hands together, as though to rid them of dirt.

"You accepted already," she said.

"Yes."

Rain clouds passed in front of the sun, momentarily darkening the living room, and a spattering of drops ticked against the windows. The room's auto lamps shimmered to on, but their light was colder, thinner, than the sun.

"I need to think about it," Kate said. "What it means."

Jessica nodded.

Another awkward paused followed.

"Would you like lunch?" Kate asked.

Jessica shook her head. "I'm sorry. I have a briefing this afternoon. That's the other thing you should know—I'm scheduled to leave in three weeks."

She knew, Kate thought. *She knew and didn't tell me.* Or maybe all that talk about Gamma was her way of warning Kate without saying anything outright.

"Then you better go," she said.

They stared at one another a moment. Then Jessica caught up her brief case and vanished through the doors, leaving Kate standing in the empty living room.

In one sense, Kate's workbench at XGen Laboratories resembled her garden. The lab allotted her a well-defined, if limited, workspace that she kept scrupulously neat. And she had her rows of tools laid out just where she needed them—some old and familiar and worn by frequent use, some of them shiny with special purpose.

Kate peered at the display, adjusted the zoom level with a few keystrokes, and studied the display again. The mask she wore over her nose and mouth itched, and she adjusted it. The customer had requested extra QA for these chips, and a high sample count to ensure the best quality. It meant more profit for XGen, but a longer, more tedious day for Kate. Still, she usually found the work soothing, working step by step through the checklist of tests, and marking down the results for each in the entry system. Today, however...

She sighed, removed the chip from the spectrometer, and placed the next one in its slot. At the next bench, Anne and Olivia talked quietly as they too worked through their allotment of gene-chips for the latest customer order. Anne tall and lean and brown, her dark abundant hair confined in a tight bun. Olivia short and skinny, with blonde spikes all over her head. The next row over, Aishia quietly argued politics with Stan and Marcel. Stan and Aishia had worked together for the past thirty years, and as far as everyone could tell, they had never once stopped arguing. Kate resisted the urge to ask them all for complete quiet, just this once.

In her distraction, she hit the wrong function key. Her system froze and blinked warnings at her. "Damn," she whispered. "Damn, stupid, damn, and damn it all again."

Anne looked up from her console. "What's wrong?"

"Nothing." Wearily, Kate punched in the key-combination to unlock the system, then went through the security codes again. XGen required several layers of identification, including fingerprint scans, these days. The clients liked that—no chance of hackers infiltrating the company and wreaking damage with sensitive products.

She noticed that Anne watched her with obvious concern. Kate shook her head. Anne was a good friend, but Kate didn't want to talk about Jessica, or the new assignment, or how they were almost fighting, but not quite.

Her system blinked a message, recognizing Kate. To her relief, it had not ditched her current entry. With a few more keystrokes, she resumed entering test codes and their results for the next chip. Concentrate on the screen and the analyzer, she told herself. Not on Jessica, who had returned late and left early, without giving Kate a chance to discuss the damned assignment. *As if discussing it would change anything*, Kate thought bitterly. She paused and drew a slow breath that did nothing for the tightness in her chest. *I should be used to it by now.*

Or not. They had never gone through the long separation most mercenary partners endured. Jessica's first few assignments had lasted only a few months apiece. The longest—a twelve month stint on the moon—had included frequent time downside. Kate had almost let herself believe that things would continue the same.

But no, terrorists didn't care about her loneliness, nor about keeping to convenient borders, such as the Middle East or selected regions in Asia. They traveled to New York and London these days. They were here, in New Haven. And now the stars.

The government draft had proved unpopular, and so private companies filled the void. In the bright new world of post Iraq, there would always be a post for a smart, brave warrior like Jessica. The money was good, the benefits even better, if you did not mind the ache of separation. And as Jessica pointed out, these companies hardly cared about her politics or her sex life. They only asked her to be dependable and discreet.

I hate it.

"Hey, Kate."

It was Anne, peering at her over the top of her console. A tiny frown made a crease between her brows.

"What's up?" Kate asked. "Problem with the spectral unit?" The new equipment had not proved quite as flawless as the salesperson claimed.

"Always," Anne said dryly. "But for once, it's not about work. Olivia and I were talking about going out tonight with Remy and some others. Maybe grabbing a bite at the new Indian restaurant, then see what's playing at the York Square. Cordelia and her husband might show up."

"I don't know…" She didn't think Jessica would like a night out, not with things so tense. Or then again, maybe a night out would help. "Let me check with Jessica."

She punched in the speed code and waited. And waited. After a dozen chimes, the phone switched her over to voice mail. Kate clicked phone shut. If Jessica were in Thatcher's high-security zones, she would have no cell access. She closed her eyes and rubbed her forehead to cover the disappointment. *Think of it as practice*, she thought, *for when Jess is really gone.*

"No luck?" Anne asked.

"Busy," Kate said. Which in a way was true. "I guess you're stuck with just me."

Anne smiled. "Hey, I don't mind."

The lab cleared out within minutes of the five o'clock chimes. But they would all be working overtime tomorrow, Kate thought, as she skinned out of her lab suit and into jeans and a T-shirt. The mask always left her hair a mess. She ran her fingers though the curls and tried to revive them.

"You look fine," Anne told her.

"Liar," Kate said.

Olivia was repairing her makeup, while Aishia recapped her argument with Stan. "He thinks with his balls," she muttered. "The right one. That accounts for his idea that God made guns so we can blow up our neighbors."

"Seems like they're blowing us up, too," Olivia said as she applied eyeliner. "Ask Remy. Her brother was on that bus in DC with the suicide kid."

"He's alive."

"Barely. A lot of others aren't."

Olivia and Aishia continued bickering as they left the lab and passed through the corporate security into the gated parking lot. Remy waited outside the parking lot, leaning against a dented lemon-yellow VW. Olivia broke off in mid-argument and waved cheerily.

"Who else is driving?" Anne said. "I took the bus today."

"Me," Aishia said. "If you don't mind the mess."

"That's fine. Kate?"

Kate barely heard them. She had sighted another familiar figure through the fence.

Jessica. She came here even without me calling.

A very jittery Jessica, to be sure, dressed even more formally than the day before—all dark gray and ivory, with polished nickel studs in her ears that winked every time she swung her head. "Hey, girl. Hungry?" she called out.

"Starving," Kate called back. She hurried through the security procedures—ID card presented to the guard, palm against the reader, the retinal scan unit. When the gate clicked open, she ran through and into a hug from Jessica.

"Time off for good behavior," Jessica murmured. "Come on. I'm starved for some good Italian food."

They retired to a diner a few blocks away, on Chapel Street. Jessica ordered an extra large helping of everything, but when her dishes arrived, she fiddled with her salad, and picked at the heap of calamari. Kate watched in silence, her own appetite slowly draining away.

"What's wrong?" she asked softly.

Jessica shrugged. "You mean, besides the usual?"

Kate nodded.

Jessica stabbed a piece of lettuce with her fork. "I hate us fighting. I hate going away for weeks and months and years. But it's what I do. And it's better for you and everyone else that my job is out there and not right here in New Haven."

"I know," Kate said quietly. "I'm sorry."

"Don't be. You didn't say anything wrong. It's just a bitch, the whole thing. So I was thinking—"

She broke off and ate rapidly for a few moments, while Kate waited, breathless, for her to continue that tantalizing sentence.

Jessica pushed her plate away and wiped her mouth with a nervous flick of the napkin. "I had another briefing," she said. "Thatcher's R&D department is testing a new device, something XGen prototyped for us last year. Do you remember?"

Kate shook her head. XGen was small, but its R&D department kept to itself. QA usually saw new products only after the customer had okayed the prototypes.

"Anyway," Jessica went on, "there's a new chip, and they want me and some others for testing. It's for recording sensory input from a soldier's body. Sight. Touch. Smell. Even subvocals. Actually, I already volunteered for the implant and... I was hoping you would, too."

"What?" Her own meal forgotten, Kate stared at Jessica. "Are you insane? Why would I volunteer for a Thatcher project?"

Jessica glanced away, her cheeks turning pink. "I thought… I'll be gone a long time, and I thought… We could use it for ourselves. It might make things easier."

Kate swallowed with some difficulty. "You're kidding."

"No, I'm not. What's the problem?"

How like Jessica to forget who else might view those recordings. "The review board," she managed to say.

"Oh, them." Jessica dismissed those concerns with an airy wave of her hand. "They read my emails and they censor my vids. I'm used to it."

But I'm not.

Jessica put down her fork and clasped Kate's hands. Hers were lean strong hands, callused from handling who knew what. Warm and gentle hands. Kate loved them. She didn't want to share them with anyone.

"You don't like it. I know," Jess said softly. "But do you understand?"

Reluctantly Kate nodded. "Yes. No. Of course I don't like it. But then, I don't like you going away."

"Neither do I. But Kate… Five years is a fucking awful long time. Even with the home visits. At least consider the idea. Please."

Kate released a sigh. "I will. Consider it, that is. I can't promise more."

Jessica squeezed her hands. "That's all I ask."

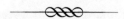

With spring's arrival came the soft soaking rains, interspersed by damp gray skies that echoed the mist rising from the warming earth. If the sun broke through a day here or there, Kate hardly noticed. She neglected her garden for Jessica's company, and avoided glancing at the calendar.

Last day, she thought, watching Jessica check over her gear. Jess wore a plain jumpsuit that announced its military purpose. Her train left at ten—one hour left. Now fifty-nine minutes. Now—

"Check and double-check," Jessica said, straightening up with a grunt. "Damn. I'm getting old for this shit. Just as well they only allow us two bags."

Two modest bags, stuffed with books and off-duty clothes and several mementos from Kate, all of them cleared by Thatcher's security regulations. Kate touched the implant at the base of her skull, the connection points hidden beneath her hair. The operation had taken more time than she expected—more than a day for the operation itself, and another three days for recovery and training, with subsequent training sessions scheduled over the next few weeks.

"I miss you already," she said suddenly.

"Hey." Jessica pulled her into a hard hug. "I miss you, too. But let's not get ahead of ourselves. We still have an hour."

"Fifty-six minutes," Kate said into Jess's shoulder. "And no, we don't have time for one more…"

She felt Jessica shake with silent laughter. "I wish we did. Come on. Help me get this stuff into the car."

Kate's internal clock ticked down the minutes as they loaded bags into the car and drove to New Haven's newly renovated train station. A winding ramp brought them over the flood zone and into the parking garage. If you ignored the trash floating on the oily waves below, the view was breathtaking. The planners had taken that into account: the moving sidewalks and glass-paneled elevators showed only the Sound and the blurred outline of Long Island in the distance. Far below, the shoreline highway curved above the open water.

Jessica slung one bag over her shoulder. She swatted Kate away from the second bag. "Might as well get used to the weight now," she said. "In six days, they won't weigh anything at all."

Thirty minutes left. Twenty-three. Passing through station security took just a few moments at this hour. Kate and Jessica sat side-by-side on the platform bench, hands barely touching in this much too public area. At fifteen minutes, the train squealed into the station, filling the air with a sharp electric odor.

Jessica quickly squeezed Kate's hand. "Hey," she whispered. "It's time."

Not yet, Kate wanted to say, but she stood silently as Jessica gathered her two bags, then pulled out her e-card for the conductor. Seven minutes. Five. Three.

"Kate."

In that one word, Kate heard a tone in Jessica's voice that she never had before. "Hey," she said.

"Hey." Jessica leaned forward and kissed Kate firmly on the lips. Kate caught a whiff of Jessica's cinnamon perfume, a fainter one of her green tea shampoo. One brown strand fell from its braid and brushed against Kate's cheek. Jessica tucked the strand behind her ear. "Six months to the first visit," she whispered.

And then the clock ticked down to zero, and she was gone.

Throughout April and early May, Kate worked to undo the early neglect of her garden. She cleared out the weeds and repaired the old border. She added fresh mulch and compost, and with judicious watering, teased the roses and irises into luscious blooms. She even expanded the beds to include a small vegetable patch, which the deer promptly attacked.

At work, she had the impression that her friends and co-workers had divvied up watches over her. Singly and in groups, they took her out to lunch (Aishia, Anne, and once Stan), or invited her to the movies (Anne, Cordelia), or on shopping expeditions (Olivia, with or without Remy).

The constant invitations irritated her at first. Over the weeks, however, she learned to accept their well-meant attentions. It helped, after all, to distract her from counting the hours, days, and weeks, without Jessica. Even so, she found herself calculating Jessica's progress away. One day of train travel. Five more days to launch. Another month until Jessica arrived at Gamma Station.

Kate had allowed herself just one letter for each week, emailed to Jessica in care of Thatcher. Thatcher would screen the contents and forward the message via satellite to Gamma Station. Jessica had fired off one brief message before the launch. Since then nothing.

She's busy, Kate told herself. *Reviewing security procedures. Coordinating her crew assignments with others in Thatcher and the military. Handling any crises...*

No. Bad idea to think about crises. Better to concentrate on the mundane tasks of personnel records and fitness reports and all the other tedious paperwork Jessica always complained about.

She parked the car in the too-empty driveway and gathered briefcase and groceries from the back seat. Following an almost-predictable schedule, Anne had invited Kate to dinner, but Kate had refused, wanting one night to herself. Maybe she could download a vid, or eat too much popcorn, or do all the things other people talked about doing when they had the house to themselves.

Still mulling over her options, she unlocked the door and scooped up the mail from the carpet. Bills. Flyer from the local ACLU. Credit card offers. A small reinforced envelope with the return address: *Thatcher Security Operations.*

Jess. She wrote.

Kate abandoned everything else in the entryway. Her pulse dancing, she hurried into the living room. A letter. A long one. Even sooner than she expected. Jessica must have saved up her letters and transcribed them the moment she arrived at Gamma.

She took up a letter opener from the letters desk and slit the envelope carefully. Nothing. Perhaps the envelope's padded interior—made from a strange soft material—blocked the contents. She shook the envelope gingerly. A micro disc tumbled into her lap.

Kate drew a sharp breath. She recognized the disc from her training sessions. Reflexively, she touched the knob at the base of her skull. No one at work knew about this device. She had not dared to tell them, not even Anne. Aishia would lecture her about man-machine interfaces and their risks. Olivia would make jokes. Anne might say nothing, but Kate had learned to read her friend's subtle changes in expression. Whatever name you put on her reaction, it would not be a positive one.

The disc gleamed red in the late sunset. Kate touched its rim—a faint dull spot remained where her fingertip had rested. Damn. The technicians had warned her how sensitive these discs were. They had provided her with a supply of special cleaning fluid, along with admonitions about overusing the stuff.

Kate vented a breath, and carefully inserted the disc back into its envelope. Again she touched the knob. *Jess. Oh Jess. What are we doing?*

She took a few moments to put the groceries away—extending the anticipation, or avoiding the disc, she wasn't sure which. Then she climbed the stairs to the tiny office next to their bedroom. The Thatcher machine stood on her desk, in the corner behind stacks of books and papers and her gardening magazines, untouched since the Thatcher tech has installed it weeks ago.

Kate cleared away the magazines and sat down. Squinted at the machine. It looked like any piece of lab equipment—a low sleek ivory box with several touch pads labeled in red. A half dozen indicator lights ran along the top edge. These too were clearly marked. She skimmed a finger along the side and found the recessed slot for the discs.

You're stalling.

Damn straight, as Jessica would say.

A touch of the power switch, and the machine hummed into life, its lights blinking through a series of test patterns. Kate cleaned the micro disc, just as the technicians told her, then slid the disc into its slot. It clicked into place.

Now the tricky part.

She touched a side panel, which slid open to reveal the connector cable with its slim square terminator. She uncoiled the cable and brushed her hair away from the knob in her skull. The terminator and her own connector port would slide open together when oriented correctly and pressed together.

She felt the click reverberate through her bones. Her skin prickled and she felt faintly queasy. Psychosomatic, she told herself. She had done the same thing a hundred times in the training lab with no ill effects. She pressed the touch pad marked PLAY.

A pale green light blinked. Kate's vision went dark.

Hey, babe.

Kate heard, felt a cough.

Testing, one, two three…

Soft self-conscious laughter followed, with an echo soon after, as though Jess sat in a small enclosed space. Her cabin aboard the shuttle? With a shiver, Kate realized she felt heavy fabric encasing her arms and legs. The air smell charged and faintly stale. She blinked, wishing she could see what Jessica saw. Thatcher had warned her she would get no visuals. The prototype

could handle them, but her particular machine had that feature
disabled. A matter of security, the tech had explained.

Hey.

Kate jumped at the sound of Jessica's voice next to her, inside
her.

*So, like. I guess this is working. Harder than vidding a message,
but damn, after going through that operation, I might as well use
the machine.*

Pause. Kate felt her chest go tight. Was that her body's
reaction, or Jessica's? Then she felt warm breathe leaking between
tense lips. A subdued laugh. The words, *Hey, babe. I miss you.
Later.*

Without warning, the machine clicked, and Kate's vision
returned so abruptly, she swayed from the vertigo. If she closed
her eyes, she could still feel the weight of Jess's pressure suit,
still taste the shuttle's recycled air. *Hey, babe,* she thought. *Don't
make it too much later.*

After some procrastination, Kate recorded a brief reply, using
the same disc Jessica sent her. She wished she could keep the
recording to play later, but Thatcher had insisted on their return.
Proprietary materials, the security manager had explained.

It took her several tries before she was satisfied. Jessica had
had it right—making the recording was far more difficult than
reading one. What to say? How to react, when every sensation
impressed itself onto that tiny disc, to be reviewed by Thatcher
research and security personnel?

In the end, Kate recorded a brief description of her garden,
one of the roses in her palm, where its velvet-soft petals tickled
her skin. *Later*, she whispered, and tapped END RECORD.

Jessica sent three more recordings over the next six weeks, all of them brief, all of them ending with a whisper-soft kiss. She supplemented those with longer text messages forwarded from Thatcher by email. Kate found the longer messages more frustrating than the brief micro-recordings; more than once, Thatcher's censors had deleted apparently random sections of text, badly garbling Jessica's meaning. Kate was tempted to add something inflammatory, but she restrained herself. Thatcher might not care about personal lives, but they were as humorless as any federal spooks. Still, the thought that Thatcher observed their correspondence bothered her. You might think that some aspects of life were private, she thought. Even now, even in these days of constant surveillance and the uneasy comprises between freedom and security.

And so, the weeks rolled from spring to summer. One hot July evening, Kate parked her car in the driveway far later than usual—XGen had another rush order from a government super-contractor. Muzzy from the long hours in the lab, she had thoughts only of dinner and cold tea, and when she picked up the mail from the carpet, she almost didn't register the envelope from Thatcher.

Then recognition clicked into place. Not just another envelope, but one with a disc. Dinner could wait, she thought. She hurried upstairs to her office and slid the disc into the machine. The terminator plug clicked into place, and the familiar black-brown veil dropped over her vision…

Hey, lover. Something new this time.

A warm hand pressed against Kate's (Jessica's?) breast. Kate drew a sharp breath as she realized that Jessica wore no clothing. What was she thinking? What about Thatcher—

The hand slid over her breast, cupped the flesh a moment and squeezed, making Kate gasp. No time wasted. The hand skimmed over her belly, and paused briefly to cover her sex. Possession, said that gesture. Kate felt the doubled warmth from her body and Jessica's at the same time. She had just time to muffle a gasp of pleasure when three fingers plunged into her vagina, slid out, and pinched the clitoris with practiced skill. Heat blossomed outward, upward. Their nipples contacted to hard painful points. The fingers plunged deeper inside. And again, but faster, more urgent. Kate's, (Jessica's) breath went ragged as she panted, *Oh, god... yes... oh... my...*

Kate's office blinked into existence.

She leaned against the desk, shivering in spite of the July warmth. Her groin ached from half-fulfilled passion, and a ripe musky scent filled the air. Very faint, almost like a memory, she could still smell a trace of Jessica's favorite perfume.

Too much. Not enough. I can't stand it.

Kate reached up to remove the terminator from her skull. Her hands shook. Deep inside, her muscles tensed, rippled, stretched, as though pleading for release. She paused and licked her lips. Slowly she reached for PLAY again.

For three days, she wavered on how to reply. She wished (again) she could keep a copy of Jessica's recording. She wished she could keep her response private. Neither was possible. Nor could she send back a simple text message. In the end, she closeted herself in the office with a glass of chilled Pouilly Fuissé and a tightly held memory of Jessica's recording.

She shucked off her T-shirt and jeans. Slid her panties over her hips and let them drop onto the floor. Though she had no audience, not even a virtual one, Kate tried to act as though she did. It would put her into the mood for what she had planned.

Perfume over her breast, at the base of her throat, behind her knees. Blinds tilted just so to let in the sunlight, but keep the room private. She had thought about lying on the floor, except the cord didn't reach far enough. She would have to make do with her office chair and her imagination.

Kate inserted the terminator, then drank a long slow swallow of wine. As an afterthought, she rolled the wine glass over her bare skin. The cold wet surface raised a trail of goose bumps that made her shiver with anticipation. She pressed her left hand over her mons. Warm and damp already. It was as though she only needed to think of Jessica, to have her body respond.

She touched RECORD.

Hey, babe. Here's something for you.

We are a duet, Jessica whispered time and again. *My fingers burrow through my pubic hair, twice over. Once with me, making me shake with desire, once with you, Kate. I'm soaked, a puddle of want. Want you. Now, girl. In and out. Again. More. Now I trail the wetness up between my breasts and paint myself with cum.*

Whatever Jessica said, Kate heard weeks later. Whatever Jessica did—how her fingers pinched Kate's nipples, how her tongue licked wet fingers and tasted her smoky climax—repeated itself in Kate's lonely office.

You are my succubus, Kate whispered back. *You take me as a ghost would, by invading my mind. As I do with you, my love. As I do with you.* She crushed her mouth against her hand, and slid the new vibrator into her own vagina. Her lips closed hard around the silky shaft. An electric pulse gripped her clitoris and rippled through her belly, up her spine. Fireworks. Hot and dazzling. She threw back her head and cried out.

Over the next three months, Kate and Jessica exchanged recordings every week. Jessica sent text messages twice a week, long rambling letters about the insipid food, the jokes her crew made, the techniques she and others used to make life in tight quarters more bearable. *Like our little not-so-secret,* she said once.

Kate disliked Jessica's jokes about their situation, but she understood them. She read on as Jessica described more about the implants.

It's a clever little toy, Jessica wrote. *Thatcher wants to run more tests once they develop their high-capacity modules, but the basic technology works. It even has a few tricks the technicians didn't tell us at first. Remember the discs and how we have to record over them? Well, the chip has a smidge of memory itself, and if you press* PLAY *three times fast, then hold down* PROGRAM *and* RECORD *together, you can store a few moments in the chip and replay it later. Here's how…*

Saturday. Kate knelt and surveyed her garden. A lush rainy summer had produced more squash and beans and tomatoes than she could give away. Now, as the season drifted into autumn, she busied herself with preparing the beds for winter.

"How much mulch do you actually need?" Anne asked. "And could you make a tongue-twister from that question?" She had volunteered to help Kate with the day's work. Later, they would go to a neighborhood rummage and art festival. Aishia had promised to join them.

"All the mulch," Kate answered, ignoring the question about tongue-twisters. "They say we'll have a colder winter than usual. Unless you think we should dig up all those bulbs…"

"Don't," Anne said quickly.

Kate grinned. "Thought not."

They set to work, Anne digging up weeds and Kate mixing the soil and compost. Kate had acquired a new supply of micro-insulating fabric that claimed a fifty-percent improvement over other materials. If she alternated mulch with the fabric, she might get away with keeping even the tulips in the ground.

"I always wished I had a garden," Anne said. "Though I'm not very good at keeping the plants alive. Where did you hear about the colder winter?"

"Almanac. Good old-fashioned almanac. Though this one is online."

Anne laughed. "And here I thought we were high-tech."

More than you know, Kate thought. She had not confided in anyone, not even Anne, about the experimental implants. *A private matter*, she thought. *As private as Thatcher allows.*

They dispatched the latest weed crop and started on splitting the lilies, which had multiplied since last year. It was easier with a friend, Kate thought, and the work soothed as nothing else could. She could almost forget the constant ache in her chest that had begun with Jessica's departure. *My garden, my refuge,* she thought as she set another bulb back into the ground. These days, even her garden seemed a less a refuge than before. Prices climbing. The shrill debates in Congress and blogs. The noisy protests at universities.

A brisk knock sounded at the front door, followed by the faint chimes of the doorbell. Kate dusted off her hands. "If that's Aishia, she's early," she said. "Unless she wants to help with covering the beds."

Anne smoothed dirt over another planting. "It might be Olivia. She said something about dropping by."

"With or without Remy?"

Anne grimaced. "Without."

Their latest and loudest quarrel showed no signs of ending. Kate could not remember when she'd last seen Remy's lemon-yellow Bug waiting outside XGen's parking lot. "Do you think it's serious this time?"

Anne shrugged. "Who knows?"

Another knock echoed through the crisp, new-autumn air. Louder. Clearly impatient. Definitely not Aishia or Olivia. "Coming," Kate called out.

She heard a man's voice. Several, talking amongst themselves. Dominionists? Surely they had learned their lessons after Jessica's pointed lecture. She gave up on scrubbing the dirt from her hands and hurried around the brick path that led through the side flower beds, into the front yard.

Three men stood on her front porch. She took in their gray suits, their humorless expressions. All of them middle-aged. All of them bland and competent, in the way she associated with bureaucrats.

"Ms. Morell?" one said. "Ms. Kate Morell?"

Her skin prickled with sudden dread. "Yes. I'm Kate Morell. Can I help you?"

He came forward and extended a hand. "I'm from Thatcher Enterprises, ma'am," he said. "I'm very sorry, but I have bad news for you. It's about Ms. Anderson."

I don't want to know. I don't. I don't.

"Go away," she said thickly.

"Ma'am."

"I mean it."

Anne hurried to Kate's side. "Kate. Maybe we should go inside."

Kate shrugged away from Anne's tentative touch, but she knew Anne was right. She could not stop them from telling her. Today. Tomorrow. Either she'd hear the news from these gray grim men, or she'd learn the details from the evening newscast. Better she heard it here, now, under the open sunny sky. "Fine. Tell me what happened."

With a glance at his companions, the man complied. Thatcher had sent their best people, ones trained to deliver their news in soft, concerned voices. Numb, and growing number, Kate listened to how terrorists had infiltrated another security firm's personnel. One, the suicide bomber, had assembled his deadly cargo during a brief stopover on the station. Moment before their shuttle was to launch for the next segment of their journey, he had detonated his bomb. Everything destroyed. All personnel dead. The method was old, as old as Iraq and Palestine and all the troubled countries on Earth.

"Nothing left," she whispered.

The Thatcher man hesitated. "I'm sorry, but no. They're salvaging whatever they can, but the explosion scattered..." His voice died away a moment, undoubtedly as he realized what images his words called up. "We have something for you, however."

Kate came alert. "What do you mean? You said—"

"A final transmission," he said. "You can refuse, of course. We've edited them for any sensitive material..."

He held out a packet. Kate took it greedily. "How much time do I have? For listening?"

Another awkward pause. "The company understands how difficult—"

"The company," Kate said crisply, "understands nothing. How much time?"

The man stiffened at her tone. "We would prefer you return the machine next week. Monday, if possible. We can schedule an operation later to remove the implant."

She nodded. "Very well. Now, please go."

To her relief, the three did not argue. Kate watched them ease their anonymous gray vehicle from the curb. The packet felt solid and heavy in her arms, like an anchor, which was good, because she had the sense of floating a few inches above the ground. Anne had not budged from her side, and Kate could sense her concern.

"Anne."

"Yes, Kate."

"Please go. I'd rather be alone."

"Are you sure—"

"Quite sure."

Anne hesitated, then with a murmured farewell, she too was gone.

A brief recording. The last ever.

Hey, Kate. Kate, my love. Kate, my darling lover. Good god in heaven, I miss you. I'm going a little crazy up here. Guess you could tell from that session. Ya think? Not sure what kind of notation they'll make in my fitness report, but what the hey. They asked for a peek inside my skull.

A shaky laugh. A pause. Kate felt and heard Jessica's breathing quicken. Was it a prelude to sex? So hard to tell. For all that the recording slipped Kate inside Jessica's skin, it showed her nothing of her lover's thoughts or emotions. Only clues, pieced together in retrospect.

I miss you, Jessica said suddenly. *It's busy here. We're having another meeting this afternoon. Commander wants tighter security. Can't say more, of course. It's just...*

Kate felt warm lips pressed against her fingertips, then those same fingertips brushed against her cheek. Her vision blurred from brown-black shadows into the dim light of her office.

One last kiss, she thought. The last one.

She closed her eyes and let the grief take over.

She called in sick on Monday. No one questioned her. Probably Anne had warned their supervisors about the situation. Kate croaked a mirthless laugh. *Situation.* What a weasel word, as Jessica would say. As bad as *incident.*

Her throat caught on another sob. *Sorry*, she thought. *I have no more tears. I cried them all away.*

She poured herself another cup of coffee. Drank it without noticing. Her stomach hurt, but she couldn't tell if it hurt because she had cried too hard, or if she was simply hungry. She sighed and with great reluctance, she climbed the stairs to her office.

The machine sat in the middle of her empty desk. Around midnight on Saturday, she had nearly pitched the damned thing into trash. Only the thought of how much fuss Thatcher would make had stopped her. Now she stared at it with loathing.

I hate you. You gave me ghosts.

Ghosts of Jessica. Ghosts of an ersatz marriage, while they waited out yet another interminable period, for yet another intangible bit of progress. Even as she hated the machine, she found herself sliding the disc into its slot and inserting the terminator into its port.

… Hey, Kate. I miss you…

She hardly needed the machine to replay that sequence inside her memory, but the machine and chip combined to give her a more vivid remembrance, with details of touch and scent and sound she could never recall on her own.

…the chip has a smidge of memory itself, and if you press PLAY three times fast…

Kate swallowed against the bitter taste in her mouth. Make some coffee, she told herself. Wake up before you do something truly stupid.

She touched PLAY. Three times fast, followed by pressing PROGRAM and RECORD together. Count to ten. A series of lights blinked success. Kate let out a breath. There. She had done it. One last kiss. Saved… Not forevermore, but for a short while, at least.

She called Thatcher at noon. By mid-afternoon, they had carried away the machine. One representative stayed behind to schedule Kate's operation to remove the implant.

"Later," Kate said.

"I'm afraid that later isn't one of the categories," the woman said with a rueful smile. "We need a more definite date."

"Next year," Kate said. "Or is that too definite?"

At the woman's shake of her head, however, she relented. "November 21st. From what your technicians tell me, I will need one day for the operation, another three or four in recovery. That means sick leave or vacation time—depending on how my HR department categorizes the operation. Whatever. My project has a few unmovable deadlines before mid-November. I'm sure you understand."

"We do," said the woman. She tapped a few keys on her cell, frowned, tapped a few more. "Yes, we can arrange something on that date. You'll spend Thanksgiving in the hospital, but I'm sure you knew that."

Kate smiled faintly. "Yes, I knew that."

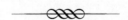

Late November. A dark cold Tuesday evening.

Tomorrow Kate would drive to Thatcher Operations. There, a technician would review the paperwork, ask her some final questions. The company surgeons would inject her with a sedative, then transport her to Yale-New Haven Hospital, where they had scheduled the operation. All very neat. No security leaks. No chance for medical mishaps. Kate had signed all the releases beforehand.

"Will I remember anything?" she had asked.

"Nearly," the technician had reassured her.

The technician had it wrong, Kate thought, as she drifted out the back door, into her winter-bare garden. If she had her druthers, she would remember…

…*nothing at all.*

She sank onto the hard frosted ground at the edge of her garden. Sheets of micro-insulation blanketed half the beds, where she had made a last attempt at normal life. The other half lay bare, with brittle stalks of dead plants poking through the dirt. One shriveled lily bulb lay where she'd left it that Saturday. Dead. Her breath puffed into a cloud. Just like Jessica. She probed inside her heart for some reaction—grief, anger, anything. Nothing. *Dead like me,* she thought.

By now she could trigger the memory without thinking. Sensation washed over her. That same familiar sense of urgency. The words *I miss you.* Kate rubbed the spot where she still felt the impress of warm lips against her hand, Jessica's hand. *She's inside me. Always will be. Doesn't matter if they rip the implant from my brain.*

Her chest felt tight, or was that Jessica's tension as she hurried through that last recording? Kate drew a shuddering breath. Blinked, and felt her frozen eyelashes prick her cheeks. The words *I miss you.* The kiss, but now her hands were numb, and she barely felt Jess's lips. *Again,* she told herself.

She had lost track of the minutes and hours when she heard a voice. A familiar one, but not Jessica's.

Go away, she thought.

The voice called out her name. A hand jostled her shoulder. Kate closed her eyes. Nothing to see anyway. The world had gone brown and black, with pinpoints of silver. In her imagination, the pinpoints whirled around, stopped, whirled again. She thought she saw the outline of Jessica's face when they paused. All too soon the image broke apart. *Show me again,* she tried to whisper, but her lips were cracked and frozen, her tongue clumsy from disuse.

Again that insistent voice. Anne's voice (good, kind, generous Anne) speaking to her, her tone anxious. It was hard to track time, here between repetitions of Jessica's last recording, and so it might have been minutes or days later when more hands took hold of Kate's arms. Voices spoke over her head in short phrases.

Careful now.

Gurney ready?

IV for this one.

Oxygen, too. Gotta bring the core temperature up.

Lucky the streets aren't slick.

We better hurry.

And then the thin, high wail of a siren.

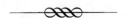

Six o'clock.

Soft chimes marked the hour. Outside, night already blacked out the skies. A dull yellow glow from the city lights seeped upward from the horizon. Winter. Even colder than the almanac had predicted, Kate thought. The air had an antiseptic smell, no matter how the nurses tried to hide it with sweet-smelling sprays.

Footsteps sounded from the corridor, then, predictably, a light tapping at her door. She said nothing. Anne would come in, or not, just as she had every day for the past three weeks.

The door swung open, and Anne leaned around the corner. Snow dusted her coat. Her cheeks were red, as though she had spent some time outdoors.

"Hey," she said softly. "Do you mind a visit?"

Kate shrugged, silent.

Anne sighed and came into the room. Kate watched her methodically unbutton her coat and hang it from the hook inside the door. A nurse peered into the room and greeted Anne, before asking Kate which meal she preferred for dinner.

"I don't care," Kate whispered. "You choose for me."

Anne frowned. She and the nurse exchanged a look. "What about the steak?" Anne said. "Or maybe the pasta—I hear the cook knows his sauces."

Good, kind, patient Anne, who never once failed to visit Kate. She had stayed at the hospital while the doctors worked to counteract the hypothermia. She came the next day when they removed the implant, and she dealt with Thatcher's representatives. Not that Anne told Kate these things. It was Cordelia or Olivia or the others who told Kate how Anne had saved her life.

As if I wanted my life saved.

But even irritation was too much effort. She sighed again and closed her eyes. She had developed the trick of pretending to sleep. If she held the pose long enough, she often did. She heard whispers as Anne evidently spoke with the nurse about Kate's meal. The door clicked shut. There was a scraping sound as Anne took her usual seat by the window.

"I stopped by your house," Anne said, just as though they were having an ordinary conversation. "Cordelia reminded me that you never had a chance to finish prepping your garden for the winter. I asked at one of the garden centers, and they gave me some suggestions."

Kate suppressed the urge to ask what suggestions. She felt a prick of guilt about her gardens, then annoyance that she felt guilty.

Meanwhile, Anne continued her recitation. "… Cordelia and I raked the yard. We trimmed back the shrubs and vines and ran those through the shredder. We even cleaned out the compost heap and finished covering the flower beds."

Kate"s eyes burned with unshed tears. Only Anne. Only Anne would remember how much Kate loved her gardens. But what good were gardens in the winter? What good were gardens if you were alone?

"… Olivia and Remy came by to help, too. I don't know if I told you, but they've made up and now they're talking about finding a house together…"

Tears leaked from her eyes. Surprising after weeks of numbness. She swiped them away.

"Kate?"

A tiny stab in the region of her heart. Insistent. Unwelcome. "No," Kate whispered. "I don't want to." Then louder. "No. No, no, no."

Her voice scaled up, louder and louder, until her voice cracked, and she burst into weeping—loud angry sobs that tore at her throat. Kate pummeled the bed, trying to beat away the grief. She didn't want tears. Or misery. None of that could bring Jessica back.

Arms gathered her into a tight hug. Anne. Anne capturing her hands so they could not scratch or beat or harm herself. Anne strong and gentle at the same time, who rocked Kate back and forth while she held her close. "I'm sorry. I'm sorry," she murmured over and over. "I said the wrong things. All the wrong things. I'm so sorry, Kate. So sorry."

"I hate it," Kate mumbled into Anne's shoulder.

"You should hate it," Anne said fiercely. "Hate me, if you like. Hate the world. I'd rather you did, than feel nothing. Oh god, Kate, I wish I could do something *real*. I wish—"

She broke off and pulled away from Kate. Shocked, Kate felt her own grief subside for the moment. Only now did she take in details she had not noticed before. How Anne's cheeks were wet with tears. And her eyes were red, as though she had not slept well the past few weeks. But Anne never wept, she thought, never lost her temper. She was the even keel they all depended upon.

"Anne?"

Anne wiped her eyes with the back of her hand. "Sorry. That was selfish of me."

No, I'm the selfish one, Kate thought.

A knot deep inside her flexed, as though an unused muscle tried to work itself loose. Instinctively she reached up and touched Anne's face. Anne flinched. Her eyes went wide and dark, and color spread over her cheeks. So many tiny clues, like droplets of watering coalescing into realization.

"How long?" Kate whispered.

"Does it matter?" Anne blew out a breath. "I should go."

"No. Stay."

They stared at one another for a long uncomfortable moment. Snow tapped against the window pane, and out in the corridor, a light sizzled and popped.

"What are you saying?" Anne said at last.

The knot inside Kate pinched tight. Too fast. Too soon. Far too soon for anything. She'd spoken before thinking.

"I'm not sure. I—I need a friend."

A ghost-like smile came and went on Anne's face. "I make a decent friend, they tell me."

So she did. Even to selfish wretches like Kate.

A person did not heal within a day or month. Often not for years, Kate thought, wiping more tears from her eyes. And yet, watching Anne's quiet patient face, Kate felt as though she could breathe properly for the first time in months. They could be friends. Good ones. More, if time and healing allowed them.

Not yet.

She could almost hear Anne's voice reassuring her, saying, *It's okay. It doesn't matter. I'm here for you.*

Unexpectedly, warmth brushed against her cheek—not a recording but a memory. Jessica.

"Hey," she said to Anne. "Tell me more about my garden. Tell me what it looks like these days. What it smells like. Tell me—" She drew a deep breath and felt the knot inside ease a fraction. "Tell me everything."

MARSDOG

Once upon a time, there was a boy named Jimmy, who lived on Mars.

Actually, he wasn't a boy and his name wasn't Jimmy. There are no pronouns in any human language for his sex, unless you made up one like Zhe or Lo. Zhe—no, that's just too damned silly, let's stick with "he." He was really a Talëdi, a six-legged arthropod. His carapace was blood red and shiny, his antennae little more than black stubs above his bright faceted eyes. The Talëdi had arrived on Mars in the far, far past of this future, so long ago their language and their mating habits had evolved well away from those Talëdi who remained in the home planetary system of Jafal. On Jafal, the Talëdi lived in dwellings open to the air, and mated without regard to caste or nest-affiliation, or even the survival of the species, while those on Mars lived out their thirty or forty deca-revolutions in sophisticated pressure suits, which they only removed in the privacy of their in-dwellings, and only with members of their mate-unities, usual three or four in number.

But that's more than you wanted to know.

Let's start over. Once upon a time, in the far, far future of the past, there lived a prepubescent Talëdi named Danu-vil-fa who lived on Mars. Let's call him Jimmy and pretend that he's a boy.

Early that morning, Jimmy slipped away from the solitary in-dwelling where he lived with his father. The in-dwelling was like a carapace itself, constructed of polished metal, with special compartments for their many rituals and more ordinary activities—one for gorging and disgorging, another for their diurnal hibernation, and an open central chamber where nest members might visit with one another. You might think that in such confined space, a father would notice his son missing for an hour or a day, but not so. His father would never notice—not today, not any day since Jimmy's mother had died, and his father had announced they would leave Yul City's glass towers for a new life on the frontier, beside the dizzy-deep canyons of Valles Marineris. His father had hired on with a specialty mining company. He worked hard, taking soundings, digging soil samples, programming the mining bots, but all that hard work left Jimmy to play alone, because there were no other mate-unities nearby.

Jimmy hurried along the rim of the canyon, scuffing up dirt into rust-brown clouds, his mandibles working in excitement and curiosity and traces of lingering grief. It was early morning yet. The skies arced clear and yellow overhead, shading to dusky peach above the horizon. A few azure patches drifted over Valles Marineris to the south, where even at mid-day the canyon's broken depths remained shadowed in bluest black, and columns of vapor rose from its unseen vents, the breath of minor demons or long-lost ice deposits breaking free, depending on whether you read the philosophers or the scientists. If you listened hard, as Jimmy sometimes did, you might hear the echo of sand grains falling into the infinity below. Jimmy usually kept well away from the crumbling edge of the canyon, but two days before,

while exploring the rock jumbles and ravines, he had sighted a
fissure in the cliff wall, right where the canyon's rim looped and
wriggled like a worm.

Treasure, he thought, his mandibles working faster. A vein of
ebony ioathamite or the impossibly rare kanoböv would make
them rich. And maybe, just maybe, his father might look up
from the everlasting red soil and see *him*, Jimmy, and not those
terrible images of hospitals and death-rites, which turned his
eye-facets gray with misery.

A sudden shrill burst of noise overhead jumped him right
out of his unhappy thoughts. He jerked up his head. A brilliant
white streak cut across the butterscotch skies. The next moment
a tiny sphere appeared, hurtling toward the ground and trailed
by miles and miles of string with a huge red and white rag
at the end that whipped about madly. It was coming right at
him! Jimmy yelped and ran as fast as he could, his pressure
suit squeaking under the strain, even though he knew it was
impossible to outrun a streak of light.

The *thing* hit the ground with a loud thump. Jimmy dove
behind the nearest rock, which didn't seem nearly tall enough to
protect him. But hey, the *thing* didn't kill him and it didn't crash
into bits. It bounced and skidded and tumbled end-over-end,
throwing up gravel and sparks, right up to the canyon. Up, up,
up....

... and over the edge.

Jimmy stared, his heart tissue beating so fast the hemolymph
thrummed behind his eyes. Dust hovered, like an old ghost,
above the flats, marking the *thing's* landing. A few feet away lay
a twisted metal rod. There was a sour smell in the air, which
reminded him of Deg beetles.

All the warnings about the canyon and its dangers flipped
through his juicy brain. Here and gone. The next minute, Jimmy
was racing to the canyon rim. He stopped as close as he dared,
dropped to his four knees, and peered over the edge.

The cliff plunged straight down for at least a kilometer. Jimmy squinted hard, but he saw nothing like the *thing* from the sky. He cocked his head and listened. Not even the faintest vibration reached his audio membranes, enhanced as they were by science and evolution. Maybe it was already at the bottom. Maybe it burned up in the air. Maybe—

Jimmy wriggled closer to the rim and slapped his clawed chelicerae onto the ground. The sticky patches on his suit gloves activated with a buzzing noise. He drew a deep breath and let his head dangle over the edge.

And whistled.

Six meters down, the *thing* clung to a tiny lip of rock almost directly below him. Three of its spiky legs dug into the vertical wall over its head; two more braced against the rocky outcropping, which was crumbling underneath its weight.

"Hold on!" Jimmy called out.

He swung his pack from his shoulder and dug out the climbing gear he had brought to explore the fissure. Lickety-split, he planted two stakes in the ground, and even before the anchors clicked out, he'd attached the extra strong plasti-metal-rope to the anchor's loops, then to his own pressure suit.

Jimmy tugged at the line to make sure it held. He took another deep breath. "I'm coming," he yelled. Then he swung himself over the edge of infinity.

Eighty-five billion thinking species do did will inhabit the known galaxies. Many of them blip into life and vanish. More than you think tell adventure stories, grand swooping tales about heart-stopping excitement (for those species with hearts, or their equivalent). There are the humans with their stories of Kim and Odysseus and Sinbad the Sailor, the Leitikaans and Kas-kilas with their multi-volume questing sagas. And let us not forget the Bibiinolavii, who have twelve sanctioned story patterns for adventures alone, which they embroider upon to each other in endless variations, recording them on metallic disks and even transmitting them across the galaxy so that far-away settlements, such as the Talëdi on Mars, have picked up the signals a thousand years later. Stand alone exposed, on the surface, and you can sense those signals vibrating within your bones, like whispers from the dead.

In other words, there are no new tales under the sun, whatever its name or whichever the galaxy. So imagine for yourself how Jimmy made his descent down the cliff's wall, how he struggled to attach his ropes to the *thing*, then to the hooks on his own pressure suit. Add a few setbacks, including one that nearly sent both Jimmy and the *thing* plunging into the canyon depths. A quick save. A few clever tricks Jimmy learned from those same Bibiinolavii recordings (for the scientists had long ago decoded their clickety-clack language, and the stories had become popular). And finally, imagine the relief and wonder Jimmy felt when the mechanism built into his suit successfully hauled both him and the *thing* up to safety. He loaded his new-found treasure into his sack (not forgetting the broken-off leg) and hurried back to the in-dwelling, arriving, as the patterns require, ten minutes before his father. He had barely time enough to hide the thing in the dusty crawl-space, behind coils of extra rope and a few abandoned machine parts.

That night, Jimmy dreamed of things and places he'd never seen before. His were arthropod dreams, of course, born of the chemicals that whorled about inside his carapace, and his stubby antennae twitched this way and that, as though seeking new alien transmissions. No luck, Jimmy boy. Your in-dwelling is too well shielded against radiation, and your father switched off the

transmitter-receiver because of those dust storm that kept him at home all afternoon. So dream of yesterday, little bug. Dream of Old Jafal and your ancestors, of the cities they built across their home planet, until there was no room for another nest and the Queen wailed in grief for children born and absorbed before they truly lived. Until the clouds of time opened, and a clawful of unities fled to the stars.

"Marsdog," Jimmy said. "That's what I'm gonna call you." Then he added wistfully, "I always wanted a dog."

Jimmy had waited until his father left on morning rounds, then hauled the *thing* from its hiding place. In the thin yellow sunlight of the early Martian morning, it looked even stranger than he remembered. It (he?) was tiny—only a meter tall at the tip of its dented cone. In fact, it wasn't much like a cone any more. All that bouncing and crashing had turned Marsdog into a semi-demi-maybe-not-so-spherical shape. All that rolling and bumping had cut deep grooves into the dull gray paint—almost like a skin—that covered Marsdog. Underneath the gray, specks of a shinier color showed through, a bright silvery-white, like the first sunflares of the day.

Neat, he thought and leaned close to get a better look.

A double row of shiny black dots circled all the way around Marsdog's head, like shallow thumbprints pressed into Marsdog's gray skin. Those had to be its eyes, Jimmy decided. More gray-and-brown spots made a freckled pattern on Marsdog's belly. These weren't eyes, though. Maybe they were special markings. Maybe it was an *alien* language.

Sssssssssssssssssssssss.

Jimmy fell over with a squawk, his arms and legs flailing.

Ssssss...s..... ...whrrrrrrr...<clickety>...

<CLICK!>

Marsdog's five spiky legs punched out in all directions. Jimmy scooted back a few meters. All of a sudden, his high-tech pressure suit felt tissue thin. All of a sudden, those stupid lectures his father gave about dangers and *why don't you pay attention, don't you remember how far away we are from civilization* didn't sound so stupid anymore.

Marsdog whirred and hissed. One leg—the longest—rotated with a grinding sound that made Jimmy wince. Still he kept a wary bug-eye on that leg, which had six jointed toes, all of them ending in wicked points. Sure, the leg wasn't long enough to reach him, but he remembered his dad's warning about the poisonous Zibi worms, which could jump seven meters even before they grew wings. Marsdog might not be a worm, but it might know how to jump, and jump fast. Maybe it would even eat his brain!

Ssssssssss...

Jimmy kept one eye on Marsdog, glanced toward the in-dwelling with his other. Luckily, he hadn't put Marsdog in between himself and the door, but who knew how fast alien things could move? And what if he did get inside, only to find out Marsdog could eat through metal?

Sssssssss....<click>....hmmmmmmmmmmm.

The hum caught Jimmy's full attention. It was almost like the after-echo of a bell tone, dark and sad and fuzzy with vibrations. "That's different," he said.

<click> Whrrrrrr. Hmmmmm?????

"Are you asking me a question?" Jimmy said.

More humming and clicking, then Marsdog opened up the claw.

Jimmy tensed, ready to jump up or down or sideways, but Marsdog did not move except to slowly rotate its claw, humming all the while. Light glinted from the metal points, and in the distance, dust whispered over the hot hard ground, as the morning breeze lifted with the rising sun. There was a spicy scent in the air which filtered into his suit—mineral fines kicked up by land rovers, or churned out by the mining bots. A vinegar smell from a very nervous Jimmy. He also caught a whiff of something sweet and oily that drifted toward him from the now-motionless Marsdog.

He's trying to trick me. Jimmy's mandibles twitched as he tried to figure out what he ought to do. He didn" trust this alien metal-thing that had rocketed down from the sky.

"Who are you?" he said.

<click> Whrrrrr.

Exasperated, Jimmy made a rude sound. "What's that supposed to mean?"

<click> Mnnnnnnnn?

Hey, maybe Marsdog repeated whatever he said.

"Say Jimmy," he demanded.

Zhhhhhhhhhhhhhhhhhh.   <click>   Mmmmmmmmmmm. <hiccup> e-e-e-e-e—

It *was* talking. Almost. Jimmy tried a couple other words, which Marsdog copied, but there were lots of times it just clicked or hummed, and it still made that awful grinding noise whenever it rotated its claw. Jimmy figured Marsdog was just stretching out, like when his Dad stretched and groaned after a hard day on the steading. Except when his Dad stretched and groaned, he ended up making happy grunts afterwards, like everything felt better, and Marsdog just clicked and hissed.

"You're hurt bad," he said. "And I guess I scared you."

<click> Hrrrrrrrt <click> Ysssssssssss.

"Well," Jimmy said, "we better get you fixed up."

After explained what he wanted to do, Jimmy rolled Marsdog over to his father's workshop building. Bumpety-bump went Marsdog, who clicked and cried at first, before it gave a scary shudder and retracted all its legs inside itself. Marsdog still wasn't round like a ball, but now Jimmy could roll and steer his new dog-friend easily. "You're a smart one," he said.

Smmmmmmrrrr....noooooo....no smrrrrt.

Huh, Jimmy thought. Marsdog was learning fast. "You *are* smart. You figured out how to talk to me, and you figured out what I was trying to do. Maybe you can help me fix you."

Marsdog said nothing except to click a few times, as though he disagreed but he was too polite to say so. Jimmy once had an aunt like that. After his mother died, that same aunt had offered to take Jimmy into her own mate-unity "just to help out." But Jimmy's father had called her a miserable old busy-body, and she left in a Grand Talëldi huff.

Jimmy spent three Martian hours tinkering with Marsdog before he finally gave up in frustration. His father had bought all kinds of tools for the steading, because out on the frontier, there were no other mechanics, and Jimmy's father knew he'd had to repair and maintain his equipment himself. Jimmy carefully took up each tool and tried matching it to any part of Marsdog. Nothing fit. *Nothing like*, as his mother used to say.

Jimmy swallowed and oozed sweaty tears from his thorax. Mom would have liked Marsdog, he thought, wiping away the secretions with the back of his chelicerae. She would have helped him look up stuff on the info-net, then badgered Dad into buying new reference books they'd never need again, just to see what they could find out. Mom was nearly as curious as he was, and she'd been all grown up.

"Mom isn't here," he told Marsdog. "You're stuck with me."

Marsdog's eyes flickered. *Zhhhhhmmmmeeee*, it said. *With-with-with-me.*

"You're funny," Jimmy said, but he felt better anyway.

He spent another hour searching through his father's tools, careful to replace everything just as he'd found it. The whole time he worked, Jimmy chatted and asked questions about everything and nothing, which he answered himself. Marsdog clicked and whirred and occasionally said something. Then the workshop clock chimed, two long sonorous tones that signaled mid-day.

"Whoops," Jimmy said. "Dad will be home soon. I'm gonna have to hide you again, buddy."

Call mmmmme Mrzzzzdog.

"Okay, Marsdog. But I still have to hide you. Dad might not understand."

Marsdog clicked and hummed.

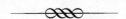

Of all the species in the Universe, few can approach the Talëdi for complexity when it comes to eating. First comes a period where the guests sample the dishes in tiny sips and nibbles, with entire sub-rituals of phrases and gestures in between, which succeeding generations have added to. Next comes a period where everyone eats in silence, filling their stomachs to near-bursting. This portion is called the True Gorging, and has not changed since Old Jafar. An interval of quiet conversation follows, with the guests continuing to sample from their favorite flasks and dishes. When that comes to an end, the ceremony of disgorging begins.

Let us pass over that part, however, which could only interest an anthropologist from old Jafar.

Jimmy and his father reclined on cushioned platforms, the dining shelf in between. The interval of tiny bites and many exchanges was past; now they ate in silence. Jimmy's antennae wiggled in excitement as he thought about what adventures he and Marsdog would have, once Jimmy repaired his new friend. And though he could not see himself, you should know that his eye-facets glittered bright gold and silver. He scooped up a clawful of noska paste but hardly noticed what he ate, even though noska paste was his favorite, and the cool grainy texture felt good after a morning under the Martian sun. Briefly he wondered if Marsdog were hungry, or if Marsdog could even be hungry. It hadn't acted weak or sick, even after crashing into the ground. But how could you tell? He finished off the noska paste and started on the glävi pie, chewing rapidly as he thought about it. What did you feed an alien dog? Maybe he could filch some laka-oil beans and see if his new friend would like those. Maybe—

All of a sudden, he realized his father was asking Jimmy questions about his morning.

"Sorry," he muttered, though his father had not scolded him.

His father tilted his head and quirked his antennae. "You look happy about something."

Jimmy said nothing. He swallowed down the glävi pie and reached for the last handful of gönü pellets.

"I'm glad," his father said. "I worry you'll get bored out here with no friends."

Jimmy shrugged. "It's okay."

A pause followed as father and son shared out the last of the mimesed juice.

"I noticed you took your climbing gear out the other day," his father said.

"Yeah. I thought I saw something."

"Not in the canyon, I hope."

Jimmy eyed his father warily, but decided his father was guessing. He didn't really know what Jimmy had been up to.

"Did you find anything?" his father said.

"Naw. Well, just some stuff."

"Stuff?"

"You know. Stuff."

"Ah. That."

His father waited a moment, then gave the gesture of resignation. (One he'd used all too often, as Jimmy approached the teenaged years.) He switched on the radio receiver, which they sometimes used when conversation flagged. A bright crackling sound invaded the engorging chamber, indicating that an electric storm danced and sparked over the rust-red plains between Yul City and the Valles Marineris. Jimmy's father fiddled with the tuning rods and sensors until, with a loud click, the static changed into clear musical voices.

"... an unidentified object sighted yesterday morning over the Amazonis Planitia..."

Jimmy stopped chewing and listened intently.

"... scientific and philosophic councils report the object emitted a burst of radio signals, which triggered both our space and aviation alarms. So far, the Imperial trackers have not located its remains, but the search continues. The incident has sparked a lively debate in the scientific and philosophical communities, coming just three weeks before the councils meet to discuss further migration options—"

Jimmy's father cut off the transmission with an angry stab at the switch. He looked both annoyed and unhappy, but not the same kind of unhappy as when he thought of Jimmy's mother. Then he gave Jimmy the Talëdi equivalent of a weak smile. "Sorry. I didn't mean to lose my temper. It's just I know they'll rehash the same arguments all over again. Do we send out nest-fledglings to the stars? Or not? Can we afford to go? Bah. As though we'd find anything outside our world except a trillion kilometers of emptiness—"

He broke off with a dry, chittering laugh. "And here I go, rehashing those arguments anyway. Maybe I need to talk to someone besides myself." He glanced at Jimmy, almost shyly. "Maybe we both do. Would you like to come along with me this afternoon?"

Jimmy's heart tissue did a funny skip. He almost said yes. He would have, except for Marsdog. With a voice he didn't quite trust, he said, "It's okay, Dad. Really. But, um, I was going to stay home and catch up on schoolwork."

He and his father stared at one another. The Talëdi do not have expressive features—the blood-red carapace that encloses their face and body segments creates a stiff mask, unreadable to most to other species. For the Talëdi themselves, however, a mere flick of the antennae, an involuntary quiver of the mandibles, express more drama than any human speech. The eye facets are the most telling—they glitter, or brighten, or turn dull; within an eyeblink, they can change to any color along the spectrum. Seeing the opaque shine in his father's eyes, the unnatural stillness of those stubby antennae, Jimmy perceived a new reserve in his father, one that found an echo inside himself. It was a strange uncomfortable thing, as though a bottomless gorge had opened between them. For one brief moment, Jimmy had the urge to leap across…

Jimmy dropped his gaze. His father sighed, picked up an oily crumb from the plate before him.

Another Martian day, another Martian dollar.

That afternoon, after his father returned to his rounds, Jimmy sat on the floor of his father's workshop and scowled at Marsdog. He wasn't mad at Marsdog, but he was frustrated, and in spite of the filters and climate conditioning units, he exuded enough sour-stink secretions to make his olafactory glands contract. Marsdog just sat there.

Nothing works, Jimmy thought with a sigh.

His father's neat workbench had disappeared underneath heaps of equipment—clamps and wrenches over here, valöf connectors, buckets of screws, rolls of plasti-patch and olabob compound, and even an old vomish meter. Nothing fit. Not even the shapes were right. The closest he could come were the stupid wrenches, but those all had six-sided openings, and the few bolt-type things Jimmy found on Marsdog's butt were all eight-sided.

"I wish I knew what to do with you."

Doooo....with-with-with-me, said Marsdog. If he had been a real dog, he probably would have thumped his tail on the floor, or poked his snout under Jimmy's hand. As it was, he continued to sit there.

"I mean," Jimmy went on, "if I were a computer whiz, maybe I could look up something on the info-net, but Dad has that all locked down tight while he's gone. And I bet that wouldn't matter anyway because you're an alien and we don't know anything about alien stuff except what those stupid Bibiinolavii recordings—"

He stopped. Marsdog was rocking back and forth. "What is it?"

Bbbbbbbb <click> bbbbbbbb <CLICK!>

"Are you trying to say Bibiinolavii?"

<click> Ysssssssssssh.

Jimmy stared. "What about them?" Then he remembered exactly what he'd been babbling. "You mean *you* want to listen to those weird recordings?"

Ja-ja-ja-ja-ja-ja-ja-ja-ja. Marsdog rocked harder.

"How can that help—"

Then Jimmy also remembered how smart Marsdog was—learning to talk in less than a day. And whoever sent him those million-gadjillion miles must have thought him smart, too. Maybe, just maybe, they could figure out something together.

"Okay," he said. "But we'll have to go inside."

Rrrrrrready inside.

Jimmy laughed. "You goof, I mean inside the house."

He reassembled his pressure suit around his carapace (a process Marsdog watched intently with his row of bright black eyes). Taking great care, he tilted Marsdog onto its side, so he could roll his friend out the door, down the ramp, then up and through the next pressure doors and into the in-dwelling. Inside he maneuvered Marsdog into the nook where his father kept the info-net console.

"Let me try first," he said. "I think I remember how to get to the recordings."

Marsdog clicked but said nothing.

Without bothering to remove more than his gloves and helmet, Jimmy settled into the sling in front of the console. He paused and his mandibles worked nervously. He had never tried to operate the console by himself, and certainly never tried to break past the locks and filters his father had set. The screen, a big square of dark blue plasti-fabric stretched inside a metal frame, stared back at him. *You can't see me,* Jimmy thought, even though that was exactly what he feared. Beside him, Marsdog . was humming softly.

There were two black mesh touch-pads to the left of the console, a single larger one on the right. Jimmy took a deep breath and pressed both his chelicerae onto the right-hand touch-pad. Immediately he felt a strong tingling sensation as the chemicals flowed past, reading his imprint, and a sweet-salty-sour taste infiltrated his brain through the fuzzy lobes between his claws.

The screen emitted a bluish-purple glow. Jimmy held his breath as patterns of squares and dots flowed past in the boot-up sequence. Next a series of tinny notes blared from the speakers. These were followed by several rank smells. (Deg beetles again.) Then the screen went blank.

Jimmy blew out a breath, frustrated. "He's locked it up, Marsdog."

Just to be sure, he went through the boot-up sequence a second time, but the screen blipped on and off right away. Darn.

Marsdog chirruped.

Jimmy glanced down at his friend, who looked agitated. Or impatient. "What? You want to try?"

Another chirrup, this one louder.

That was definitely a *Let me try* noise. Jimmy pushed the button to retract the sling and moved his friend closer. Marsdog sat still a moment, his black eyes flickering. Then he extended one skinny arm toward the right-hand touch-pad. The claw opened flat and thick short bristles emerged. Marsdog brushed the bristles over the touch-pad. A rapid pattern of black and emerald green dots appeared, so bright and fast his eye-facets hurt. Then came a dreadful pause, during which Jimmy feared he and Marsdog had broken the console. He was so going to catch it his from his father…

A honey-sweet smell filled the in-dwelling. The screen flickered and turned butter-yellow. One by one, icons popped into view until they made a gaudy border around the edge.

"You *are* smart," Jimmy breathed.

They were into the system, and skimming through the info-net. Jimmy tapped his claws over the three smaller touch-pads. New combinations of chemicals zinged his sensitive lobes, and the patterns of squares and dots flickered like the tiny luminous zü gnats that made the desert twilight so lovely. Jimmy hardly paid attention. He was trying to remember exactly where those recordings were. Even though his father never let him use the info-console alone, Jimmy had often peeked over his father's shoulder.

"Here it is," he said pointing at the screen.

Marsdog reached out and started tapping on the smaller touch-pads.

"Hey," Jimmy said. "Stop that. You're gonna screw things up—"

Then he snapped his mandibles shut. The Bibiinolavii icons had vanished, replaced by a lot of wriggly blue lines. Marsdog kept tapping, blinking, tapping some more. On the screen, the wriggly lines scrolled up and down, zoomed larger, then vanished to a new screen filled with tiny dot patterns. Jimmy recognized a couple words here and there. It looked like one of his father's extra-super-technical manuals, the ones he pulled out when the steading's electronic machinery needed repairs. Smart didn't even begin to describe Marsdog.

Finally Marsdog stopped tapping and chirped, *Prnnnnnt?*

"Huh? Oh, you want to print what's on the screen?"

Yzzzzzzzz. Prnnnnnnt.

Jimmy wondered how Marsdog knew about printing, but then he figured Marsdog had read that from the screen itself. "Here's how," he said, and showed his friend the sequence for the bottom left-hand touch-pad. Before you could say Bibiinolavii three times backward, ribbons of scented plastic started to scroll out the console's printer slot. Soon they had a large jumble of them, which Jimmy collected onto a spool.

"Is that enough?" he asked Marsdog.

Yssshhhhhizzzzzeeeenuf.

Now they could really get to work. Jimmy rolled Marsdog back to the workshop, where he and his friend tinkered and argued and fiddled with his father's tools, making them do things Jimmy didn't know was possible. First they replaced Marsdog's broken leg. Marsdog stood up and walked around the workshop, pulling items off the shelves, handing them to Jimmy. A couple times, Marsdog rewired a device in a way that made Jimmy cringe. Maybe he could tell his father that dread Ravönii bandits had attacked the in-dwelling.

A loud click jerked his attention back. Whoa. Marsdog had suddenly sprouted a couple of cylindrical shafts, like miniature rockets, and Jimmy had to blink six times before he could believe what he saw.

"Wow," he said. "What are you? Some kind of space ship?"

"That's not the question I would ask."

Jimmy's father stood in the entryway of the workshop. His eyes were shiny-bright. His antennae poked forward stiffly. Only the spiny hairs along his upper chelicerae quivered. Jimmy swallowed. He had not even heard the outer locks chime, or the inner doors whoosh open. He felt a sudden drop in pressure as his father continued to stare at him.

"I...I can explain," he whispered.

Jimmy's father shook his head. "What do you think you were doing?" he said, as though Jimmy hadn't spoken. "This isn't a toy. You might have hurt yourself. Or other people. You should have told me right away—"

"When?" Jimmy yelled. "When *could* I tell you? You're always *working*."

"At dinner," Jimmy's father went on, heavily. "But you don't talk, you don't listen—"

"—I *did* listen. I listened so hard for months and months and you didn't say anything until last night and—"

Jimmy broke off with a sob and sat down hard on the floor. More sobs followed and he oozed sticky secretions from his thorax that made the whole in-dwelling smell bitter. Marsdog leaned into him, humming deep and loud, and Jimmy hugged him tight. "I wish Mom were here."

Jimmy's father sat down next to him. "I wish that too," he said quietly. "Every day."

He gave a gusty sigh. Glanced from Jimmy to Marsdog. Jimmy clung to Marsdog tighter, not sure what his father might do.

What his father did was to reach over and run his gloved chelicerae along Marsdog's back. Soft and gentle and sure, like when he checked over a much younger Jimmy after a bad fall. Marsdog twitched, then held very still. "He's an odd one, isn't he?"

"He's... he's a space alien," Jimmy said, subdued. He wiped away the secretions from his cheeks and thorax.

"Hmmmm. Maybe he is." Light flickered over his father eye facets.

Marsdog's eyes blinked and flickered back.

"Ho. What is he trying to do? Send us radio signals?"

"He doesn't need to. He knows how to talk."

Talk-talk-talk, said Marsdog.

Jimmy's father started in surprise. "I never thought—Well, never mind what I thought. He does talk, and talks pretty well. Can you tell us who you are, my friend?"

Mrzzzzdg.

"Murzdug?"

"No, Marsdog," Jimmy said. "I named him."

His father's mandibles quivered. "A good name. So, Marsdog, where do you come from?"

Whirrrrrr <click> <click><click><click>

"He hasn't done that in a while," Jimmy said. "Only at first, before he could talk."

"Hmmmmmm." Jimmy's father made a humming noise much like Marsdog. "Maybe he'd let me take a look at him? What do you think, Marsdog?"

Marsdog clicked a few more times, then hummed back.

"I'll take that as a *yes*. But I'll need your help, Jimmy."

Together, he and Jimmy gently explored Marsdog's surface with the soft fuzzy lobes between their claws. It was Jimmy's father who discovered that brushing Marsdog's belly made Marsdog stutter and click. (*He must be ticklish, Jimmy thought.*) And his father also figured out that a couple quick taps on Marsdog's butt made his legs retract completely. But it was Jimmy who, when he tickled Marsdog underneath its eyes, made the biggest discovery.

Marsdog plopped down onto the floor of the workshop. A thin panel in his midsection slid open, and light poured out, a round translucent beam that caught the whirling dust specks in the air. In the middle of that silvery bubble, eight tiny figures appeared.

Jimmy's antennae quivered with unbearable excitement. "Who are they?" he whispered.

"Holographic projections," Jimmy's father said. He was whispering, too. "Maybe these are the people who built Marsdog."

Whoa. Jimmy leaned closer, hardly daring to breathe. The tiny figures, barely a half meter tall, were like nothing he'd ever seen before, even in the weirdest net zines. They were all different shapes and sizes and colors, from livid purple to brownish-red to the palest ivory, like bones left to weather on a hillside. But all of them were covered with strange leathery skin, not carapaces, and they all had long bendable necks and eight legs, each with eight long flexible toes.

Eight! Jimmy thought. *Just like those bolts on Marsdog.*

The tallest purple figure stared directly at Jimmy and his father. It lifted one arm (leg?) to its flexible trunk, right where Jimmy imagined its heart might be, and made a low trilling noise.

(*What's it saying?*)

(*I don't know.*)

....*whrrrr <click> <click> <click>*...

The trilling noise hiccupped into real voices.

"... twenty-nine thousand kilo-light years from your world..."

(*Hey, Dad—*)

(*Hush. Marsdog is translating...*)

Another loud click interrupted them. Speckles and waves distorted the light bubble for a heartbeat, then it snapped into focus once more. Once more the tallest purple figure gazed directly at Jimmy and his father, but this time, his voice deepened to a lower, more musical register. And his words...

"We call ourselves the Edälom. Our world we name Mauris Una. Ours is the solitary planet of the star named Maurenas, which lies on the outer rim of the Corvallis star cloud. Based on previous scans and transmissions, we estimate that we are twenty-nine thousand kilo-light years from your world. We cannot ourselves visit, I regret to say. It was just two generations ago that we discovered tiny wormholes, which allowed us to send out scouts within our star cloud, then later to distant worlds such as yours."

(*Ours?*)

(*Quiet. He's not done talking.*)

(*How do you know—*)

"... but we hope that within another ten generations, which are like six of yours, we dare to launch our first voyagers to the stars that we might share our knowledge with yours and others. We ask, as you ask, are we welcome?"

With a faint click, the voice fell silent, the figures within the bubble froze.

You are, are welcome. Please come. Yes. Come.

Ever afterwards, Jimmy could not say who had spoken, he or his father, or some other voice within Marsdog itself. He only knew he had thought those words, as loud and fiercely as he could. What else could he say, they say? Forget us? Leave us to wonder at the universe's vastness, where a single raindrop vanishes in the immensity? No, that was impossible.

The light clicked off. The panel slid shut. Marsdog *whrrrred* and its black-black eyes twinkled in a syncopated pattern.

"He *is* a scout," Jimmy's father said softly.

Jimmy's heart thumped faster. An alien scout. This was better than any adventure tale he'd ever read or listened to. Then he remembered the broadcast from yesterday. "Does that mean we supposed to call the scientists?" he asked in a small voice.

"Probably." But his father did not make a move to stand. Instead he picked up a tool and cocked his head at Marsdog. "So, Marsdog. Anything else needs fixing?"

Hmmmmm. <click> Yzzzzzz.

Under Marsdog's direction, Jimmy and his father repaired the last bits. They carefully popped out the three biggest dents. A new panel slid open to show a couple loose wires, which Jimmy's father reconnected. Then Marsdog tilted himself so that Jimmy's father could examine the strange cylindrical shafts. Jimmy's father ran his chelicerae over the ribbons of printout Marsdog had obtained from the info-net. "These look like boosters."

"Then he's not a dog," Jimmy said. "He's a rocket, just like I thought."

"Rocket. Dog. Sounds like he's a little of both."

Jimmy's father made a few more adjustments, before they took Marsdog outside. With all his legs working, Marsdog lumbered and jumped and hopped over the hard-packed Martian dirt, sending up tiny red dust clouds when he landed. The whole time he was buzzing and his clicks sounded louder than ever. But these weren't hurt broken clicks. These were happy excited ones. When they reached the steading's main road, Marsdog took a few galloping leaps that made Jimmy laugh. "What is he doing?"

To his surprise, his father was shaking his head. "I think… I think he wants to fly."

"Fly?" Then Jimmy realized what his father meant. "Like, away from us?"

"Why not? He's a scout. And away from us means home for him."

Jimmy stared at Marsdog, who had stopped and swiveled around, its eye lenses blinking in the harsh afternoon light. "Do you?" he asked. "Do you want to go home?"

Hmmmmmm.

"But... but..." Jimmy's mandibles worked. "What about me? Don't you want to be my friend?"

Marsdog trundled back to father and son. *Friend,* he said clearly.

Jimmy blinked against tears. "But you're going away."

Hmmmmmm.

Home. All that humming was really Marsdog talking about how he wanted to go home. Just like Jimmy wanted to go home to Yul City someday. *If I'm really his friend, I should understand that. I should let him go.*

Gently, he touched Marsdog's bumpy head. "Will you come back someday? Maybe?"

<CLICK> whrrrrrr <click>

That sounded so much like a negative, Jimmy's antennae slumped in disappointment.

"Maybe he doesn't know," Jimmy's father suggested. "Twenty-nine thousand kilo-light years is a long way, even with worm holes and fast rockets. You might be all grown up before he comes back."

"I know. I just—" Jimmy swallowed hard. "I'll miss him."

Marsdog bumped against Jimmy's arm and whirred softly. *Zhmmmmeee frnnnnnd. Remmmmbrrr meeee.*

"I could never forget you," Jimmy said fervently.

Marsdog extended his arm with the claw flattened out. With a glance at his father, who nodded, Jimmy touched his gloved chelicerae to the bristly pad.

Rmmmmmbbbbbrrr you-you-you.

"Promise?" Jimmy whispered.

Promise. Try-try-try to come back.

It was yet another pattern within the greater tapestry of adventure stories recognized by the Bibiinolavii and so many other species. The strange alien visitor. The lonely child. Their tightly-bound friendship disrupted by a necessary departure. The promise of an eventual reunion. (Or not.) Even as Jimmy acknowledged these truths, he wept great thick bug tears and gripped his father's leg segments as hard as he could.

Marsdog rocked and swiveled around. Whirring and clicking, he lifted each leg one after the other, extended it with a hiss, then set it back down, as though working out the kinks. Jimmy's heart squeezed tight as he watched his friend trundle back to the steading's road. Marsdog paused. His cone-head tilted forward. His legs bent slightly. Jimmy was about to call out when Marsdog started a bounding run directly toward the Valles Marineris.

"Won't he fall and crash?" Jimmy said anxiously.

"No, he won't. Watch."

Marsdog leaped into the air. Four stubby wings burst out from his sides, and a bright hot flare exploded from his rocket thrusters, making the air shimmer with crimson and gold. For a moment, Marsdog wavered over the canyon's void—Jimmy held his breath so hard, his thorax ached—then with another burst from his thrusters, Marsdog was high, high in the air, streaking toward the skies.

Jimmy let out his breath with a sob and waved as hard as he could. *Bye, Marsdog,* he thought. *Bye.*

The small bright dot that was Marsdog wavered in the sky, as though Marsdog had tilted its wings in farewell. Jimmy blinked away his tears. When he could see again, Marsdog was gone, leaving just a trail of smoke and glitter behind him.

"Do you think he *will* come back?"

Jimmy's father fluttered his antennae. "If he can. I think he's someone who keeps his promises. After all, he did once before."

The story does not end here, of course. As the Bibiinolavii would say, each variation of each story pattern links to the next and the next, like a string of stars across the sky, so that when you reach the end, you find the beginning all over again. But this particular chapter of this particular story ends here, with Danu-vil-fa and Degbalid-

vil-no watching the bright point of light that was Marsdog fade from view. So much about them, the Talëdi, is so like us, and yet so different. No matter how many centuries I have observed them from my ghostly plane, my human speech falters when trying to convey what I see. But come, I hear the wind rising, and as night falls, I sense faint signals from the distant stars, vibrating within my bones, like whispers from the dead.

A Handful of Pearls

*I*t was said in folk tales that the world came to be when Ame-no fell sick from a pomegranate offered to him by the Monkey-god. Greedy for its sweetness, Ame-no ate the fruit in a single gulp, only to discover the Monkey-god had filled it with poison. He sweated and groaned and heaved up the mountains. He sweated and groaned and spewed forth the oceans. When the sickness at last faded from his belly, Ame-no spat upon the ocean to show his contempt for the Monkey-god's evil tricks.

And from every drop of spittle there appeared an island.

Three dark smudges broke the endless green horizon, just below the faint white discs of the twin moons. Yan Dei leaned over the ship's rail and squinted through the warm ocean spray. The sun was just slanting behind the expedition ships, and the waters ran red and silver from the liquid sunset. Between the mist and the approaching twilight, it was hard to make out if those were storm clouds rising above the waves, or if at last they had reached—

"Land!" a crew member called out. "Land, ho!"

Almost immediately, a clamor broke out behind Yan— shouts and laughter and delighted cries. Half the crew, those not strictly on duty, and all the scientists crowded the decks, everyone chattering excitedly. Yan squeezed his way from their midst and took refuge behind the ladder to the upper decks. Here the ship's metal skin hummed as the electric engines shifted into a lower gear. A hot tinny smell rolled up from below decks, making his stomach heave.

Hari Dun strolled over to Yan. "Not interested?"

"Hard to breathe in that mob," Yan said shortly.

His friend smiled. "Understandable." He glanced toward the ship's bow, which was hardly visible through the hordes. "And I can't blame them. It's been a long voyage. Give them another few minutes, and Doctor Mar will have them back at their posts. Then we can get a glimpse ourselves."

A ripple of movement passed through the crowds, and those nearest Yan and Hari pressed back as Bej Saihan, the expedition's lead tracker, made his way toward the bow. He paused, standing head and shoulders above everyone else, and scanned all points of the horizon, seemingly unaware of the small clearing that formed around him. As Bej swiveled his massive head around, Yan caught a glimpse of the man's blunt features.

Not quite a man, or so the rumors claimed.

Bej's massive jaw and squashed nose looked crude, unfinished, as though someone had haphazardly shaped his features from a muddy lump of clay. It was said in whispers that Bej counted the *pemburu* among his ancestors. That Kun Mar had rescued the man from prison, and had given him jobs that used his uncanny hunting skills. The *pemburu* were the hunters—half-cousins to humans—and looking at Bej's face, Yan could easily imagine him in a jungle, or in the ruined coastal cities, where a few pockets of *pemburu* survived.

Now Kun Mar, the senior biologist and expedition leader, strode into view. "Back to your posts," he shouted. "We'll see land soon enough. Team leaders, I'd like to see all of you in the main boardroom. Now."

The crowds quickly scattered. Yan expected Hari to go immediately—he was the senior biochemist for the expedition—but Hari went forward to the rails and lingered a few moments, gazing southward. "The pearls of the southeast," he murmured. "So the poets called them. I like the old legends better, myself."

"Spittle from the heavens," Yan said, wrinkling his nose. "I know the tales."

Hari grinned. "Do not despise them, my friend. Spittle and vomit are the working tools of the scientist. And from these we will make pearls." The grin faded, and his eyes narrowed to a speculative look as he studied the horizon. "Six months of paradise," he said quietly. "Six months of discovery and exploration, masquerading as hard work. Hmmmmm. I think I smell land. Can you?"

Yan took a tentative sniff, then a deeper one. Yes, just beneath the heavy salt tang, he detected a sharp biting scent that reminded him of crushed leaves. "Trees and bark and mud and swamp."

"Shit and musk and old rotting things."

"Hah. You can't smell all that."

Hari laughed. "No. Only Bej Saihan could claim that ability. But soon—tomorrow at the latest—you and I both will. And like the lucky seventh son in the folk tales, let us hope we can turn all the shit we find into gold." He pushed off from the rails. "Well, I best go before Kun starts bellowing. Take care, Yan."

Yan nodded. He had not missed Hari's subtle hints. Work hard. Be a good member of the team. Even that comment about shit and gold meant something, for that was the point of this expedition, a joint venture between XiangGen Pharmaceuticals and the Tai Jing Federal Council on Scientific Research. If their research led to even one medical breakthrough, it meant acclaim for every member of this expedition.

Or even just a second chance, Yan thought. With his department head at the University. With Mei.

He smacked both palms against the railing. *Not my fault.
Not—*

Yan clamped his lips shut and glanced around. Slowly he let
his breath trickle out. Good. No one had seen that tiny outburst.
It would not do to make the wrong impression, not here where
every interaction found its way into the official reports. Best to
forget Mei. His future lay just ahead, within those islands.

He turned his attention back to the horizon. In just the past
few moments, the bumps and smudges had turned into distinct
masses, like a handful of mismatched pearls, scattered by the
gods over the far seas. He could even make out a jagged peak
that might be a volcano. Above them, the twin moons stood
out sharper against the evening sky, and a spray of pale stars
emerged. A creaking sound vibrated through the air, as the ship's
solar sails folded for the night.

Yan flexed his hands and breathed in deep lungfuls of the
ocean air. The smell of crushed leaves was stronger now, mixed
with the unmistakable scent of rotting fish. A strange paradise,
indeed.

The tightness in his gut eased. *This time I will not stumble.*

The expedition's three ships navigated cautiously past
the rocks and shoals that ringed the island chain. Their first
destination was a shallow harbor belonging to the island
designated as XTI-19S137W-1A.

Using maps from the earlier survey teams, Kun Mar and his
advisors chose a level site beside a wide swift-running stream,
half a klick inland. Under their direction, the crews cleared away
the brush, dug trenches, and transported crates of equipment
from the ships. By the sixth morning, a miniature settlement
existed where before only scrub trees grew. Various technicians
still worked to set up the laboratory equipment, but the main

work was complete. The other ships withdrew their crews and began preparations for their departure.

Yan spent most of the day transferring the last of his belongings from the ship and setting up his sleeping tent. Late that afternoon, he joined the rest of the microbiology team at their lab site, which occupied the southern quadrant of the enormous camp.

"You will work in pairs," Doctor Au told them. "One senior member with a junior—a teaching partnership, if you will. We are here to find practical applications, but Doctor Mar tells me there is no rule against expanding our knowledge, as long as we do our work."

Smiles on several faces. A few laughed dutifully.

"We start work tomorrow," Au went on. "You've read the materials and reports, and you know my ideas for how to approach our task. So. For the rest of today, I suggest you familiarize yourself with our immediate surroundings. You will not have the leisure for that later. At least I hope not."

More laughter and some obvious delight at being released, if only for the afternoon. Doctor Au handed out slips of paper with the partner assignments. Yan read the name *Lian Luo*. One of the graduate students from the State University, he remembered. He had come across her once or twice aboard the ship, always in the company of other students. He glanced around and found her sitting with a few friends, all students and technicians, discussing their assignments. Easy enough to read her thoughts, though she greeted him politely when he approached her.

"You are stuck with me," he said. "Sorry about that."

Lian offered him a tentative smile. "Don't be. I hope to learn a lot from you, Doctor Dei."

She was a pretty girl. Long wispy dark hair, barely contained by her hair clips. He smiled back, in what he hoped was a pleasant manner. "We can learn from each other."

An awkward pause followed. Lian gave him another quick smile. "If you will excuse me, I must go and see about my tent."

The rest of the team went their separate ways. Yan returned to his sleeping quarters. He unpacked a few items, then stowed his trunk out of sight. A dozen books and several photographs of his parents and two brothers made his small bookshelf look less empty. He wished he still had photos of Mei, but she had removed them all from their apartment.

My apartment, he corrected himself automatically.

Once theirs together.

Yan closed his eyes. The air pulsed against his skin, making his head throb. Steady, he told himself. It was the heat, the tent's closeness, the excitement of landing. That was all. Nothing to worry about.

He took himself to Hari's new headquarters, where he found a dozen technicians checking rows of vials against their printed labels. Hari and his senior assistant, Che Lok, were bent over one of the worktables, reviewing stacks of reports.

Hari glanced up. "Yan!" he exclaimed. "Excellent. Please rescue me from my too-vigilant assistant, Doctor Lok. You do know each other, no?"

Che was a tall angular young woman. Taking in her severe, tight braid and lack of makeup, Yan thought she must be afraid of looking pretty. He already knew about her from Hari's frequent references. Che had just earned her doctoral degree, and Hari had hand-picked her for this expedition.

Che met Yan's gaze briefly. A slight crease appeared between her brows. "We've met."

"We did?" Yan said. "Was that on board ship?"

Che shrugged. "Where else?"

Yan had no answer to that. He turned to Hari. "I'm hardly making a rescue. Are you busy, or would you like to take an early dinner?"

"Hmmm. Not too busy. A walk first, old friend. Or perhaps walk and dinner at the same time. After all, Doctor Lok has our lab well under control."

At the second mention of her new degree, Che's smile became genuine. "You are too kind."

"Never," Hari cried. "Doctor Mar emphasized that we are to be hard, cruel taskmasters. To that end, would you please check over the reagents? And have the technicians unpack the larger beakers and pipes. We shall want to run some preliminary tests tomorrow morning."

"I won't keep him too long," Yan said to Che.

Che gave him a cryptic look, but did not reply. Yan hesitated, thinking he should say something more, but Hari was already propelling him out the tent.

At the kitchen compound, they selected a handful of self-heating food packs and headed down the beach. Several groups made picnics by the stream's mouth, but further along, they found themselves alone, treading a curving, looping path between the seas and vegetation. Quiet settled around them, broken only by the hush, hush, hush of the waves. Ahead, the shore stretched, an untouched expanse of pale green sands made of tiny particles of semi-precious stones that glittered in the fading sunlight. A short distance out, their ship stood out against the violet skies, its solar sails folded like awkward wings. Lights from the portholes winked on and off. A faint hum from the electric motors rippled over the water.

"I love this time of the day," Hari said softly. "It's as though we are walking through borders. Sunlight and moonlight. One day and the next. The rules are different at twilight, the old folk tales say. A magical hour when we might accomplish anything."

"Are you talking about miracles?" Yan asked.

"Practical ones," Hari answered. "A drug to cure senility. A fuel more powerful than coal or sunlight, and more plentiful than oil. Even an engine that lets us fly to the stars. You might laugh, Yan, but someday we will."

"Someday," Yan said, though he wondered at Hari's sudden pensive mood.

A massive man-like shadow erupted from the sands, not ten meters ahead. Yan started, then recognized Bej Saihan. He glanced toward Hari. Hari touched Yan's arm with a light hand, but he had not shifted his gaze from Bej. Interesting. So Yan was not the only person unsettled by the tracker.

Bej seemed not to notice them, or he didn't care. He tilted his head back and breathed audibly, as though tasting the air. Yan could not restrain a shudder. It was said the *pemburu* were Ame-no's dogs, shaped before he made humans. They were the god's hunters, sent to exact justice where necessary. Folk tales, Yan told himself, but it was easy to picture Bej as something primordial, mythical, a creature larger than life.

Bej snorted and trotted off into the darkness. Hari laughed softly, as though amused by something, possibly his own reaction to the man. The thought did little to comfort Yan. He finished chewing the meat paste and took a swallow from his water bottle. "Hari, why does Che dislike me?"

Hari shook his head. "She doesn't. She's just… cautious."

"Well, it's clear she likes you."

"We get along." A slight pause, then, "Are things going well with you so far?"

Yan kept his voice as neutral as Hari's. "Better than before."

Better now that he and Mei were several thousand kilometers apart. The thought of Mei immediately brought Hari's assistant to mind. In truth Che looked nothing like Mei. She was much taller and skinnier, and her lips thin dark lines, where Mei's mouth curved full against her honey-brown skin. Nevertheless she and Mei both had the same quick frown, the same wary expression. It was uncanny.

He shrugged away the thought. "So what tests are you starting with, Doctor Dun?"

"Dull stuff," Hari said dryly. "We're running several standard analysis sequences with our equipment to check the calibration. But then things get interesting. I was thinking, and Kun agrees with me, that we should do a thorough breakdown of the various trees. It would be lovely if we came across another biological treasure like the ones Anwar Enterprises discovered. What about you?"

"Water samples first," Yan said. "Then soil samples, etc. But what really interests me are the tests Au wants to run to check for antiviral compounds..."

The conversation swung back and forth, much like their path skirting the tidal edge. As the sun sank behind the horizon, the breeze shifted, blowing in from the opens seas. Yan felt the day's accumulated sweat evaporate, and he breathed more easily.

The Tau'ini Po'a Islands. Nicknamed A Thousand Pearls. Located 19°52S, 137° 56W. Includes hundreds of islands ranging from tiny footprints to sizeable land masses stretching thirty or forty kilometers in length. Even the smallest shelter pockets of sea grass, while the largest ones support dense forests of shrubs and low trees.

Unlike the remote Hăna-măna islands, where recent scientific expeditions uncovered the rare tikaki human subspecies, there are no known settlements in the Tau'ini Po'a Islands. Numerous stony reefs ring the island chain, and a peculiar twist in the Kailuang Current makes any approach difficult. Native tribes populate the island chains 150 kilometers to the north, but as far as any scouts could determine, there are and have never been any signs of human habitation in this world within a world.

Over the next month, Yan established a comfortable routine. Throughout the morning, he and Lian Luo worked in the laboratory, running tests on their samples. In the afternoon, they wrote up their results and attended meetings with the other team members to discuss the next day's experiments. Evenings he spent in Hari's company or alone, reading. Che remained aloof from him, but he gradually formed tentative friendships with other team members. Once or twice, Lian joined him for lunch. *Six months of paradise*, he thought more than once. *Perhaps Hari was right.*

The first morning of the second month, the rhythm broke.

Lian Luo poked her head into the laboratory tent. "Yan, come see," she said. "Something new."

She vanished before Yan could ask anything. He hurried after, but immediately found himself engulfed in a stream of scientists and technicians and support crew. From a distance, he heard Kun Mar bawling out orders for people to keep back, dammit. Yan ducked into the forest and circled around until he came to the front of the crowd.

Kun Mar stood in the clearing next to Bej Saihan, who gripped the leg of a small, skinny monkey.

Not a monkey. A child.

A child that was all bones and brown skin, its legs mottled with scars, its face hidden behind a snarled mass of thick black hair. Young. Maybe eight or nine, though it was hard to tell. He could just make out its eyes and mouth, stretched wide in terror. It was filthy.

"What's going on?" Hari whispered, coming up behind Yan.

"I don't know," Yan whispered back.

The child cried out and launched itself away from Bej. Bej swiftly captured the child's other arm and subdued his captive. Again, the child made a grunting, howling sound.

"It can't talk," Che said softly. She had appeared from nowhere, and now stood next to Hari. Yan glanced down and saw their fingertips brush each other. Ah. When had that begun?

"Back to work," Mar said brusquely. "Come on, people. Five months isn't forever. We are on a schedule."

The remainder of that day was not a productive one. Distracted, Yan had to run several tests twice over, and from the Lian's grumbling, she was having the same difficulties. Finally, by mid-day, Yan gave up and sought out Hari.

He found Che and Hari in the otherwise deserted biochemistry labs, talking in low undertones.

"I sent them away," Hari said, obviously weary. "No use working today."

He meant the child, of course.

"Where did Bej find it?" Yan asked.

Che glanced at Hari, who sighed and told Yan what he knew. Bej Saihan and his trackers had decided to make a sweep of the island's northern tip, searching for signs of certain small reptiles notes by the original scouts. The trackers had just crossed over the stony ridge that divided the island, when Bej heard a noise.

"He thought it might be a snake," Hari said, "hiding in a patch of brush near the ridge. But then the child burst from its cover. Old Bej thought he'd flushed a monkey until he caught it. Fast little thing."

"It fell," Che said abruptly. "It stumbled over a root, or slipped on the loose rocks. Whatever. It sprained its ankle. Now Kun is trying to decide what to do with it."

"But what about its parents?" Yan said. "Surely—"

"Dead," Hari said softly. "Bej found their bones."

In spite of the heat, Yan's skin prickled with a sudden chill. He had read about such practices among various native tribes, who sometimes abandoned a criminal on desolate islands. Often, the children of those criminals were exiled along with their parents.

"The gods only know how the child stayed alive," Hari went on. "There's plenty to eat, of course. Shellfish. Roots. Those chewy tubers in the marsh—"

"They cut out its tongue," Che said. "They mutilated a child and left it here to die. And you both talk about the poor thing as though it were a specimen."

She pushed back her chair and stalked from the tent.

Yan made an abortive move to follow. Hari signaled for him to stay put. "Let her go. She's upset. More than I would have thought." He blew out a breath. "So am I, come to think of it."

So were many others in the expedition, though the tension revealed itself in odd ways. Hari and Che quarreled about procedures. Doctor Mar and Doctor Au broke off their late night card games. Lian made excuses when Yan asked about lunch, and several technicians requested changes in sleeping quarters. The fresh-cooked food tasted off, as though spoiled by heat and the cook's inattention.

After a second rebuff from Lian, Yan kept to himself. Once or twice he glimpsed Che in passing. Each time, her gaze flicked away from his, then a cool remote expression settled over her thin face. But she said nothing to him, only hurried on her way.

The third time their paths crossed, twilight was darkening toward night. The twin moons floated above the dark blue ocean, leeching all the color from the emerald green sands. A warm close evening, when the salt tang overpowered the scent of crushed leaves.

Che stopped and changed directions. Yan hurried forward and laid a hand on her shoulder. He felt her shudder through her thin shirt.

"What do you want?" she said.

"To say I'm sorry."

She shifted her gaze to his hand, resting on shoulder. "For what?"

Yan licked his lips. "For speaking the way I did about the child Bej found."

No answer. Just that cool remote expression, as though he himself were a vial of chemicals to analyze. Then, "I knew Mei."

That startled him. "You did? Then you know—"

Her lips thinned. "I know how you bullied her. Oh, you did nothing wrong. Nothing outright. But I know your type. You better watch yourself, Doctor Dei. Even if Doctor Hari Dun is your friend."

With a suddenness that took him by surprise, Che knocked away Yan's hand and pushed him aside. Yan fell against a tree trunk. It took him only a moment to recover his footing, but Che was already far beyond him, hurrying, almost running, toward the camp's brightly-lit center.

Just like Mei, running to a waiting taxi.

"Dammit!"

Yan smacked the tree trunk with his open palm. Damn Mei. Damn Che. What did she mean, *Watch yourself?* As if he had ever stopped watching every word and gesture he made. Damn the stupid heat that pushed and pushed against his patience. Tenure or not, he could not last another five months in this swamp.

He slumped against the tree trunk, breathing hard. His hand throbbed. The palm stung fiercely, scraped raw by the tree trunk. He brushed away the dirt and bits of bark from his hand. It bled slightly, but it would keep until he could talk calmly with the camp physician.

Walk it out, he told himself. That always worked.

He circled the camp and headed toward the beach, only to hear the sounds of laughter and cheers. Evidently, a group of the younger technicians had made a bonfire. A few were singing off-key, and Yan caught a whiff of roasted meat and wood-smoke.

With a muttered curse, he veered onto another path that led along the eastern edge of camp. Here the tents and wooden shelters were deserted, lit only by a few cool-lamp bulbs. He flicked on his pocket lantern. The soft trill of insects made a blanket of soothing noise, punctuated by the high-pitched chirp of the small frogs in the marshes.

And a soft persistent whimpering.

He paused and located the source of that whimpering—it came from one of the supply tents.

The child.

He had not seen it since that first day. After protracted arguments between Kun Mar and Bej Saihan, Mar had at last agreed to arrange for its care. "We've no damned anthropologists," he'd muttered, according to Hari. "And no damned nannies."

But that was enough for Saihan, who had cleared one of the supply tents for the child's sleeping quarters. Away from the main laboratory tents, close enough for casual supervision.

Yan hesitated. He retraced his steps and ducked inside the supply tent. A sudden scrambling broke out to his left. Yan lifted his lamp and shone the light over the interior.

The tent was a mess. Dirty bowls were scattered about. Three or four gray-green blankets made a nest in one corner. The whole thing smelled of sweat and filth. Then his light caught the child, who had squeezed behind a few cardboard boxes in one corner.

A girl, he thought. *A little girl.* He had not noticed before.

She was naked, but clean. Much cleaner than that first day, when Bej brought her into camp. Scars and bites covered her legs, her feet and hands were rough with calluses, but her eyes were like brilliant black stars. Thick glossy hair spilled over her face.

Yan crouched down. "Hello. Bej left you all alone."

No answer. No sign she even had heard him.

"What's the matter? Are you deaf, too?"

Odd that they left no one to supervise the child. But then, Mar didn't want distractions, and Bej had his own duties. She was a pretty thing, Yan thought, now that they had washed her.

He reached out to brush the hair away from her cheek. To his dismay, the girl flinched away from his touch.

"Hey, I'm not trying to hurt you—"

The girl launched herself away from him, but collapsed with a hoarse cry, clutching at the thick cast around her ankle. No wonder she had not run off. Yan took hold of her arm to help her up. With a quick twist of her head, the girl bit his hand. Yan gave a muffled shout and smacked her hard across the face. Again that grating cry. "Stop it," he hissed. "Stop making so much *noise*."

The little beast was weeping and snarling. Someone would surely hear. There would be questions. Yan could explain, but no one would listen. They never did. He grabbed for the girl's arm and managed to capture one wrist, then the other. Now he had her on her back, his hand over her mouth. All the while he was muttering, "Quiet. Quiet. Quiet."

Without warning, the girl went limp. Yan stared down at her, his chest rising in time with hers falling. His heart beating against hers. Her eyes wide and dark with terror.

Yan pushed away from the girl. "No," he whispered. "No."

He stumbled back to his tent, still shaking, and crawled into his cot. No one had seen. No one. Please dear gods. He had done nothing. Nothing wrong. He needed this job. Needed this second chance…

That night, he dreamed of midnight skies above still black seas.

The next morning, he woke groggy and underslept. He drank down a pot of strong tea and set to work examining a series of microbe cultures that Lian had prepared for him. When Hari dropped by for lunch, Yan waved him away. "I think I'm onto something."

"I hope so," Hari said cryptically.

Yan barely heard him leave. He worked through the noon hour, quitting only when the heat became unbearable. He switched off the equipment and stared through the tent's fabric at the glaring sunlight outside. *I lied*, he thought. *I'm not onto something. No one here is.*

Progress reports from the other two research sites had arrived that morning. In spite of his absorption in his own work, Yan had heard mutterings from the other members on his team. *Valuable data*, said all the reports. *But so far, no practical applications.*

Yan rubbed the sweat from his face. Lian. Che. Hari. Mar. They had all foolishly hoped for the same success as Anwar Enterprises's first expedition that had discovered the miraculous *tikaki* people and their regenerative blood. It was hope that made their disappointments even harder to bear.

He retreated to his tent and stayed there for the whole afternoon, his shirt off, with an electric fan blowing directly on his face, as he reviewed the printout of his latest tests. Odd and peculiar microbes inhabited XTI-19S137W-1A's soil and water. He might—could—make the case that microbes here represented a separate evolutionary chain, itself a valuable discovery for the scientific world, but so far, it was all speculation. He had uncovered nothing that could turn a profit for XianGen Pharmaceuticals or its government friends.

The rest of the day vanished into a haze of frustration. That night he dreamed that enormous creatures hunted him through XTI-19S137W-1A's scrubby forests. One in particular, a massive beast with blunt, yellow fangs, chased him along the island's stony spine. Yan kept glancing back—he could not help himself—only to see the beast gaining on him. His foot came down on a loose rock. He slipped with a garbled cry…

… and woke covered in stinking sweat.

Yan wiped his hands over his eyes. Impossible to catch his breath in this thick air. Impossible to sleep. He got up from his cot and pulled on a pair of loose trousers. A swig of water cleared the sour taste from his mouth. He splashed more water over his face and rubbed himself all over with a wet cloth. Hot. The air as thick as mud. His heart beat erratically, as though he had run for his life.

A walk. He needed a walk.

Yan picked up his pocket lamp, shoved his feet into his shoes, and headed out the tent. Just a walk, he told himself. He'd go upstream and sit on the rocks. Listen to the water rill past until he got sleepy again.

His path took him past the supply compound. All was dark and silent, around the tent where they housed the girl. Unconsciously, he rubbed his hand between the thumb and palm, where the girl had bitten him. Stupid girl. Hardly any difference between her and Mei, come to think of it. Both squalled if you looked at them the wrong way.

Yan paused, breathing heavily.

Don't do it. Don't think about it. Don't—

He lifted the flap and ducked inside. The girl did not stir. Only when his hand covered her mouth did she start awake. There was a brief struggle, but Yan was stronger and bigger. "Quiet, quiet, quiet," he murmured, though he knew she could not understand. "Be good. Be quiet."

She went limp, and did not move as Yan unbuckled his trousers. No response as he insinuated his tongue into that emptiness that was her mouth. Only when he pushed her legs apart and forced himself inside did she fight back. The stump of flesh, all that was left of her tongue, worked against his, as though she were trying to speak.

That night Yan dreamed of the scent of crushed leaves. The rich ripe sweat on his body. His mouth on hers. Her eyes, her wide dark eyes, just a few inches from his.

"They've named her Ah-ne," Hari mentioned a few days later

He and Yan sat together on the beach, eating their mid-day meal. Yan could see the remains of the bonfire—burnt logs, discarded cups, and the blackened empty shell from an enormous sea turtle. A few clouds smudged the southern horizon, suggesting that they might have rain showers later.

"Why Ah-ne?" Yan asked.

"From the sounds she makes. It's strange. She was a wild little creature when they caught her—and I can't blame the poor child—but now she's as quiet and calm as anyone would like. Just makes that grunting sound when someone comes into the tent. Ah-ne. Like that."

Yan nodded, only half listening. He raked his hair back from his face. His skin felt sticky, even though he had just bathed, and there was a heavy cloying scent all around that reminded him of Ah-ne.

He had avoided the supply tent these past few days, and immersed himself in work. It was work he needed. Work to block unhappy thoughts about Mei or Lian or Che. Work to numb the temptation. To his relief, the dreams had gradually faded. That same morning, Doctor Au had spoken with Yan privately. He was impressed with Yan's meticulous attention to detail. He was especially pleased with Yan's dedication in the face of growing rumors about the expedition.

"We have all contributed valuable knowledge," he said. "Especially you, Doctor Dei. If you care to join the research division at XiangGen, I would be happy to recommend your name."

With a start, he realized that Hari had stopped talking. "Sorry," he said. "I was thinking about next week's experiments. Another month and I might have something to make Doctor Mar happy."

Hari shot him a strange look. "Didn't you hear? Kun is talking about moving our site to another island. Next week we might all be packing our equipment."

Yan suppressed a start. "Next week? What about—"

"Your experiments? If Au agrees, take samples with you. Or start fresh with the new island. I heard Kun mention XTI-19S142W-8C. If that's the one, he's gambling on its isolation."

Hari rambled on about the characteristics of their possible destination, which was unique among the Tau'ini Po'a islands. Isolated from the others, with higher, older forests according to the survey teams. Most likely, Kun would order the other ships to new islands as well.

It was for the best, Yan thought, as Hari continued to talk. Mar would release the girl back into the wild. She would return to the life she knew. He thought again of her eyes, her wide dark eyes that took in everything Yan did, and his pulse gave an uncomfortable jump. How much would she remember? Would she even recognize him again?

Within another day, Doctor Mar announced the long-expected departure to another island. Two weeks, he told the senior scientists, who reported the news to their teams. Two weeks to wrap up their experiments and pack their equipment.

Yan remembered little of those two weeks. He spent long hours cataloging their existing microbe cultures, making duplicates of his reports and Lian's, discussing possible changes in procedure with Doctor Au. By evening, his bones had turned to water, and he dropped into his cot, exhausted. If he dreamed, he did not remember.

"Good news," Hari said to Yan during one of their rare visits together. "Kun has undergone a heart transplant and shows signs of actual humanity. Let us hope it doesn't ruin his abilities to manage the expedition."

"What are you talking about?" Yan said. In spite of the long hours, and hard work, his mood was hopeful. Lian's earlier remoteness had faded, and she had agreed to have dinner with him.

"I'm talking about Ah-ne," Hari said. "Kun is sending her back to the mainland on the next supply ship. He thinks they might do something to restore her voice. Probably there's a grant involved, but it's not like him."

Cold washed over Yan's skin, in spite of the heat. "No, it's not. I thought—" He broke off and managed a weak smile. "I rather thought he'd leave her behind."

"Hmmm. He's a practical man, not a brute. But yes, I'm surprised, too, at how much he's willing to do for the poor thing. Perhaps Doctor Mar thinks to impress the anthropologists after all. Think what the girl could tell use about her early life."

"Yes. Just think," Yan said softly. Dimly he listened to Hari's talk about major breakthroughs with voice box technology, pioneered by that same Anwar Enterprises whose success had inspired this expedition.

Ah-ne. Ah-ne talking. Not just with her eyes, but with her mouth, that soft empty mouth that now could grunt and sigh, but never shape the words for her thoughts.

Yan stood up abruptly. "Sorry, Hari. Got to lie down. Headache."

He stumbled away, not waiting for Hari's reply.

In his tent, he searched through his supply of medicines. He was not lying, he thought as he opened the bottle of aspirin with shaking hands. His head ached. His eyes throbbed in time with his pulse. Another moment and his stomach would heave up his lunch.

He swallowed the aspirin and then a double-dose of sleeping tablets, ones he had not used since Mei first left him. Two pills, not any more. He was upset, not ready to die. The sleeping pills almost stuck in his throat. He gagged and forced them down, then drank water until his stomach hurt. He stretched out on his cot and closed his eyes, waiting for oblivion.

... moonlight flickering between the branches of swaying palm trees. A pack of dogs chased after him, their tongues licking the air, as though tasting his scent. All of them were huge—Ame-no's hunting dogs, the pemburu. *He recognized them from old paintings, from carvings on temple walls, from his nightmares of two weeks past...*

He woke to full night. A hum from the insects drifted through the air. Yan stood, shaky from hunger. More water helped to revive him, but his stomach still felt pinched, and his skin itched. Images from his nightmare flickered through his brain, and merged with yesterday's memories.

Ah-ne. Ah-ne talking. Ah-ne telling everyone what happened to her.

He was halfway to the supply tent without even knowing what he intended to do. Talk to her. Try to persuade her. She had to understand how he had not meant to hurt her. Not that way. He found himself muttering, *hush, hush, hush,* as he crawled inside and fastened the flap shut so that no one could see. Ah-ne lay curled into a tight ball, hands laid together beneath her cheek.

Yan touched the girl's shoulder. "Ah-ne."

She woke with a start and scrabbled away from him, making panicked grunting sounds. Yan caught her by the arm. "No, Ah-ne. That's not why I came here. I came..."

How to explain?

"I came," he started over, "to ask you something."

Ah-ne struggled against his grip. She was breathing hard, making that soft grunting sound. *Ah. Eh. Ah. Eh.* No sign that she understood. How could she? Had she ever learned to speak before her people cut out her tongue? Maybe—

No, he could not depend on that.

"I can't talk here," he muttered. "Come with me."

He bundled her from the tent and hauled her to her feet. Her ankle had healed enough that she could stand, though she limped slightly as Yan dragged her away from the campsite. She tried to bite his hands. He gave her a hard shake and a slap. "Be quiet."

She went limp a moment. Thereafter, she stumbled after him, silent except for her labored breathing.

A short distance from the camp's edge, Yan plunged into the forest and aimed for the marshes. No one kept any watch, but couples sometimes prowled about, looking for privacy. He wanted no unexpected encounters with other members of the expedition.

For a while, the going was difficult. Once he passed the criss-crossing paths made by the expedition, he had to fight his way through the thorn bushes. The air was unusually close, here among the trees, filled with a musky scent from the leaves. Moonlight flickered through the branches, reminding him uncomfortably of his dreams, but he pressed on.

Gradually the trees thinned to an open patch of rough grass by the edge of the marshes. Yan stopped and knelt before Ah-ne. The girl's face was wet with tears, he realized with a start.

"Ah-ne," he said softly.

She stared at him, lips pushed out. Watching. He could feel her watching. Feel the tension in her skinny arms.

He tried again. "Ah-ne. They will take you away. Make you talk. They might... they might ask you questions."

He closed his eyes. Who was he fooling? He could not make her understand. Could not until she learned their language and for that she needed her tongue. And if she had her tongue—

Without warning, Ah-ne wrenched away. Taken by suprise, Yan almost lost his grip on her. He yanked her back around. She spat in his face.

A wave of red swept over his vision. He pushed Ah-ne to the ground and fell atop her. Ah-ne tried to twist away, but Yan captured her fists and crushed his mouth against hers to silence her grunts. Still thrashing, the girl whipped her head around and caught Yan hard on his temple. Stunned, he collapsed to one side. The next moment, Ah-ne had wriggled free and was on her feet, running.

"Ah-ne." Yan lurched upright and immediately stumbled over a root. Damn, damn, damn. She would run to camp. Kun Mar would find out. He'd dismiss Yan from the expedition. Au would withdraw his offer and notify the University.

Then, above the pounding of his heart, Yan heard a splashing sound, then a soft thudding as Ah-ne gained firm ground. She was heading for the ridge, where Bej Saihan had discovered her.

He ran a few steps. Stopped.

A girl. A savage beast-girl like that. She could disappear into the wild. She had lived there her entire life after all. And this time, she might know to avoid the trackers. Even trackers like Bej Saihan, whatever his background.

With a last glance toward the ridge, Yan started back to his tent.

"No sign of her?" Yan said.

A weary Bej Saihan stumped back into the campsite. "None." He took off his hat and wiped his face, looking entirely human, and not at all like a creature of the gods. "We checked the valley. We checked all the ravines in the area. We even dredged the marshes, just in case. Nothing."

More search teams returned throughout the morning, but already the expedition members had turned their attention from Ah-ne's disappearance to the final preparations for departure.

Stacks of crates awaited transport to the ship. Crews dismantled
the remaining tents. The settlement had vanished, leaving a bare
clearing and scattered trash heaps. Yan had packed up the last
of his own belongings, and now oversaw the transfer of the lab
equipment onto the ship.

Only when he was about to board the ship did Hari return
with Che at his side.

You could tell he was more disappointed than Bej himself,
Yan thought, taking in the man's stained shirt, his mud-caked
boots, and the dark bruises beneath his eyes. "I'm sorry," Yan
said softly.

Hari shook his head. "We tried. She wanted to go."

Che took Hari's hand. "Come," she said softly. "We all have
work to do."

Hari smiled at her wearily. "That we do."

Yan watched as the two walked through the empty site
toward the ship. Then he turned to his own chores. Che was
right. They all had work to do. And Lian would need help with
storing and labeling the last of their samples.

Within the hour, the last crates were aboard, the last
transport skiffs hauled up. The ship's motors chugged to life, the
solar sails expanded to catch the sun, and the ship slowly backed
away from the shallow bay. Yan leaned against the rail, watching
the island shrink slowly to a small point on the horizon.

In five or six days, they would arrive at the new island. More
work lay ahead—it would almost be like starting over—but Yan
didn't mind. A new island meant a new chance. Who knows,
perhaps it was best that Mei had left him. He should forget
about her entirely and concentrate on someone new. Someone
like Lian, who seemed to appreciate him better.

The winds shifted and blew hard against his face. He drew a
deep lungful of the cool salt-laden air. Already he could breathe
more easily.

Watercolors in the Rain

Shades of green and white colored the hospital room, bleeding from verdigris shadows to a bright frothy snow. The halls were quiet in this midnight hour, the patients asleep, and the visitors gone. Only the occasional nurse passed by on her rounds.

Evann Douai sat in the bedside chair, hands folded together, anxiously studying his wife's face. No change in the last hour. No change in the past three days, and yet he could not bring himself to go home. For what? He could not sleep, and it was too late to answer the many phone messages.

He sighed and rubbed his hands against his trouser legs. Light from the corridor leaked through the half-open door and fell across Gwynn's bruised face. Fair Gwynn, he had called her when they met, thirty years ago. Gwynn with her laughing gray eyes and hair like sunlight.

Ah, Gwynn. What went wrong?

An unreasonable question. He knew what had gone wrong, but every time he asked himself, Evann so disliked the answers that he asked again.

149

Gwynn stirred in her dreams. Strange images floated past her inner eye—those of witches and castles, of thick thorny vines, of light flaring from a needle's tip. Gradually, the dreams gave way to awareness, and her eyes blinked open.

The bed felt strangely unbalanced. Empty and quiet. Evann must have gone already. She turned her head. *Not gone*, said the plumped-up pillow and smooth quilt. *Never there.*

She blew out a breath. He must have worked late and spent the night in a hotel. It wasn't the first time.

Ignoring the tightness in her throat, Gwynn threw back the covers and got up. At least it was Saturday, she told herself sturdily. She could spend the morning gardening, clearing the weeds from around the roses. The need to work meticulously, to avoid the thorns and other hazards, would distract her.

Thoughts about drainage and peat moss and phosphorus absorbed her as she dressed and gathered her hair into a knot. She slid her feet into sandals and flung open the bedroom door.

And squeaked in surprise.

Gone were the familiar doors and hallways of her house. In their place, a marbled passageway stretched into the distance, lit by rows of torches, whose light rippled over the blue-veined stone. In the distance, a solitary bell tolled.

Gwynn let out a shaky breath.

I'm dreaming. I have to be.

Or was she? Vertigo swept over her, a feeling at once exhilarating and terrifying. Only then did she realize that her left hand gripped something heavy. She glanced down. It was a leather satchel, like an overnight bag.

Gwynn licked her lips and tasted a sweet perfume in the air. Roses. Hundreds of roses bloomed somewhere close by. If this was a dream, it piqued her curiosity. She shifted her grip on the satchel and stepped into the corridor.

Her hands were warm to his touch, but unresponsive. "Gwynn, Gwynn," he murmured, cradling them within his. "Can you hear me?"

Nothing except that elusive heartbeat. He did not count the monitors with their vivid green lines, nor the faint wheeze from the tubes that kept Gwynn breathing.

The police had called his cell phone. An accident, they said. A combination of black ice and fog. But Evann knew that Gwynn's presence on that road, at that hour, was no accident. They had given him a painstaking description of the scene— the sharp curve, the old blue Honda crumpled into a stand of trees, the suitcases and cardboard boxes scattered along the road. Evann had collected the wet and broken items from the police station. Spread over the living room carpet, they looked like a jumble of memories—stockings and hats and skirts, Gwynn's favorite shoes, the jewelry she made at the craft studio. And, of course, her books. The books had suffered the most, their pages wet and the ink smeared, so that Dunsany and Austen and Dunnett were all mixed together. Underneath the books, he had discovered the plaster gargoyle she'd acquired years ago in Paris, carefully wrapped in scarves. When Evann unwrapped the figure, he noted a deep crack along its base.

What if? he asked himself, vehemently. *What if I had come home early?*

What if? The most useless question in the world. He closed his eyes and rested his forehead on his hands, which still clasped her limp one. The cloying scent of roses filled the hospital room, from the many bouquets sent by neighbors, by their grown children (two children, not three), even from the local church, though neither had attended in years. *What if?* he asked, more quietly, and with its repetition, some of the sharpness of his anguish dissolved, like watercolors running and bleeding in the rain.

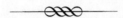

Gwynn drifted along a passageway lined with paintings and tapestries reminiscent of those she'd seen during their holiday in France. Biblical scenes. Portraits of angels, saints, and martyrs. A woman dressed in sumptuous velvets, her throat wrapped in pearls, her chin lifted as she gazed at her supposed audience. Gwynn paused, struck by how well the artist had captured his subject. In the wavering lamplight, you could imagine her chest rising with a breath just taken.

She let out her own breath, and felt an ache deep within.

Bridget never had a chance to breathe.

Tears blurred her eyes. She thought she was done with tears. Evidently not. She ran a hand over her face and turned away from the woman's portrait. Stupid useless paintings. Who dusted all these frames anyway?

Restless, she kept walking down the corridor, oblivious now to whatever paintings or tapestries or statues decorated the walls and niches she passed. What if? she thought. What if Evann had remained with her that long-ago day when she miscarried? Ah, that one was too painful to contemplate. What if... What if he had chosen a different, less-demanding career? What if he had spent more hours with her and their other two children? (Two, not three.) What if...

But she had not. And he had not.

She slowed, aware that her surroundings had changed. The paintings had vanished. In their place stood a series of looming statues, and the marble walls had become rough stone blocks that glinted red in the torchlight. The place reminded her of the Cluny, with its centuries-old foundations, where the cold dusty air still tasted of antiquity. Her pulse beat quicker, though nothing disturbed the stillness. It was too quiet here, too empty, even for a dream.

She stopped and closed her eyes, suddenly afraid.

If you can't see the monster, it can't see you.

A shaky laugh escaped her. Feeling foolish, she opened her eyes.

And drew a quick breath.

The passage had vanished. She stood in an octagonal room with doors set into three of the walls. Overhead, an elaborate chandelier hung from the ceiling, but otherwise the place was bereft of any decoration.

Gwynn blinked, but the scene did not change. She turned around slowly. Three doors. What lay behind them? Something new? Something... better?

The sense of giddiness returned, as though she stood upon a new threshold. *Choose anything,* she thought. *Choose for myself. Choose because it doesn't matter anymore.*

A childhood rhyme came back to her. *Ingle angle, silver bangle,* she recited, pointing at each door in turn. *Out goes you.*

Left then. She undid the latch, which lifted smoothly. Just as she pushed the door open, a shadow flickered over the walls. Startled, Gwynn turned around. Nothing stirred except the dust, whirling and glittering through the lamplight.

With his eyes closed, Evann could almost imagine that he sat in another room—anywhere but that sterile hospital, any time before Gwynn's accident. Think of a happier day, he told himself. Of that holiday in France, climbing among the ruins of a castle, which time had covered with rose vines. Think of himself, not as a vague, unreliable man, but as a knight errant, come to rescue his lady fair.

Silent laughter shook him. Still, he held the image of that castle in his mind. It stood upon a grassy sunlit ridge, while behind him rose a dark silent forest. Roses, vines, and thorns covered the castle's stone walls. Here and there, he glimpsed a carved figure, but otherwise the castle was invisible, cloaked in dark green leaves and scarlet blossoms. A solitary bird circled overhead—a crow or raven.

Evann dismounted from the horse (what horse? Oh yes, all knights rode horses) and drew his sword, which gleamed a ruddy gold in the late afternoon sun. He strode toward the nearest vine.

Six times Gwynn noticed shadows gliding over the walls. Six times, she turned but saw nothing. The exhilaration had subsided, leaving her weary and uncertain. She no longer felt like a carefree traveler. She was lost in a maze, somewhere within a strange castle.

"Waiting," said a voice. "For a rescue that never comes."

Gwynn spun around. The alcove behind had been empty; now a tall woman, dressed in swirling robes, stood within. She had pale luminous skin, her lips were the color of rose petals, and her eyes, like her robes, were a blue so dark, they seemed black. She was beautiful, Gwynn thought with a pang. Beautiful and strong in a way Gwynn had always longed to be.

The witch smiled, as though amused by Gwynn's silence. "Well?"

So she wanted an answer. Gwynn swallowed against a suddenly dry mouth. "I'm not waiting."

"No," said the witch. "Not anymore."

She held out her hand and spoke a word. Light flared, and a vial appeared in the witch's hand, filled with a pearly white liquid. The liquid smoked, faintly, and Gwynn caught the scent of summer grass, warmed by the sun. "Magic," said the witch. "Magic to ease your distress, to take away your indecision. To free yourself for all time."

Curiosity pricked at Gwynn, followed quickly by suspicion. It was too easy, this magical offer. Witches always demanded a price, even if they called it something else.

The witch studied her closely. "You don't like my potion."

"I can't tell," Gwynn said cautiously, trying to keep the tremor from her voice.

"Nor could you tell what lay ahead, when you chose the left-hand door."

She saw me. Cold prickled her skin. But of course the witch had observed her. This was her domain—that of dreams and fairy tales and enigmatic conversations.

The witch tilted her head. "You understand in part. But you don't see the implications yet. I'll ask again later."

With a quick gesture, she flung the vial upward, spinning it end over end. Its contents scattered into a glittering spray. Instinctively, Gwynn reached up to catch the vial. Before she could, it blinked out of sight.

So too had the witch.

Sweat dripped from his brow and stung his eyes, but Evann did not pause to wipe his face. Twilight was falling, and he wanted to reach the castle before full dark. He took aim and drove the sword into the next vine.

Clear red fluid spurted from the gash. The vine shrieked, its leaves unfurling like mouths.

Evann shuddered and closed his eyes a moment. He'd hacked through twenty such vines, and still their cries made him queasy. He gripped the sword hilt, tugged the blade free, and swung again. Once. Twice. On the third stroke, the vine abruptly went limp. Evann paused, panting heavily. His hands were sticky from the strange blood. His head still rang from the high-pitched cries.

"Christ and Buddha and Mohammed," he muttered, as he stamped toward the next one. There was such a thing as taking imagination too far. And yet, he never considered turning back.

"Why not?" said a voice. "You've done so before."

Evann peered through the thicket of vines. He could just make out a woman's pale face, framed by blue-black hair. If he were a fanciful man, he'd say it was a witch.

"I am," said the witch. Her mouth quirked into a smile. "And why not give up? Because you think to find your wife inside this castle, Evann Douai?"

Evann didn't question how she knew his name or his business. He was dreaming, after all, and such things happened in dreams.

"I have my reasons," he said shortly. "Why is not your concern."

She laughed and flicked her hand upward. The nearest vine whipped into life, catching Evann around the throat. He yelped in surprise and dropped his sword to grab the vine, but the thorns were already digging into his flesh. More vines twined around his arms and legs. They crept up his chest and covered his face, their leaves opening and closing like hungry mouths.

Damnable witch really wants me to stop. He gave a harsh laugh, in spite of the thorns. He'd cut through far thicker, nastier obstacles in his life.

"Maybe the true obstacles aren't visible," said the witch.

She spoke a word, and the vines recoiled from Evann's body. He lay gasping for several moments before he touched his throat with a shaking hand. No blood, but a ripping pain when he swallowed made him think the encounter was real. The witch had disappeared.

He pulled away the now-dead vines and stumbled to his feet.

Go. Turn back. Give up.

But he had never given up before, never backed away from a challenge. Never, he reminded himself, except once.

He sucked in a lungful of air and hefted his sword. Working like an automaton, he hacked and slashed at the vines, pausing only to push away the shriveled masses of leaves, never minding the thorns, which tore at his hands. When he finally cleared away the last one, he stood, dazed and swaying slightly. It took a moment before he could focus on the door itself.

It was a massive wooden slab, twice the height of an ordinary man, with bolts and hinges that looked stiff from rust and disuse. Evann put a hand against its smooth surface. *How on earth am I to open that?*

The door swung open. Evann braced himself for another confrontation.

A puff of stale air blew against his sweaty face. It smelled of dust and smoke, with a trace of rose petals.

Evann waited but nothing else happened. He leaned inward, one hand against the doorframe. The castle's interior was smothered in dark, and like water poured from a bottle, the shadows flowed outward to merge with the deepening twilight. An illusion, just like the others. But he could not rid himself of the sensation that he might drown in that darkness.

Turn back, the witch had said.

"Like hell," he breathed, and walked inside.

The hall was not entirely dark. Rows of windows, diamonds and squares and circles, were visible high above. Still, Evann found it difficult to see. He moved forward cautiously, his footsteps echoing from the dusty tiles. Far overhead, he heard the rustle of many wings.

"If this is a fairy tale," he said. "I'd expect magic lights. A servant, at least."

The air went taut. Evann caught his breath, thinking how the witch might challenge him this time. A heartbeat later, torches blazed into life.

His first thought was that he'd stepped into a fantastical summer sky. Blue marble tiles covered the floor. Huge columns, decorated with figures of men and beasts, rose upward to the domed ceiling, which was also blue. Unlike the fairy tales, there were no sleeping servants, nor a feast preserved by enchantment, only an empty castle, with halls extending off in all directions and one grand staircase leading upward.

The next time Gwynn encountered the witch, it was in a bell-shaped chamber, whose walls were decorated with mosaics of courtly scenes. Though Gwynn had not climbed any stairs, she had the impression of having ascended to a great height. The air here felt cooler, clean of dust and smoke. Only a faint trace of incense lingered.

"One last warning," the witch told Gwynn. "Turn back now, and you can ride into oblivion, the eternal traveler."

Gwynn had had enough of riddles. "What happens if I go through there?" she said, indicating the door.

"The choice is yours."

"I don't believe you. Whenever I choose, the opposite happens. At least, that's been my life so far."

The witch shrugged. "You do have choices. What comes after, however, might be difficult to control."

Gwynn hesitated. The witch had given her a deliberately oblique answer. Did she mean that Gwynn could choose a different life? And if she did, could she choose its direction as well?

Choose what you like, said the witch.

Easy for you to say, thought Gwynn.

She set down her satchel and opened the last door.

Six times he nearly stopped before he reached the tower room. The witch had gone. More unsettling, he realized she had removed every obstruction. He had light where he needed it. When his throat closed from dryness, a flagon of cold water appeared at the next landing. He even heard low sweet chords of music, as though to urge him onward.

She made it too easy, he thought. With every physical obstacle gone, he had only himself to fight against—his own natural hesitation, his tendency to glide around the difficult patches, or to avoid them altogether.

So he wasn't surprised when the next landing contained a padded bench, its curved back and smooth broad armrests calculated to please his tastes. Evann sank onto the bench, trembling. The witch knew him too well. He'd wanted to rest, to consider what he was doing.

Turn back, she had said.

It would be easier if he turned back. Easier to give in. To let the future have its way. After all, Gwynn had made the choice when she left him. Wasn't it selfish of him to pursue her?

He leaned against the wall and tilted his head back. Far overhead, the stonework made a spiral, overlaid by shadows in another pattern, equally complex. One hand ached where a thorn had pierced his palm. Absently, he rubbed the wound, which had scabbed over.

Two children, not three. Years had leached some of the anguish, but not all. Never all.

What if? he thought. *What if I had wept at home and not alone in my hotel room, that week?*

But he had not. Not that week, nor the next. However much he wished, he could not change today without altering his entire past. And the past, he reminded himself, was immutable. Only the future remained.

The future. Yes.

Evann stood up. Abruptly, the bench vanished and a jangle of trumpets reverberated through the tower. Ignoring that, he mounted the stairs quickly, passing landing after empty landing until he arrived at the top.

An arched doorway stood opposite the stairs. Hardly knowing what to expect, he passed under the arch to enter an airy room with tall windows open to the skies. A full moon lit the scene, and by its clear blue light, he picked out the sleeping figure within its alcove.

Gwynn.

She lay upon a bier draped with green and ivory silk. A breeze stirred Gwynn's long hair, which took on a silvery cast in the moonlight. Heart beating faster, Evann crossed to her side and looked down. Gwynn, fair Gwynn. Her face was unmarred, her lips curved in a faint smile.

Kiss her.

The witch's voice sounded clear within his mind. He looked up in time to see a shadow outside the window and heard the slow heavy beating of wings.

Never mind the witch, he thought. He'd do what he liked, without regard to her schemes.

He bent over Gwynn and kissed her softly.

The taste and scent of summer clover. The warmth of her breath tickling his cheek. Gwynn's eyes blinked open; in the moonlight, they gleamed like silver. "Evann," she murmured. "Have you come to share my dream?"

"If you like."

Gwynn frowned. "I don't know what I like. I almost did."

Somewhere in the background, Evann heard muted laughter. Here was the true obstacle. Not the thorns, not even the long trek through this deserted castle, but in this room, facing Gwynn. Hardly knowing what he did, Evann held out a hand. "Stand up. We'll both think better."

After a moment's hesitation, Gwynn allowed him to help her down from the bier. They stood in uneasy silence, then, studying each other from a few paces apart.

She looked beautiful to him. He looked strangely battered.

"What happened?" she asked.

Evann glanced down. Dirt stained his trousers; bits of leaves clung to the rest of his clothes. There was blood underneath his fingernails, and more spattered down his shirt front. "Ah. I had some trouble getting into the castle."

Her smile was pensive. Trouble. How like him to understate the matter. He must have encountered the witch, and she wondered if he had managed to offend her. Was that a bruise around his neck?

Evann looked anything but amused. He rubbed a hand through his hair and vented an unhappy breath, before he finally met her gaze. "Gwynn, I'm sorry."

"About what?" she said warily.

"Everything." He made a sweeping gesture. "I wasn't—It wasn't right of me to leave you alone after Bridget died."

Her heart stilled, and for a moment she could not breathe or speak. "It's not—It's not just Bridget."

He nodded, a quick jerky motion. "I know. I—"

"If you knew, why didn't you say anything before?"

Evann flinched. Gwynn held up both hands, as though to recapture her words. "I'm sorry," she whispered.

We're both of us worn out, Evann thought. *Both of us over-sensitive and ready to flee.* But he'd promised himself to make one last attempt. He'd gone over the words a dozen times as he climbed the stairs, reviewing and rearranging them in his mind, wanting to say it just right.

"What if," he said. "What if we try again? What if we stop trying to change yesterday and change tomorrow instead?"

Unconsciously, he'd reached toward her. She took his hand, careful of his injured palm. "Isn't it too late?"

"I don't know. But it's worth finding out."

They heard the rush of wings outside, followed by a thin reedy note. It might have been a flute, or the wind gusting over the stonework. Shadows rippled upon the stone walls; Gwynn heard whispers, and Evann sensed the company of other people. It was as though the castle had drawn a breath.

Again the suggestion of music floated through the air, and a familiar voice said, *Dance.*

The witch. Gwynn smiled. Evann tilted his head, his expression unexpectedly shy. "Will you?" he said. "Dance with me, I mean. It's not so bad an idea."

She hesitated. "I'm not so good with dancing."

"Neither am I. But we could try."

Try. And stumble. And know that every step would constrain her, and in turn, would constrain him. He must have read her thoughts from her expression, because he withdrew his hand and turned away with a sigh.

"Wait," Gwynn said and reached toward him.

He looked half-afraid, she thought. As well he might. She hadn't given him much encouragement.

"Please," she said. "You said yourself we should try."

Now it was his turn to smile. "So I did."

Evann circled her waist with his arm. Around them, the tower room stretched outward to become a ballroom. The breeze quickened, its keening transformed into the first notes of a dance. Wing beats marked the time.

"I remember this song," Evann said. He moved to take the lead, then paused. "You start."

Less sure of herself, Gwynn took a first step. Evann moved in counterpoint, awkwardly but without treading on her toes. Another followed. Gradually the urge to quit receded from their thoughts. Step reflected step, painfully conscious at first, and then becoming more natural as the music lifted into a polyphony of horns and drums and sweet-toned violins. On and on they danced, whirling across the polished floor, until the music reached its glorious crescendo, bright and dark chords cascading over them.

They paused, his lips close to hers.

"I love you," he said and kissed her.

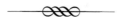

"I love you," Evann said, turning his cheek against Gwynn's wrist. Her skin smelled of powder and disinfectant, but underneath was a trace of her perfume, a sweet cinnamon scent that spoke not of this hospital, nor of death, but of Gwynn herself. *Sweet Gwynn. Fair Gwynn. Gwynn, my one true love.*

A shadow flickered against the wall—one of the night nurses, no doubt, checking on her patient and the visitor—but before Evann could turn around, the nurse had vanished.

Evann kissed Gwynn's hand, his touch as light as air. A strand of hair had fallen over his eyes. In their courting days, the strand would have been a glossy black, now it was streaked with gray.

"Will you dance with me again?" he said. His eyes were bright and no longer shy.

Ghostly figures twirled around them, like memories of older days. The music too had not stopped. The castle had awakened, and the music would continue, Gwynn realized, no matter what her answer. Only Evann remained still, waiting.

Do what you like, the witch had told her.

Choose. Today and tomorrow and ever after. No longer a solitary traveler but perhaps just as free.

Gwynn touched Evann's cheek. "Dance with you again? I would like that."

He smiled and drew her close. And again they began to dance.

Medusa at Morning

S cent came first on awaking—the fragrance of rain on autumn leaves, though trees no longer grew by her cottage. Was it memory or a dream? she wondered. Or simply regret?

She lay a moment longer with her eyes closed. Muted sounds intruded through the open window: the surf hissing over sand and rock, a tern's shrill cry. Nearby, a floorboard creaked, as though a ghost trod through her empty cottage. No use, sleep was gone.

Reluctantly, she rose and went to the window. The seas were a dark murmuring mass, but above them, dawn had turned the sky transparent. A breeze, laden with salt tang, blew in from the south. From its damp caress she judged the day would turn wet. She smiled. *I should have been a sailor myself, instead of loving one.*

As if in response, her hair rustled. *Be still,* she told it. With a practiced twist, she bound the hair into a loose braid, and wound it once around her head, where it lay silent.

She pulled on a thick sweater and loose pants. Habit carried her from bedroom into kitchen, where she took a coffee tin and glass carafe from the cabinets. Her thoughts only half on her task, she measured coffee and set a kettle of water on the gas burner.

So. He was gone—had been for two weeks—leaving her with a cottage and the solitary grandeur of this ocean view. Oh yes, and the company of her sisters on the neighboring islands.

She expelled a painful breath. *No more self-pity*, she thought, swiping the tears from her cheeks. The abrupt movement dislodged her braid, and a strand of hair slithered across her breast, the dark copper glinting in the sunrise. So she had loved, risked her heart, and lost. What else?

A sputter, then a pop—the water was boiling over. She snapped off the burner and poured the water over the coffee in its filter.

My courage, she thought, continuing her daily monologue. *My sense of balance. Of self.*

Good memories and bad. She remembered him laughing, his ruddy face alight with excitement. She remembered his red-gold hair, thick and springy between her fingers. His moods, those electric and unpredictable moods that left her breathless and off balance.

That was how he had infiltrated all her defenses. She remembered that first wild kiss, his breath on her cheek, and his warm spicy scent. *Love me back*, he had whispered. And then, *I dare you.* His favorite challenge.

She had dared, believing herself courageous and generous both. Thinking she saw a need behind that shield of bravado.

The aroma of coffee filled the air. She poured herself a cupful, added a splash of cream, and stirred the bright whorls into smoothness. Cup in hand, she left the cottage for the rocky cliffs and settled herself on the highest of the slate rocks. Sea and sky stretched out unbroken before her. Ink-blue shadows obscured the coastline, but a blood-red dawn stained the far horizon, and light brushed over the dark swells like an artist sketching in the day.

Trees had once lined the coast—she remembered them from her childhood. Disease had taken them all years ago, leaving only a few husks preserved by the salt water. In their most bitter argument, the last one, he had compared her to that blight. Her look, he'd said, could wither men and trees alike.

"How can you say that?" she'd whispered.

His dark brown eyes had turned opaque. "You ask too many questions."

When had questions become threatening? When had trust, freely given, changed into demands, both his and hers?

Her throat squeezed tight. She swallowed and took a gulp of her coffee. *Strong and scorching hot,* she thought with a breathless laugh. *And the sunrise flawless.* Her two standards of perfection now so pointless.

The last night, he had taken her into his arms. "Beloved," he had murmured, in a tone that reminded her of their early days together.

"What do you want?" she'd asked. "I'll give it."

"Freedom," he'd said, kissing her gently. "For us both."

His words, like an executioner's sword, had severed the last strands of hope. By morning, he had gone, catching the weekly flight to the mainland.

A breeze rolled in from the sea. She drew in a breath and tossed her head back. Her hair uncoiled from its casual knot and tumbled free. *Freedom is a painful gift,* she thought.

I dare you, he had whispered.

The snakes stirred. This time, she did not stop them.

Jump to Zion

*D*ays lon tan, days long-ago, our mothers and fathers sang about the promised land. They sang in secret, in the slave quarters, of a city where the ancient kings ruled. They sang of Zion, whose towers glittered in the sun. Oh, but Zion was more than a city lapped in jewels and gold. She was like the catch of laughter, a lover's kiss, as sweet as honey, as strong as wine. She was the mother who heals all wounds.

In Zion, the gods told us, we would be free.

They lied to us, those gods.

Through my open window floats a hot high breeze. It carries to me the stink of donkeys in the market square, the sweet perfume of hummingbird flowers and the musk of the jungles, not so far away. My shop lies near the harbor district, and if I listen hard enough, I might hear the hush of waves against our island shores.

"Youn, dé, twa..."

I count the bills from my money-box. So very few, each one precious. I think, if I had money like the rich, like a river, it would not be so difficult to let each bijet go. From the street below comes an echo of little girl voices. Like bells they are, high and clear, and they are chanting.

Jump the child, jump so high, jump the snake and run away.

It is twenty years—more—since I jumped the rope with my sisters and m' zanmi yo de kè, my friends of the heart, but memory comes back strong each freedom day. These girls below—I have no need to see with my eyes. They do the same as I did. They laugh, they skip and leap, heels flash like black birds on the wing, as they sing their song.

Jump to Zion. To libète. Jump all the slaves to La Trinète.

I have no use for the old songs. Pa jamè. No, not ever. Not on that day each month I pay my freedom tax to M'sieu Vide, before sunset and sabbat close his doors.

"Uit, nèf, dis…"

Ten livres royales lie in a row, printed on crisp new paper, as the custom tells us. Ten times the face of Sekou Omar, our President and King. For a moment I regard them, these ten soldiers of wealth. The paper is cheap, the ink dark blue and smeared in one corner from the sweat on my thumb. Ten livres is what I earned these past eight days from mixing herbs and powders—charms for luck, potions for the sick, and good strong physicks to ease the heart. In the center of each, Sekou Omar's face is like a spider web of blue-black lines, his eyes blank dots. Is there a heart inside the man?

I think not.

A woman shouts outside. The girls' voices stop, and they scatter like small black birds on the wing. My mouth tilts in a smile, remembering how I once did the same, but my smile is not a happy one.

Manman e papa e twa sèsè yo. Youn frè. Mother and father and three sisters. One brother. All gone these past ten years. Now, only my daughter, only Raziya remains.

My daughter. For her, I count out ten more livres. Ten belong to my master for my own freedom tax. It is the price I pay for these rooms, this shop. For a life that is almost my own. Ten more livres are for Raziya, so that one day she too might fly free. I touch each square of paper, dis e ven, before I close the shutters and prepare for my duty.

With fresh water drawn from the well, I wash the sweat from my face. I untangle my hair from its braids and pour sweet oil over my head. With swift fingers, I tie the hair into tight rows, then into thick braids that hang down my back. I dress in my good white blouse and clean red skirt, and cover my head with a dark blue scarf—all this to show respect to my former master and the gods of La Trinète.

Six bells ring from the market towers as I lock the door to my shop.

The livres royales lie against my heart. They speak soft with rustling voices.

The beads in my hair and around my neck speak aloud as I walk. *Klik e klik e klik.*

Hot it is, outside, the air wet and the skies dull with the coming rains of spring-time. In the market, old women pick through baskets of the tiny red chiles, the bananas and sweet potatoes, and the winter sugar beets. Farmers have brought their best produce, their fattest lambs, for the Carnival season upon us, and soon everyone will feast and drink and dance, and sing the old songs about Zion.

Above our city of Azil rise the three peaks of La Trinète. The masters call them Father, Son, and the Holy Servant. The rest of us, slaves and freedmen, call them the Twa Manman. Truth? Does not matter, I think. Their faces are gray and blank, their haunches clothed in dark green skirts. They watch without comment over the wretched pageant below, much as they did ten years, dis ane yo before.

I do not lift my gaze to the mountains. I squeeze between the vendor stalls, only thinking how M'sieu Vide will beat me if I am late, and that alone if I am lucky. Just as I break free of the stalls and cross the wide open plaza, a hand stops me. One brief touch—hot, like an iron upon my skin.

The scent of horses and sweet jasmine floods my senses.

I swing around to see no one.

No one except a tall figure in robes striding away through the crowds.

My breath sticks sharp inside my chest. *I know him.*

In my ears, I hear my name echo like a chant from dreams long ago. *Adjua, Adjua, Adjua.* I see a man in white robes, the white robes of a priest of the old temples, coated with red dust, and close my eyes against the tears. It is no good, ne jamè. I am dreaming the old bad dreams.

M'sieu Vide is a goldsmith. That means, for those of you who do not comprehend the implications, he is rich. Rich and with influence. Twenty slaves live under this roof to cook and wash and serve the master. Thirty more labor in his accounting house, recording the moneys that flow inside, the fees and payments that slither out in bribes and fees. For me, Adjua Dia de Vide, his status means that I pay this man ten livres royales every month, because he showed mercy in permitting me to live apart from his domain.

I present myself at the slave doors. I take the wooden stick from its socket. Once, twice, three times I knock.

Within moments, a young man appears. He is dressed beautifully in white linen breeches and a jacket tied with a crimson sash. Two rubies pierce his ears; another hangs like a drop of blood from his lip. His name is Kafele, well-beloved of his master in many ways, and we know each other from the days when I too lived in the same household.

"Lagras," he says. "Grace be to you." His dark brown gaze brushes over me, as cool as the night breeze, as soft as the silk I will never wear.

"Lagras e lonè," I reply. "Grace and honor to you. I am here for my duty."

He nods. We understand each other, well enough.

I step into the shadow-filled passageway. The tiles of the floor are cool and damp against my bare feet, and the air smells of earth and drifting clouds of wood smoke. Through the open doorway into the kitchen, I hear the girls banging pots in time to an old song as they chop and slice and fry the good onions. Once I worked in that same kitchen. It was old Oji, the cook, who taught me what else herbs and powders might do, who gave me the key to my almost-freedom.

"He works late today," Kafele says, so soft.

I say nothing. Whether M'sieu Vide works late or not is egal to me, who must pay her tax this day or fall back into slavery.

My face is blank enough for the masters, but Kafele is slave. He does not need lamp or letters to read my heart. He sighs and the coldness drops away from him, leaving a weary boy.

"Follow me," he says. "I know where you may wait."

He takes me to a tiny set of stairs that climb up to another secret corridor where slaves hurry to their tasks. Some carry buckets of water to wash the floors; others bear stacks of clean linens atop their heads, to make fresh the beds for their master and his guests during this Carnival season. My gaze flickers over them, but I do not see my daughter.

We come to a closet off a larger hall where M'sieu Vide has his office. Here Kafele leaves me.

The closet is small and dark, but it contains a stool, upon which I sit. I expect to wait a long time—a thing I am used to. Through the doorway, I glimpse the familiar sun-filled hall with its statues of Mère Mariama Maria and her daughters. Below them sit the smaller figures of toads and lizards and rats. The old gods of La Trinète and the new gather around the goldsmith's office door, or so the old man believes.

Ah, woman, you let yourself think too free.

It is these two, almost three years away. I forget—almost—how to keep my wild thoughts tied up in a knot and buried deep inside my heart. Others, they have forgot completely. M' papa e manman e twa sèsè yo. My brother who joined the rebels and who died with a bullet in his heart, sent there by Sekou Omar and his bloody soldiers.

Inside my blouse, my twenty livres rustle. Speak soft, they say, and freedom will be yours.

They lie. And still I listen. What else should I do? I breathe out hate and anger and desire. I pass a hand over my face and wipe myself clean of all expression. When Kafele returns with word that M'sieu Vide has a moment, I am like this young man, as cool and empty as the night.

We glance at one another. Our faces say nothing. Our hearts, so much.

And so I walk through the doors.

The law does not require me to give these ten livres to my master with my own hand. The law only cares that I have my receipt to give the judges. Oh, but tradition requires much more. It is for tradition that I enter the dark shuttered rooms of my master's office, eyes cast down and hands crossed over my breasts. It is for tradition that I spread my skirts and kneel and touch my forehead to the wooden floor. Then I take the livres from my blouse. They are damp from my sweat, and smelling sweet from the oils that soak into my skin from my work. I stretch out my hands with these livres in supplication—to Mère Mariama Maria, say the priests, but in truth to M'sieu Vide—and bow down to the floor once again.

My master loves this, the tradition.

"Adjua," he says. His voice creaks and groans. He is an old man. He was old, then, when he first took me to bed.

"My master."

"Non-plu," he says. "You are free."

After so many years, the lie does nothing more than sting against my conscience. I draw myself to sitting. It is dull and dark in this great room, with only six bars of golden light falling through the shutters. A single lamp upon the desk shines its ugly light upon my master's face. He is old, his dark face lined by his seventy years, dusky and dull. His eyes, however, are like polished brass coins. He reminds me of the toads statues outside the office, which gather around Mère Mariama Maria's feet. They too are old. And dangerous.

M'sieu Vide beckons to me. "Stand. Give me the tax."

The livres hiss, as if they object to the transaction. Or maybe it is my own heart that speaks. I shut my ears against these thoughts and lay the *bijet yo* upon the broad polished desk. One stack, two. The old man, the toad, catches them up with his shriveled fingers. I draw back three steps and bow my head.

My master mutters the numbers as he counts the sum. When he reaches the number *dis*, he sets those bills aside. "No more."

I am so surprised, I stare. "But…"

He stares back at me. His toad-eyes are bright and glistening. I remember myself. I sink to my knees and press my forehead to the wooden planks once more. Hard, because I am trembling and I do not wish my master to see.

There is silence between us. Through the shutters, comes the sing-song of the marketplace, but quiet and far away. Much closer is the wheeze and groan of my master's breath.

"You were a good girl," my master says. "You gave me no trouble, non. So I will tell you that a man offered me a fair price for the girl. She goes next week."

For a terrible moment I cannot move. His words cut like the lash, a pain so sharp even when you brace yourself against it.

Where? I cry deep inside. *Where have you sold my daughter?*

I do not speak those questions aloud. Freedmen are slaves with a different name, goes the saying, and so I pretend that I am some stranger, listening to this old man speak about another stranger girl. If I am quiet enough, he will say more.

He does. "I will speak with her new master. Ask him to allow your visits. It is only right for the mother." Then he fiddles with the livres upon his desk. I can hear them whispering. "And, eh, it is no big thing, but you will have credit for the money you have paid me already for her."

I do not want my money. I want my daughter, old man.

Another impossible thing.

For almost thirty years I was a slave. For two more, a freedwoman, which is a slave by a different name. I have the practice of my life to keep me from screaming my rage, to lock it tight inside me with the key invisible. I stand and bow to this toad. His mouth curls as I do so. He does nothing more. Only when I reach for the second stack of bills does he stop me. "Sa se pa nesesè. You may leave that money with me."

The thief. My breath vanishes, and I would strike him if we were both two free souls. But I cannot. Raziya lives within this household still. For every libèrte I take, my daughter would suffer. And so the trembling stays inside me. I bow to my master and back away from the room.

The young man Kafele appears at once to guide me back to the slave doors. The master does not wish a freedwoman to speak with the slaves of his household. It would make for unhappiness, or so he would say. I am not truly free, non byen sèten, but I have a kind of freedom these others do not share. I understand and so I do not refuse.

By the kitchens, however, I pretend a great faintness.

(*Not so much a lie. That man will sell my daughter.*)

"Might I, souplé, drink a cup of water?" I whisper.

Kafele knows too much. He does not argue with me.

"Sit," he says. "I will ask the cooks to fetch what you need."

There are no chairs or benches near the slave door. I find a crate that once housed lemons and limes. I sink upon it, oh, so carefully, and close my eyes. A girl from the kitchens brings me a tin cup filled with sweet cool water. She brings too a plate of biscuits, dripping with honey. A special treat. It is not enough to pay for my daughter's freedom, but it is all that a slave like Kafele can do for me. In my heart, I thank him.

Water, so pure and cold. It leaves a taste of flowers and earth upon my tongue.

Biscuits, each bite like a burst of sweetness inside my mouth.

I eat slowly to savor them. A tiny packet of joy amidst the rest.

"Manman."

Raziya kneels before me. Fifteen, she is, but tall. Her face is the clear bright brown of a polished coin. Her eyes are dark and soft, her lips the color of the rose, the dark-brown rose that grows inland on the mountains. Our stories tell us the rose came with us to La Trinète, in the old days, days lon tan, when Zion was real, or so we believed.

My daughter reaches out to touch my cheek. Her eyes hold pity, her mouth sorrow. So young, I think, and yet she is not. Underneath the thin cotton of her blouse and skirt, it is clear to see she has a woman's breasts and hips. Only fifteen. It is too soon for her.

(*And yet, I was fourteen when M'sieu Vide took me to bed. Fifteen when I took my first and only lover. Sixteen when my daughter was born.*)

I brush away those memories. They do me no good today.

We speak swiftly. We have little time.

"He told me," I say. "Do you know where?"

"The palace," she answers.

There is but one palace on all the island—Sekou Omar's.

My throat pinches tight in sudden anguish. *Oh, oh, oh. Non, pa jamè.* Sekou Omar and the men of his palace take women and girls like ripe plums to chew and spit away.

"Manman." Raziya rests a hand upon my arm. "Manman, are you sick?"

"No," I whisper. "Tired, cheri."

But my daughter is a clever young woman. She knows how to read a slave's face as well as I do. Better. "Oh, Manman," she says. "It is too late to save me from that."

They say that we were slaves before, in that other world, far beyond the seas of La Trinète. That our masters were demons— pale ghosts from lands so cold the water fell in frozen teardrops from the sky. They took us from the hot desert, from the sweet sweating forests, and carried us in vast wooden prisons over the ocean to islands much like La Trinète.

Some of these stories are like the ravings of those who drink the bitter black wine—but the rest? Well, the rest I can believe because I see the fingerprints of truth each day. Just like our judges, those white men bound us with incantations called the law. And when the law herself was not sufficient, they cut our backs with the whip, they raped our children, they called us savage beasts—as if that wiped their souls clean of the savagery they visited upon us. Even our own language they burnt from our memory. We have only their tongue, and a few words, like precious jewels saved from a great disaster, from the land called Afrik.

All that was two, maybe three hundred years long ago. The number makes no difference to me. All I know is what the songs tell me. That one day Kweku Ananse came to my people and promised to carry us all to Zion, away from the white demons.

And so he did. He gathered our mothers and fathers from long-ago into great ships. He gathered us from Haiti and Trinidad and many other islands. When he had gathered as many as he pleased, those ships sailed through a bright gate, from ocean to ocean, from world to world.

But he never promised to make us free.

The memories of my people from long-ago fade into the warm damp night of today, of now. I settle onto my knees in the soft soil of a new grave. This is not, you understand, the graveyard of the rich like M'sieu Vide or his compatriots. All around me are the tiny stones that mark where we bury the ashes of slaves and freedmen.

I take a knife from the leather bag. Next, three small sacks of cornmeal, flour, and bricks ground fine. A handful of bitter herbs gathered in the previous dark-time, the day when Mother Moon hides its face from Father Sky. Three white candles dipped in sweet honey-suckle wax. A bowl cleansed as the rituals require. The knife shines bright in the full moonlight, a silver flame brighter than any candle.

Holding one candle close, I strike a flint against the nearest gravestone. Sparks fly over the damp earth and rotting leaves. The candle sputters, then catches light. When it burns steadily, I light the other two from its flame and set them in the points of a triangle. Now I have the white of the moon, the yellow of candlelight.

"Mère Mariama Maria," I say. "Listen to your daughter. Hear her cry for justice. For this, I set the gift of my body and my heart before you."

As Oji the cook showed me, in those other lessons, beyond cooking and healing, I make the *veves* to draw the gods and spirits closer. I draw a circle from the cornmeal. With the white of flour, the dull red of brick, I add the shapes within, the ones that belong to the spirit I would summon. My hands tremble, making the shapes waver before my eyes. I have performed this ritual just once before—that first time M'sieu Vide said he would sell my daughter. I came to this same graveyard and called the same spirit. That was before I understood the price the orisha would demand of me. That spirit saved my daughter, but in her place, M'sieu Vide sold my three sisters to the palace.

It is not the same, I tell myself. *I have no more sisters to lose.*

Still, a sour taste fills my mouth as I contemplate what must come next.

I must. If I do nothing, Raziya will die.

With a cry, I snatch up the knife and slash my arm from wrist to elbow.

The metal blade burns my flesh. Blood pours into the bowl. I want to vomit my soul onto the earth before me, but I do not. The ritual requires that I maintain control of my body, or else the gods will not hear. Me, I have no idea if the gods care if I spew upon the dirt or not. I only know I dare not risk any disrespect. Not tonight.

My thoughts collect themselves. I swallow and my stomach holds herself intact. Byen.

The ritual continues. I crush the green herbs between my fingers and drop the crumbs into the blood. Next come certain powders, collected that afternoon from the shadow market, behind Mère Mariama Maria's grand white temple. Powders ground from the murder-man's bones. Roots dug from this same graveyard and dried under the full moon. A lizard's tongue which turns to dust between my thumb and finger.

All of this I stir into the blood with my fingertips. It is thick, like mud, and smells of animals, of death.

"Mère Mariama Maria, hear me," I say, and paint the mixture over my lips.

"Yemaja, hear me," I say, and suck my lips into my mouth.

My mouth fills with the flavor of blood and bones. But I am not done, no, not yet.

"Legba," I whisper.

Mère Mariama Maria is the mother god of the Chretiens. Yemaja is the savior of our children. Oh but it is Legba who opens the doors to the spirit world. We must speak to him with blood or not at all.

Eyes closed and head bowed, I sing the prayer old Oija taught me years ago, lon tan, when I first asked her help to call upon the spirits. That year when M'sieu Vide thought to sell my young daughter, and instead delivered my sisters to the palace.

Please, great god. Please to hear my prayer. I am less than the ants in the dirt, less than the sand upon the shore, but I would beg you to hear me...

A finger touches my cheek.

Adjua.

A chill pours over my skin. This voice I remember oh so well. Not Yemaja or Mariama. None of the Chretien gods, nor those we knew from Afrik. This orisha never told me its name. It belongs to La Trinète alone. Hearing its voice now, my heart grows cold and heavy inside me.

The shadows wrap themselves into a figure with golden lizard eyes. My breath scrapes from my lungs and I cannot speak at first. The orisha laughs to see this. The sound is like beads shifting inside an empty gourd.

Adjua, says the voice again. *You have come to worship me at last?*

Have I? Truth is important when speaking to gods and demons both.

I fall onto my face, into the soft dirt of the new grave. "Yes," I whisper. "If you will but save my daughter, I will do anything you ask."

A very long moment passes, like the quiet before the storm waves crash onto shore. Then, a strong wind from nowhere rushes through the jungle, shaking the trees around this graveyard. Leaves hiss. The candle flames jump, go dark. The orisha's voice echoes inside my skull.

I shall save your daughter, Adjua Dia de Vide. My sacrifice I take when the time is full.

Darkness washes over me—so thick, it smothers my eyes and ears. I cannot see anything, I cannot hear anything, not even the tattoo of my own heart.

Orisha? Yemaja?

I whisper the names of my gods, but no one answers.

He has lied to me. They have all lied, gods and demons.

I sink down and weep. I have no more strength to pretend, to believe.

"Adjua."

The voice, whisper soft, breaks through my grief.

My heart goes still. This is not the voice of the orisha. This is a human voice—a man's. I know it well from ten years long ago.

"Casmir," I say. I do not say it happily.

A shadow emerges from behind the banyan trees. Not a thing of smoke and spirit, like the orisha, but a human. I can tell by his shape, by the flutter of his robes, by the scent of a man who has spent weeks in the jungles of La Trinète.

Casmir approaches me, nervous, as one might approach the old gods. I tuck my lips into a smile, then wipe it clean. "What do you want?"

There is little I can see of the man I once loved those many years ago, but a few signs remain. So tall. His face like ebony set in planes. The sweet scent of the clove cigarettes he smoked in spite of our master's prohibitions. We made a hurried love at night, in between our obligations. I remember how his eyes turned bright, like the flames of a bonfire, when I told him of the child.

I have no time for memories, even sweet ones.

So I am cold and hard to this man, as he was hard to me, once.

"You call yourself Ijabo," I say. "You live in the jungle. You are a great man among those who follow you. Those people—" I spit upon the dirt. "Those people who pretend they are above the miserable slaves who cannot wrench themselves from the cities or the farms. Poor, poor souls, who cannot see how great you are. What have *you* to do with *me*?"

Casmir, who is also Ijabo, wipes a hand over his face. "We need your help, Adjua. Sekou Omar—he has lost too much money to keep the soldiers happy. And his plantation masters are not certain, no longer, that he has the power to keep their lands secure. We think we have a chance..."

No more slavery. No more freedom tax. Everyone free, as our ancestors dreamed. I have heard the arguments before and cannot answer at first. He tells me of a great meeting between Sekou Omar and his generals and the richest men of La Trinète—plantation owners, men of the banks, the great merchant houses—a hundred men who rule the island between them, all gathered in the palace. Casmir and his people have spies there. Not enough to kill these hundred men and their guards with guns and knives, but enough to take control in the confusion of their deaths. They have made contact with rebels on the north side of the island. Others, too, have promised to join their cause. Most important, they even have trusted people in the kitchens...

Ah. My breath rolls out like the tide as I see the shape of their plans.

"You do not need me. You need powders and poisons—"

"That is not true—"

"You *lie*. You always have."

We stop, both of us hot and furious and impatient.

We have had this argument once before, ten years ago, when my daughter was but five and Casmir thought to lead a revolt against Sekou Omar and the masters. We would all be free, he had promised. My sisters were dead in the Palace. M' manman, papa, e frè believed him. They are all dead. Only I and my daughter survived. And that because I did nothing.

My grief takes me by the throat. I cannot think about my daughter.

We remain silent a few moments longer, we two children of slaves, among the graves of more dead slaves. The frogs and toads of La Trinète raise their voices in shrill chorus to the midnight moon. The air stinks of dirt, the thick scent of my blood and the bitter tang of my fears. From far off comes the sweeter scent of jasmine and orchids, the richness of the jungle. High above the clouds drift past, those vast birds of the heavens, and I wait, hoping, hoping, hoping…

My hope fades. I let loose the air from my chest and talk to the man who was once my lover.

"You want my help," I say flatly. "Poisons—quick and strong so these men do not cry out to their guards."

He nods, a faint movement of dark against dark. "Yes. Adjua, I know what you think, but it is time and past. We will be men. Free."

"And women?" I ask dryly.

He makes a throw-away gesture. "Yes, of course, the women, too."

And now my rage flickers bright and hot. "You care nothing for women. You care only that the other slaves worship you."

Casmir stares at me, his face stiff with anger. Only now can I see that he is not the young man who kissed me of a sudden that other moonlit night. We are older, he and I. Older and angrier.

The proof comes in the next moment, when he speaks.

"You always did want quiet."

"I wanted my daughter."

"You have lost her, too," he says, and walks away.

At home, I wash my arm with herbs and water to cleanse away any sickness, then bind it in clean cloth. The flesh aches, but no worse than any beating. Tomorrow it will be worse, then slowly better. Much like my heart, which aches from an older wound.

There is little sleep for me this night. The next morning in temple, I sit and stand and chant as the priests tell us. Then I return home to my shop. Sabbat is done for me. The rich, they sit in their fine houses and drink wine or tea. The poor must work.

The sun pours through my shutters. The room where I work is a furnace. I wipe the sweat from my eyes with an old rag and set to work, grinding the good black peppercorns into dust. Pepper is for strength, Oji taught me. For clarity of thought. And so it was trè chè, very expensive. It came with us on the ships from the old islands. Before that from old Egypt, and before...who knows where? I have a small planting in my shop, where I keep trays of dirt so that no one can steal from me.

Grind, grind, grind.

He has stolen my daughter. He has robbed me of my joy.

I pour the pepper into my smallest measuring cup. Enough. I set the cup upon a sheet of paper and slide a knife across the top. The cup I pour into my mixing bowl. The rest, just a bit, I pour into a great glass jar for those recipes that do not require the strongest ingredients.

He has taken her to bed himself, and now he would sell her for a profit.

Sweat burns my eyes. I do not weep, oh no. Tears are useless, but the sweat, she comes from hard work, and that alone will save us. Or so manman told me. My mother is dead, however, and I cannot argue with her.

My hands do not shake as I set the pepper jar on its shelf. I am a good worker.

You gave me no trouble, non, says an old rough voice.

Now I take down another, this filled with fine white powder—the teeth drawn from a living shark. Sharks are Legba's first children—old and terrible and strong. It is said that a potion that contains their teeth trebles in power. What I make is for an old woman who needs her strength, she says, to care for her grandchildren, so her son and his wife might work in their shop. She is a freedwoman who will not see true freedom in her lifetime, but Mère Mariama Maria and Yemaja willing, her grandchildren will.

I will have no grandchildren, no not one I might gather to my breast to sing a lullaby.

And why did I not guess months before that he would treat my daughter as he treated me?

A woman does not die from one old man's lust. I did not, though I wanted to die from shame and anger. But what if he had sent me to the Palace? To Sekou Omar's soldiers? Would I be alive today?

What can I do? I am a slave. A woman. I have no voice.

Casmir escaped. He lived. You saw him yesterday.

Oh but I would have to give up my shop, hide in the mountains as he did. And pray the soldiers did not hunt for us.

On and on I work, chopping and measuring and mixing, while my thoughts whisper inside my skull. Outside is the quiet of the afternoon. The little girls do not jump their rope or chant. Those in the marketplace sleep under their tents. All La Trinète slumbers through this hour, even the ocean breeze.

All but one.

Ulululuuuuuuuuu.

From far, far away comes a thin high wail. A faint cry at first, but it grows in strength, like the winds from a *siklòn*. It is the godspeaker. The prayer is from the old-times, from before our captivity. The godspeaker calls to the gods to remind them of our presence, to lift our voices to heaven and rejoice that we live. Nafula is an old woman, but her voice does not falter. Her cry floats through the market square, rising up and up, to my window and my workroom. It touches my memory and I shiver, thinking of last night, when gods and demons and my past confronted me.

Casmir came to me the night before the revolt. He begged me to join him with the others, to rise against the masters. Raziya was but five. I refused. I said I would not lose my daughter to a war without purpose.

He was right. I was right.

I remember when my people rose up against the masters, dis ane yo before. The day that sun rose, Azil and all the other cities of La Trinète cried out to the gods, the air stank of blood and gunpowder. Two, three hundred slaves died. I lived and my daughter, too. Casmir vanished. I thought him dead until rumors spoke of a kingdom in the jungle.

Now, now my daughter will die, too, and for no grand purpose. Only to feed the hunger of Sekou Omar's soldiers.

The godspeaker's voice dies away. The bells ring three times. The city Azil draws its breath and wakes from sleep. In the marketplace, a donkey brays. One dog barks. Others yammer back. And down below the little girls gather from the shadows to start their game.

"Youn, dé, twa…"

Me, I close my eyes and wish the afternoon were done so I might drink a cup of tea and eat my bowl of beans and rice, which waits for me. But I hear the stair boards creak, announcing a customer. So I wipe my face with my rag, smooth away the grief, and prepare to smile as the door opens.

Oh, oh no.

Casmir enters my workroom.

Beth Bernobich

He is dressed in long white robes, flecked with red dust. Tiny blue stitches decorate the hems and collar—protection against evil spirits—and more stitches over his heart ensure that his soul remains secure from more serious assaults, of lust and greed and other temptations of the flesh. It is the perfect habit of a priest. I saw it yesterday in the marketplace.

"You," I whisper. "You came here."

He raises a hand. "Lagras, m'dame. Grace to you. I have come to purchase a charm."

A secret visit, then. My hands shake as I set my grinding stone and bowl to one side. He thinks to involve me in his plans, even after last night. Even after all the words we never spoke these past ten years.

"Lagras e lonè," I say. "What charm do you seek?" I gesture at his robes. "You are well-protected against all common attack. Do you need assistance with your prayers, you who are so secure with the gods?"

His chin jerks up. Ah, he is angry. Good.

"I am but a human as you are, my daughter," he says.

He makes a familiar gesture, the one for speaking in private. I recognize it from my days in M'sieu Vide's household. The memory catches at my throat.

"Speak," I say.

"Make me a charm first," he says. "Dried rose blossoms to help me sleep."

It is a common charm, and not so extraordinaire. A good reason for a priest to visit me.

I make the charm with rose petals from my second-best jar. One small scoop. I add a pinch of jasmine petals, and one of cinnamon. These I bind into a cotton bag and tie them with a rough string, long enough that man might hang it from his neck. I speak a few words to bind the petals to their purpose.

"It does not take me so long to make a charm," I observe. "Do you have more to say?"

He accepts the bag and gives me a single livre royale.

"Too much," I say.

"Then you must fetch my change. Adjua," and his voice drops to a soft, silk whisper that I remember too well. "Adjua, I am sorry I spoke so rough last night. It is true, I have come, did come for your help, but if you cannot—if what I ask is too much, then so be it. Today I ask nothing. I come only to say that the president's meeting takes place in three days. We will act. We must. I tell you so that you do what you must to be safe."

I shake my head. "Why have you told me this?"

"Because I trust you. Because I heard—"

"Heard what?"

He makes a swift gesture, like birds in flight.

"That Raziya, that she has troubles."

I nearly laugh. What a delicate way to say it. Now I know he lives in the jungle, because no slave would be so careful. They would say, *Your daughter, the master wishes to sell her body.* Or even, *Your daughter, they make her a whore. She is pretty enough. Too bad she will die from the fucking, or from the children she must bear, or even the medicines they force upon her to kill the babies they make inside her.*

There is nothing to say, however. I count out a handful of coins from my moneybox.

Casmir takes the coins and tucks them inside his sleeve. "You might save her."

"I have told you. I will not make poisons for you."

He catches my hands and grips them tightly. "And I heard you clearly. I do not ask you for anything. I tell you because we loved each other once. And, Adjua…"

With a great sigh, Casmir lets go my hands. He scoops up the charm from my worktable and hangs the string around his neck. His hands tremble, so hard the coins jangle in his sleeve and a dark flush along his cheeks betrays the passion underneath. It is not enough, I tell myself. We had passion like the ocean before. It did us no good.

So I turn away and make as though to order my shelves and worktable. Behind me, Casmir makes no move to leave. He is a patient man, but I too have learned how to wait and wait. It is something that all slaves must learn. *Even when we call ourselves free.*

At last I hear a creak of the floorboards. He takes the two steps to my door and stops. "If you wish to save Raziya, go to M'sieu Baudouin's printing shop. Tell him his friend Dayo sent you. He will arrange everything. You do not need to do anything for us."

I know the name well. Matunde Baudouin is a rich man, free just as his father was free and his grandfather, all the way back to the ships themselves, three hundred years before. He has a good trade, printing newssheets and books. He has no fear of any judge or freedom tax. Casmir guesses my thoughts because he says, "It is not only slaves who hate slavery."

Now the door opens. I cannot pretend any longer.

"Casmir."

My voice catches on tears I dare not shed. Casmir pauses once more.

It is hard to speak the truth, but he will not wait much longer, this man, and so I speak quick and harsh.

"I do not know she is your daughter. I have no way to tell."

I had to say it. In case he doubted later and thought I meant to deceive him. So no matter what, he would not blame Raziya for her mother's silence.

I hear a sigh from the man who was once my lover.

"She is the daughter of my heart, Adjua," Casmir says softly. "Nothing else matters. You should know that."

I should know it. I had not before.

And now I am too late.

I finish the potion for my grandmother who needs her strength. I grind and mix and measure, count coins, and instruct my patients on the medicine I have prepared for them. They are grateful for my care. I am grateful to keep so busy that I have no time for recollection.

At last the sun sets. My signboard I turn to show the moon, to show my shop is closed for the night. My door I lock with trembling hands. Outside the market square empties, and the moonlight rolls over the shores and up toward the three mountains of La Trinète. A few joyous souls sing and dance, though Carnival does not start for three more days.

At last, I must think about this matter I do not want to think about.

I scrub my hands with soap to cleanse them of the oils and powders of my trade. It is impossible, though, to erase all traces. Roses scent the creases of my finger joints. Sharp ginger has soaked into my skin. When I sweat, I sweat pepper and honey and lemon and limes. And when the sun shines down sharply from the sky, you see the fluttering outline of demons in my shadow.

I go into my bedroom. There I light a candle.

A golden tide washes away the darkness. I kneel before the wooden box in the corner.

Six wooden blocks stare back at me. Each carries a single name, for manman e papa e twa sèsè yo. Youn frè. Between them sits a clay pot with earth mixed with their ashes (what little I could gather) and a knife that gleams clean and sharp in the candlelight.

One swift cut on my thumb, which is thick with scars from the many other nights like this one. I squeeze the flesh and let six drops fall into the pot, where they mix with my family's ashes. I do not pray to the gods. Tonight is for me to think.

And so I think as I have not allowed myself to, these ten years past.

I think of M'sieu Vide and his bed.

I think of Casmir, who is also Ijabo.

I remember the night Casmir came to me, dis ane yo before, when he begged me to join him in the mountains—I with our daughter, who might not be his daughter, only mine and M'sieu Vide's.

I have made the wrong choice before. No, that is not true. I cannot go back to my young and frightened self and truly say, "Go. Kill the masters. Take your daughter to the jungle. If, that is, you both live through the night."

So. Yesterday is gone. Its truth does not matter. Tomorrow is what I must decide.

Tomorrow comes in a red flame upon the indigo skies. I have hardly slept between the tears and dreams of my family. But today is not like yesterday. My daughter is not five, a child scarcely past the milk years, who cannot live apart from her mother. She is a young woman and faced with life at Sekou Omar's palace. In a way, M'sieu Vide has made my decision easier.

As if such a choice could be easier.

I chew my breakfast and drink a cup of water. When the godspeaker calls out the morning prayers, I set off through Azil's sun-painted streets. The day, it is hot already, and dust rises from the streets. In a week or ten days, the spring rains will fall and wash the city, the jungle around us, the tall stone slopes of the island, but today, I breathe air thick with winter and a dying year.

My path takes me through the narrow lanes, across the many market squares. Soon I come to the richer quarters, where the merchants and shopkeepers live. Here, in a tiny courtyard under the shadow of La Trinète's three mountains, I find M'sieu Baudouin's house and printing shop. There is no slave door—I search both sides of the house—only the grand door for visitors of worth. It must do. They cannot blame me.

My hand is heavy. It takes all my will to lift it, to take the stick from its receptacle and beat upon the door. *Youn, dé, twa.* The noise echoes from the other houses. I hear shutters rattle, feel the weight of eyes upon my back, but I do not flinch. I am here for my daughter, and thus everything is simple.

A boy opens the door. He is dressed in plain gray breeches and a shirt as white as the summer clouds. Not a rich man's servant. An apprentice?

"Lagras e lonè," he says.

"Lagras e lonè," I reply. "Grace and honor to you. I have come with a message for M'sieu Baudouin." Recalling the name Casmir gave me, I add, "From his friend Dayo."

The boy's eyes betray nothing. Perhaps he does not know about his master's other business. But he politely invites me inside and shows me to a small room with fresh herbs strewn over the floor and a cushioned chair. There is an altar with statues of Mère Mariama Maria and her daughters. Paintings show the older gods of Afrik. This is a man who worships all the gods. I remind myself that so does M'sieu Vide.

As the boy runs off to deliver my message, a girl comes through another door with fresh strong tea and biscuits. They must think I am a woman of means.

It is not only slaves who hate slavery.

So Casmir said. I sip my tea cautiously, expecting a bitter brew. Non. This tea is hot and sweet and invigorating. The biscuits are light and crisp. These are not the gifts for a slave, or even a lowly freedman. Could it be that this man treats all men and women alike? The idea disturbs me. I gulp down the rest of the cupful. The tea, this room, light a warmth of hope inside my heart, even as I shiver at the implications.

"M'dame Adjua."

An old man stands on the threshold. His hair is white and like a spider web caught around his bare skull. His skin is the color of sun-dark nuts; his eyes are warm and brown. And yet I do not mistake this man for a kindly old grandfather. Oh no. This man studies me with a knife-sharp gaze, even as he greets me with *Lagras* and *Lonè*, with all the grave formality our mothers and fathers taught us.

I set my cup on the table. "M'sieu Baudouin. Your friend told me that you have a good word for my daughter."

Matunde Baudouin regards me with an unchanging face, still kind, still gentle, but I can see how he holds himself still, as still as a deer in the forest. Then he sighs. "So much trouble in the world. Our friend told me you might visit. Come with me, M'dame."

He takes me through a long corridor, past oh so many rooms filled with rich carpets and cushioned chairs, past more rooms crowded with shelves and those shelves overflowing with books—so many I have never seen before. After the libraries and parlors, we pass through other rooms filled with great machines that stink of oils and grease. Men work at the machines, enormous metal wheels, which spin over and over, spilling a waterfall of paper gleaming with fresh ink. The wheels roar and clatter, the men shout orders to each other. It is so loud here I cannot think.

At the last of these rooms, we go through a small door into an office. The door shuts and silence falls over us.

"Ah. Quiet." M'sieu Baudouin smiles—a true smile this time. But the smile fades quickly. He gestures for me to sit. When I shake my head, he sighs. "Byen. These are not time for pleasant visits. Very well. Let me speak to the point. Your daughter— Ijabo tells me that her master has sold her to the palace. You wish for her to escape."

He is blunt. I like that. "Yes. She goes next week. Casmir— Ijabo tells me you are able to arrange everything."

"Who is her master?"

He no longer seems so frail, this old man with his seamed face and halo of white hair. He is strong, this one. A man who understands the dangers we all face.

"She belongs to M'sieu Vide," I tell him.

Baudouin nods. I can see his thoughts *klik* like beads.

"It must be tomorrow night," he says. "They will not miss her before the morning, and that morning is Carnival. So, M'dame—"

"I am no m'dame. I am a freedwoman."

If so much.

Baudouin does not argue with me. Perhaps he thinks we have better to discuss. "You must get word to your daughter tomorrow morning. Can you do that?" He does not wait for me to speak. He goes on, his words spilling like the rolls of paper from his machines. "Get word to her tonight or tomorrow morning. No later. Tell her she must find an excuse to go outside after sunset. She should bring nothing with her. I will send a woman to meet her. And we shall arrange for a distraction, if necessary."

He stops and waits. At last I understand he expects an answer. "I can do that."

"Byen." He holds out both hands to me. His clasp is brief and warm. "These are bad times, M'dame. I wish you and your daughter bon chans."

I thought I would forget his many instructions, but I remember them all.

I return to my shop, but not directly. First, I go to the market and buy six kinds of herbs. I buy other things, too—saltfish and green bananas, dasheen, a pumpkin to bake later, in the cool evening. *We must hope that no one has followed you to my house,* Matunde Baudouin said to me. *I think not. Still we must provide a reason for you to be away from your shop so long this special morning. Here is what you must do...*

And so I wander through the morning market with the other women. I buy a few items with great brass coins he placed in my hand. Not too much, to be sure—I am no rich woman with many livres to spend—but a few centimes for this, a few for that. Besides, I am well-known too. The farmers are not surprised when I add cotton root bark, and yams, and the green papaya to the plain woven basket the old printer gave to me. They know the women come to me for such things.

Before the bells strike mid-morning and the godspeaker calls us to prayer, I am at home in my shop. There is no one who watches me now, but I pretend the police and their spies are sitting outside my window. I put the saltfish and green bananas, the dasheen and the pumpkin to one side. I clear a space on my table and set out the many other things I have bought in the market. I break the cotton root bark and measure the heap into six packets of linen. One packet for each time she gets with bebe. She will not need these packets, but Matunde Baudouin has insisted. *Everyone must believe she goes to the palace. There must not be one who doubts, no, not a single one.*

And so I mix the tea for my daughter. I wrap the yams and green papaya. I pack my basket once more. Then I take three livres from my money box and tuck the bills inside my blouse. Youn livre to give to Kafele, to speak alone with my daughter. Dé e twa for my daughter, if she needs to bribe a servant, or simply to take with her into the jungle and her exile.

Three livres and a handful of brass centimes—youn, dis, e ven—remain in my money box. It is not enough for my rent or food, but I think of the coming riots and wonder if I shall live to see the next month.

I will live, I will. And I will see my daughter again in libète.

The day leaks the hours very slowly. I work. I talk to customers. One has heard of Raziya's troubles. She touches my arm. Her eyes are bright with tears. She does not say anything, but I know her heart weeps with mine.

(*Sister, my sister. May we all weep together under the stars. For Zion and freedom.*)

The songs of my mother fill my heart as at last the sun glides toward the sea, like a spider down its thread. It is the hour after supper, when M'sieu Vide takes a cup of wine in his rooms. Later, he will call for a girl or boy, as he once called for me, but for now, the slaves are free of his presence. They work, all of them. They wash the dishes. They light the candles. They do small tasks to make this household pleasant for the master.

I go with my basket to M'sieu Vide's grand house. I knock at the slave door.

My clothes are plain—this is no freedom tax day—but my blouse is fresh, my scarf is clean and pressed with hot stones. I show respect to my master, but nothing extraordinary, nothing that might attraction attention from the police. It is not a strange thing, I tell myself, that a mother would wish to give her daughter such a present, but the basket weighs so heavy, and my heart is like a butterfly inside my chest. When the door opens, I must use all my slave memory to keep my face smooth.

Kafele stares at me from the shadows inside.

"Grace and honor to you," I say. "I have come to give my daughter a last gift before she leaves this household."

All the words I have practiced crowd upon my tongue, but at this boy's strange blank expression, they crumble into dust. He stares and stares, and my throat turns dry with fear. "What is it?" I whisper. I think of the bribes I must give him, of Matunde Baudouin's cautions, of—

"She is gone," he says. Then, "He sent her away this morning. They wants more girls for—" His face pinches into a terrible frown, as if he realizes what he was about to say. "I am sorry. So sorry."

Sorry. Oh no. Oh such a word. Sorry.

I want to strike him, but my arms, my knees are like water. I find that he has taken my elbow and led me inside. *No, no,* my heart cries. *Do not bring me inside to this murderer's house. Do you not see the blood that paints the walls?*

Kafele cannot hear my heart, the child. He settles me upon a bench. He brings me cold water. As if water could save Raziya. But I drink it, three cups, shivering as if I were suddenly transported to the land of the white demons who once held us captive. Slowly the world comes back to me, or I to it.

"She is gone," I say.

He nods.

"I must go."

He takes my wrist. "Do not be foolish."

I want to laugh, but then I see his eyes—so dark and old, though he is but a young man. *I am a slave,* that face tells me. *I am angry too.*

"You see, I do understand," he says.

He does. I take my basket and leave the household.

There are stars in the soft late winter sky. There are men drinking on the steps of their houses. They call out to me, *Hey, m'dame. You are trè bèl.* Their voices are warm and friendly but I cannot comprehend the words. One steps in front of me and lays his hand on my arm. *Sister,* he says. But then my gaze lifts to his, and he drops his hand. *Ah,* he says. *Ah, pardon. Respect. You have my sorrow, m'dame.*

"You will have your poison," I tell Matunde Baudouin.

It is early the next day. I have slipped between the houses at dawn and waited until the first lamps appear like fireflies in the windows of the printing shop. The boy admitted me without question to the inner office, where Baudouin sits amidst a stack of papers.

He wipes his eyes with one thin hand. "M'dame—"

"I am a slave," I snap.

Almost I regret my harshness. His face folds in upon itself, like an old letter. But then he lifts his gaze toward mine. His eyes are bright and hard. Again I think of the oldest ones on La Trinète, the gods and orisha who were here, long before Kwaku Ananse lured us onto the ships, and carried us to these islands. Before we divided ourselves again into slaves and masters.

"You are a woman," he says. "A human like me, and even Sekou Omar. He was a man like us all, once," he says, his voice stronger than before. "Before the strong drink of power sent him into madness."

I say nothing. I have no power.

Close behind me, I sense the monsters of madness. They whisper at me in their dead voices.

Be still, be quiet, I tell them. We shall have our revenge.

Unaware of my monsters, M'sieu Baudouin shakes his head. "No matter. You say you will make poison for us?"

"I will."

He sighs and makes the sign of the Chretien worshippers, a swift cross over his breast, and fingertips to his eyes, which signify our blindness in this world. "I do not like this, this murder. And yet, I see no other way. If you are certain, M'dame, bring me the poison tonight—"

"I need a day to prepare it," I say.

He nods. "Early tomorrow, then. I will tell our friend. Come to me when you are ready. I will arrange for everything."

Poison.

I sit before a garden of poison.

Under the windows stand three trays of pepper plants—my treasure, and harmless. Before me, six trays of castor bean plants—the plants as tall as I am, their beans hanging low, the color of dried blood. Another six of datura, the pòm de diab, its stout green stems like so many forks set one upon the other. Pressed cold, the castor beans make a useful oil for the skin. Tea from the pòm de diab brings sleep—how heavy depends upon its strength. Too much, and the sleeper never wakes. Both are trè danjere, very dangerous.

I am a woman who heals, but I must know the dangers of each medicine I brew.

Death or death? And how quick?

Casmir's words come to me. They must kill the president and the generals in an instant—like a candle pinched between two fingers—so that no one gives the alarm. That decides me. I draw the cotton gloves over my hands. I set the cotton mask over my mouth and pluck the castor beans into my basket. I take as many beans I shall need to kill a hundred men.

Again the madness whispers to me. Take more, it urges. Those men are not only guilty ones on La Trinète. There are the guards, the other officers. The plantation owners who are not as rich, but who are twice as vicious. The masters, like M'sieu Vide, who take young girls and boys to their beds. Kill them all and then you shall be free. That is what all slaves dream.

My blood beats like drums inside my skull. Death and death and death, say the drums.

My hands drop to my lap. I am shaking. Again I taste the bitter blood in my mouth, the same as when I called upon the orisha. I hear its words from two nights before: *My sacrifice I shall take later.*

Oh yes. Now I understand what the sacrifice it demands. It will save my daughter, but taking blood for blood, and not just one but a thousandfold. Again I hear the shouts and cries, the sharp crack of guns, that night ten years ago.

We will all die. Oh ma manman. Oh Mère Mariama Maria. What can I do? How can I save my daughter, my people?

From far away comes the call of the godspeaker, a thin high song that rises above the island.

Death is not an answer, said that voice, as clear as if the godspeaker stood beside me, one hand on my shoulder. *Not for you. Not for Zion and libète.*

I stare down at the heap of castor beans. She speaks the truth. Death is not the answer, but there is a kind of death that will answer.

I pour the beans into the trays. They will sprout later, for other, for better reasons. I bend the nearest stalk of pòm de diab and draw the knife down. My purpose now is not to bring death to these men, but sleep. After that, we shall see what we can do for libète.

By sunset I have my vat of sleeping potion. While it cools by the window, I cook a batch of jele. That too I set upon the window sill. A long time apre, I cook my dinner of saltfish and green bananas. I eat and think upon my childhood. I sing and chant memories from the days with my sisters e m' zanmi yo. Tomorrow is Carnival. Tomorrow is a day of new birth.

By midnight the jele is stiff. I mold it with my fingers into pellets. I fill them with just so much of the devil's apple brew. I am very careful. Too much Sekou Omar and his people die. Too little, and we slaves and freedmen die as rebels and traitors. My eyes and fingers ache before I am done, but when I am, I have three hundred capsules set in a row, one each for Sekou Omar and his guests, the rest for their guards. The pellets will break with just a pinch, but until then, the jele keeps my potion safe from others.

There is no sleep for me tonight. I dare not. I have no slaves to wake me.

And so I clean my shop and the room where I sleep. I tend my trays and water my plants. I spend a fortune in candles to do this, you understand. Will I need a fortune tomorrow? I do not know.

When the dawn floods the eastern sky, I wash my face. I dress myself with care in my blue skirt and blouse. I hang my red beads around my neck, and tie a sober black scarf over my head. I pack the pellets in my basket and cover them with a cloth. The streets below stir as I leave my shop and lock the door.

Many years before, when I was a child, I danced for Carnival. The drums beat like hearts of the mountain. The girls cried a high sweet ululullu, the men chanted the old, old songs from Haiti and Trinidad and Louisana—from all the lands where Kweku Ananse gathered us onto the ships. Songs from Afrik, our mother and home of golden Zion.

Today the girls sing softly. They do not dance, though they are dressed in bright red and green and orange skirts, and their scarves are like a garden of colors. It is early, and the men have not drunk enough to forget their anger. Was it always so? I wonder. Did I never see before, because I was a child? Or have the many years changed others as well as me?

The same young boy opens the door. This time, he takes me himself through the many hallways, through the cavern of machines, which stand like silent mountains today. My feet glide over the smooth damp wooden floors. My beads go *klik e klik e klik*. They echo from the ceiling, like tiny crickets in the forest.

Matunde Baudouin sits behind his desk. His face is slack with weariness, his hair lies in damp patches upon his skull. He makes two brief gestures. One for me to sit. The other to the boy, who leaves us without a word.

I do not sit. I stand with my basket tucked under one arm.

"You have it?" he asks.

I nod. "But I have one more request, M'sieu. I must take this poison to the palace myself."

He pauses. "Your daughter…"

"I would deliver these goods to the palace myself, M'sieu. That is my request."

We argue. He tells me I do not understand the risk. I shrug. He speaks of spies and counterspies and those who will act for the cause, only when they see no danger for themselves. His voice does not condemn these people, you understand. He speaks of them as he might a machine that cannot perform a task because its builder did not create it so. But there will be danger, he warns me, even if Casmir and his friends succeed and Sekou Omar dies. Especially then.

I repeat my words. "I must do it. Or else I take these poisons away."

Baudouin leans back and rubs a hand over his eyes. He is an old, old man, and he has not slept this past night or two. I watch him carefully. He could summon his servants to take the basket from me and throw me into the street. I must not let him.

He drops his hand. His gaze remains fixed upon his desk, as if he cannot bear to see this angry mother. "It is dangerous."

"You think I do not understand that?"

"Non, but—"

"But it is my right. It is my daughter who dies drop by drop inside that palace."

I have no more arguments, none, except the tears in my eyes, and he will not look at me, this man with his rich house and many books. My heart whispers that I am not fair to him, that he has risked himself to free the slaves, but I have no room within me for fairness today.

At last M'sieu Baudouin lifts his gaze to mine. "You insist? Of course, you do. Ah, byen. Listen to me now. Listen and remember."

He gives me special words to give to each set of guards. He orders me to repeat them until I say them perfectly, no hesitation. Then he describes the way to the kitchen, where I must go directly to a man named Fahim. To him alone I should give the poison. He does not tell me to run away. He does not give me any other instruction about my daughter.

I bow my head. "Thank you."

Matunde Baudouin rises and bows to me. "M'dame. May we both see the suns of tomorrow."

The same words our father and mothers spoke, three hundred years before.

I hurry away from the empty printing shop, through the streets—now noisy with song and revels—to the grand stairway that leads upward to the palace. With every step I whisper the passwords, the name—Fahim—of the man I must speak with, the many other instructions Matunde Baudouin gave me. My throat chokes upon fear. But I do not think, not once, upon my daughter. I cannot, or I should fall weeping to the ground.

Two hundred soldiers march in the square before the palace, which is like a gleaming white anthill. A hundred more stand guard around the gates. Sons of mothers every one, brothers to sisters. It is hard to remember that when I think of my own dead family.

You must do what is not possible, the godspeaker told me.

It is always the mother who must bleed tears, I think. If I live, I will write new prayers about priests and gods who must suffer a hundred years of labor, while the mothers lie in comfort. If it were not today, I would laugh at the thought.

There is a small dark street to one side. There I find the slave door and give the proper words. A weary woman points down a shadowed corridor. *Go*, she tells me. *You will hear the kitchen soon enough.*

The kitchen thunders with pots and pans, with voices raised to shout orders, with all the roar and timpani I came to know at M'sieu Vide's but multiplied by ten dozen more slaves. A gray-haired woman tugs at the basket. I clutch it to my stomach and shout the name Fahim. She must understand because she thrusts the basket back at me and scuttles away into the crowd. A moment later and large man with a blood-stained tunic appears before me. His eyes are like dark stones in his smooth brown face, his shoulders like the mountains of La Trinète. He wears a white turban.

I give the final password. Fahim stares at me a moment, as if he doubts, but then he beckons for me to follow him. We thread our way between the work tables, where women skin and bone chickens, where others chop the good onions, and others still are measuring the strong-brewed coffee into great carafes to serve Sekou Omar and his guests. Small boys dart between us. Girls fetch trays with the coffee and bread, the cool water with fresh-squeezed lemons. So many people, all of them so busy. No one can watch everyone. We do have a chance.

Fahim stops by a table with twelve great stone jugs. An older woman frowns at me as I approach. Here the noise is not as great, or my ears are better used to it.

"She is not the right one," the woman is telling him.

"She has the right words," Fahim says back.

"But she—"

"I am a friend of Ijabo," I say quickly. "I bring what you require." And then, because I want her to pity me, and because it is the truth, I add, "My daughter came to this palace yesterday. I hoped to find her before, before..."

It is not necessary to say more.

"Ahhhh." The woman sighs. "M' konprann, my sister. Come with me."

Their plans are what I guessed. Omar and his guests eat their breakfast while they talk of payments to the army, of favors to this rich man and that, and how those generals and rich men would support Sekou Omar and his government. *We serve wine the next hour, so they might celebrate their grand accord*, the woman tells me. *They will all drink together.*

"You must allow me to measure the ingredients," I tell the woman. "I know how much in each. Too little and they will not die quickly enough. And," I say, "I will come to serve the wine with your women. To see my daughter."

The woman studies me. I think for a moment she will refuse me, but at last she nods. "Yes. You may do that."

She leaves me to add my potion to the wine. Twelve stone jugs. A hundred men. My hands sweat and tremble as I calculate how many pellets for each jug. When I am done, I have two hundred left. "Do you serve the guards water?" I ask the woman. "Wine?"

She grunts and points to a barrel of water. I whisper prayer to Yemaja and pinch them all swiftly between my fingers, then drop the pellets into the barrels. They will sink to the bottom, and I do not want to lose even one drop of the liquid I have brewed.

Girls fill great jugs from the barrels and go to serve the guards. Now we move swiftly, the woman and Fahim and I. We fill a hundred wine cups. I and a dozen other girls hurry toward the grand ball room with our burdens. *Vit, vit, vit*, the woman tells us, then she falls away as the doors open and we girls and women enter.

My breath escapes me at the sight. The room is vast, like a cavern in the mountain. Golden chandeliers hang from an egg-white ceiling, each one set with a hundred candles, all of them ablaze, though it is full morning and the sun of La Trinète pours through the glass windows. Sekou Omar sits at the head of an immense table. Forty chief officers make a row down one side. Dozens of rich men—bankers and plantation owners—make a second row across from them.

Through a half-open door, I see another room. I hear a girl's laugh—high and thin. So close to tears, though these men would never hear it. I want to see if Raziya is that girl, but I cannot. Master and guests and soldiers must drink together.

We set a glass beside each man. We draw back, invisible, to the walls.

The wine trembles as the men lift their glasses to Sekou Omar. They shout. *Glory to our leader. Glory to La Trinète.*

They drink and slam the glasses onto the table. I watch, unable to breathe, to look away. Minutes fall away like rain. My blood thrums inside my head. I think I hear faint laughter, like dried seeds in a gourd. Has the orisha touched my poison, made it harmless? It might. It wanted a sacrifice. It demanded blood.

Beside me, a woman lets out an almost-silent ahhhhh.

I see why. The men sit stiff in their chairs, their eyes are wide and dark. Sekou Omar pushes himself to standing with both fists, but the effort is too much. His mouth opens as though to shout for his guards, then he falls to the floor. Another man reaches toward the president. His head drops upon the table. The rest collapse this way and that, like puppets without their strings.

From the next room comes a terrible thump, thump, thump. But not all the guards fall as their masters did. I hear the rattle of many swords. Men shout, their voices slurred by the pòm de diab. Moments later, I hear the crash of the doors. A gun roars—so loud I think the walls must shake—but through that half-open door, I see a swarm of bodies.

Raziya stumbles into the grand dining chamber. Blood covers her face. Her eyes are wide and white in her face. More blood covers her dress, which is ripped and falling off her shoulders.

I run to her and catch her before she falls. "M' cheri."

She is gasping. "They are killing… the guards…"

Then she sees the tumble of bodies in front of her. Slowly she rises to standing. She trembles, but her eyes are bright and fierce. Then she turns toward me. Sees me truly for the first time. Her mouth forms the word *manman*, and she grips me in a tight embrace.

The noise of fighting dies away. The palace is quiet. From far away comes the echo of old songs, the ones our mothers and fathers carried away from old Afrik.

It is a false peace, I know. The next moment, I see the proof of my thoughts. Dozens of men appear in the doorway from the next chamber. All of them carry machetes. I see Fahim from the kitchens. Behind him, Casmir. His mouth is swollen in a great bruise, his shirt is bloody, and he too carries a machete. He glances toward me and Raziya, only for a heartbeat, but in that blink of time, I see a new world in his eyes.

The moment winks to nothing. We are in the middle of a revolution, after all. Raziya and I draw back to the walls, away from the men with their machetes. Casmir slides around the others to the head of the table, where Sekou Omar sprawls across an empty plate.

His fingers clasp the man's wrist. He frowns. "Adjua—"

"He sleeps," I say quickly.

The other men pour into the room. They lift their weapons, all except Fahim.

"I did not lie you," I say to Casmir alone. "I gave you medicines, just as you insisted."

"But—"

"But if you murder these men, you paint your hands with blood, and Legba will wrap your souls in chains. You will be another kind of slave. Take them prisoner, yes. Make a trial for all La Trinète to witness, rich and poor. And if you must, execute them for justice. Then, oh then, you are truly free. *Then* we shall have Zion."

I turn away from him. Where I go, where I take my daughter, I cannot tell. I can only think that Raziya and I must leave this palace, and quickly.

Casmir touches my arm. "Adjua."

"Do not ask me for anything more." My voice cries out like a bird.

"I would not," he says. "I would do what is right. For you and our daughter. For La Trinète."

His eyes are bright, like the sun rising to a new day. Again I see a new world, and my breath catches in my chest. For the first time in ten years, I think, *Yes, oh yes.*

And inside a voice, which might be the godspeaker's, might be Yemanja's herself.

Justice. Honor. Grace.

Air and Angels

As everyone knew, Lady Miriam Grey's soirées were the most exclusive in all London. Members of Parliament, literary icons, eligible daughters of the rich, even a spare noble or two could be found on Mondays and Thursdays in her exquisite drawing room, there to partake in brilliant conversation or to sample the delectable fare. More fanciful rumors said Lady Grey had seduced, then abducted her amazing French cook. Of course *that* was mere foolish speculation, but as Lady Grey herself said, Society loved its stepchild, Gossip.

It was for all these reasons—the gossip, society's expectations, but most especially the eligible daughters—that Stephen Eliot nearly sent his regrets. Nearly, but not so. His parents had made the consequences all too plain if he did not attend.

Dear Mama. My respected Papa. Stephen mentally tipped them a bow as he mounted the steps to Lady Grey's townhouse in Berkeley Square. He was unpardonably late, he knew. The bells from St. George's were ringing half past nine. The day's vivid October sunset had bled into twilight hours ago, and the edge of full night advanced swiftly upon the city.

A butler admitted him into the entry hall. Stephen was turning over his hat and gloves, when he heard a delighted cry.

"Stephen!"

Lady Grey glided toward him. She was dressed in a distinctly Continental mode, in dark blue Chine-figured silk draped about with lacy scarves. Exquisite as always, and with the grace and energy of a far-younger female, but Stephen could not escape the distinct impression of age overtaking a beautiful woman. He covered his sudden confusion by bowing and kissing her proffered hands.

"I am so glad to see you again," she said. "I missed you terribly."

"And I you," Stephen replied. "It is because of you I am here."

She laughed softly. "You lie beautifully, Stephen." Then, in a lower voice, she added, "So beautifully, indeed, I wish I had seduced you years ago, when you were younger and I more foolish in these matters."

"Ah, but you never had any inclination for younger men."

"Just as well. Now we can comfortably be friends instead of disappointed lovers." She took him by the arm and led him into the drawing room. "Come, let me introduce you to several other friends. Their acquaintance will go far to soothe your parents."

Stephen soon found himself exchanging greetings with the secretary of a rising politician, a recently appointed ambassador to Germany, a financier. "Influential men," Lady Grey murmured as they continued through the room. "You might wish to call upon them tomorrow. No, do not protest. You have time enough to make your choices later. But now, to make this evening more pleasant for you and for another young guest...."

They had come to the other end of the drawing room. An arched doorway led into a small elegant parlor where a few men and women listened intently as an older white-haired gentleman expounded on the state of England's African and Indian colonies.

In another corner, a famous actress, whose name was sometimes connected with that of the king, held her own court. Lady Grey continued past them to a quiet nook at the far end. A young woman sat there alone. She was dressed in a simple mourning gown, with her hair drawn back in a loose coil. She was writing in a small notebook with the stub of a pencil, oblivious to the company around her.

"Miss Dubois," said Lady Grey. "What are you doing, scribbling like a schoolgirl when you should be enjoying yourself?"

The young woman gave a start, then laughed. "Lady Grey. One might think you were seriously scolding me."

"I am never serious, except when it profits me. Mister Eliot, I would like to introduce you to a dear friend of mine, Miss Eva Dubois. Her grandfather was also a much-valued friend."

Eva Dubois's eyes were a deep rich brown, the exact shade of her hair. A flush edged her cheeks, either from amusement or embarrassment, Stephen could not say. He noticed smudges of lead on her fingers, where she gripped her pencil, and one beside her mouth, as though she had rubbed her thumb there in abstraction. He bowed. "Miss Dubois."

"Mister Elliot." She closed the notebook, but not before Stephen glimpsed a complex diagram and closely written notes filling half the next page. How very odd.

"Mister Eliot has just returned from a few years abroad," Lady Grey said. "Studying mathematics and the human nature, though the latter was not necessarily a formal program. Eva, I believe you will find each other excellent company. Stephen, I must see to my other guests, but do speak with me before go."

She departed for the drawing room. Meanwhile, Eva Dubois was studying Stephen with an unreadable look. Unsettled, Stephen took a seat next to her on the sofa. As soon as he did, she slid her notebook into a handbag at her feet. "So," she said, "you are studying mathematics?"

Stephen shrugged. "I was, after a fashion. Are you interested in the subject, Miss Dubois?"

Her lips twitched. "After a fashion," she replied archly. "Or would you rather talk about your travels? If not that, we might discuss the October weather, or the possibility of the sun rising tomorrow. I'm certain we might discover some topic of sufficient interest to us both that we could satisfy conventions."

He flushed. "I am sorry. I never thought you would—I mean, I never thought—" He stopped and shook his head. "I'm sorry. I was rude. Rude and unthinking. I… Miss Dubois, it's doubly uncivil of me to say so, but you are not what I expected."

If he expected her to show dismay, or outrage, he was mistaken. Eva Dubois smiled, a warm genuine smile. The change was so sudden and acute that Stephen blinked in surprise. "You were not uncivil, you were honest," she said. "Unless you believe, Mister Eliot, as my father did, that honesty is another form of insolence."

Her voice had all the surface qualities he associated with well-bred young women, but something in the slight emphasis on his name, the shadow beside her mouth, suggested a much older, much more sophisticated person, as though an angel had come to visit this world in the guise of an innocent.

He shook away the strange impression, and was about to reply, when his attention was caught by another entering the parlor. But *enter* was too insipid a word—this woman strode through the arched doorway like a man, oblivious to the curious looks of the women, the frank appraising stares of the men.

Her gaze swept the room and alighted upon Stephen and his companion. "Eva," she said. "You remember our previous engagement, do you not?"

An aunt, Stephen thought, or an older cousin. He could tell by the cant of their eyes, the echo of line and color in their features. He rose and held out a hand. "Delighted to meet you," he said. "You must be Miss Dubois's—"

"—sister," Eva said. "Mister Stephen Eliot, my sister, Lily Dubois."

Lily Dubois favored him with a brief, uninterested glance. There were faint lines beside her eyes and mouth, and her complexion lacked the creamy radiance of Eva's. What intrigued him more were the white scars over her fingers and the back of her hand, which caught his attention when she impatiently tucked a loose strand behind her ear. He glanced down and saw the other hand was equally scarred.

"I am so glad you find me worthy of close inspection, Mister Eliot," Lily said. She turned back to her sister. "Eva, enough with the pleasantries. We must take our leave now."

Eva Dubois rose at once and tucked her bag with its mysterious notebook under her arm. "My apologies, Mister Eliot, but my sister has it right. We are promised elsewhere, and must hurry or we shall be unpardonably late."

Her fingertips brushed his, then she was following her sister from the room, a stir of whispers following in the wake of their passage.

"So," Gilbert Wardle said, "the prodigal son has returned."

"I had no choice," Stephen said. "My parents wish me to marry and start a career. I wanted another year abroad to complete my studies but—"

"—but they threatened to cut off your allowance and you were not about to play the impoverished student."

They were sitting in one of the upper rooms of Gilbert's club. The hour was late; most of the other members had departed for home. A few remained to enjoy a whiskey and cigar, as Stephen and Gilbert did, and the haze of their smoke drifted through the room, making the air close and stale. Stephen ran a hand across his eyes. He felt an incipient headache coming on.

Gilbert watched him through narrowed eyes. "I've offended you, haven't I?"

Stephen shrugged. "Yes. No. It's true I made a mess of my studies. Perhaps my father had the right—that I liked the role of student better than the actual work."

"Now you are being merely foolish," his friend said. "You were handy enough at Cambridge. What happened to send you off course?"

"Oh, the usual. I let myself become distracted by novelties. I was on the point of…" Stephen broke off with a smothered laugh. "My apologies. Excuses are tedious. Suffice to say that I neglected my classes in favor of drinking and wenching—in short, the ordinary run of vices. And that is all the self-pity I shall inflict upon you. How goes your own work? You landed a plum of an appointment with Lord Randall, if I recall."

Gilbert gave an elaborate sigh. "The same as always. Boring. A bloody boring sinecure, pardon my language. But at least it keeps me in funds."

There was a pause while they both sipped their whiskeys. The room had emptied out in the past few moments. Even now the last two members trailed out the door, leaving behind a silence and a solitude that made the room's air seem even warmer and closer than before. Stephen swirled the whiskey around in his glass, and considered ordering another, perhaps with less soda. His discretion overtook his urge; he set the glass aside and rubbed his forehead again.

"You know," Gilbert said, "you might like the work I do. It's not so very taxing, and it would give you the means to live independently. You would have time enough to pursue mathematics on your own. Are you interested?"

He spoke in the same languid tones Stephen remembered from their university days. Still charming, still handsome, with the deep blue eyes and patrician features so loved by women, he was like a Dorian Grey, only without the vice, Stephen thought.

And yet, watching him now, Stephen thought he could see shadows underneath the glittering exterior.

"Mind," Gilbert went on, "there is no guarantee, merely a suggestion. I shall have to speak with my superiors. But I did not wish to meddle unless you agreed."

A sinecure. It did not sound very appealing, but Stephen did not wish to refuse outright. "I shall have to think about it," he said.

"Fair enough." Gilbert drew a long breath on the cigar and breathed out a stream of smoke. "So tell me, fair one, how did you like Miss Eva Dubois?"

"How did you—"

His friend waved a hand. "Rumors," he said lightly. "They fly like eagles, swifter than leopards and keener than wolves. Or something like that. In this particular case, the leopard was young Littlefair. He too attended Lady Grey's soirée and saw you talking with the girl. Did you like her?"

"I hardly had time to make her acquaintance. Why? Do you?"

The smoke rippled as Gilbert shook his head. "Hardly. Sweet young virgins do not appeal to me. And before you make the suggestion, I have no interest in the sister either. A freakish creature, that one. Have you heard the story? No? Ah, now I remember. You had departed for the Continent a few months before the scandal broke. I must enlighten you, then."

Without asking Stephen, he called for two more whiskeys. When the waiter brought them, he asked the man to see what kind of night it was outside and, if the weather had turned wet, could he summon a cab for them. Stephen watched, silently, noticing that Gilbert did not resume speaking until the waiter had retreated from the room. A wisp of breeze from the closing doors stirred the smoky air.

"About the Dubois family," Gilbert went on. "The grandfather had his moment of fame in the Royal Society with some well-received papers on astronomy. The father took to law, where there was more money. He—the father, that is—had hoped for sons, but when Fate offered him daughters, he attempted to do the right thing. Governesses. Sizeable dowries. He married the elder off to a colleague two years ago. A decent man who allowed his wife to indulge in her odd fancy for chemistry, but the girl showed little gratitude and ran away several times. At last the man divorced her, and she vanished from society until two months ago. Rumor says that Lady Grey lent the girl money so she would not be on the street, but no one knows."

"What about the younger?" Stephen asked.

Gilbert sipped his whiskey and made a face, as though the drink did not meet his expectations. "Our friend Rumor is curiously silent on that matter. All I know is that she lived in the country with her parents until two months ago, when the mother and father died suddenly in a carriage accident. The elder girl returned with indecent haste to oversee the property, and from time to time, she and her sister visit the city."

"You seem to know a great deal about two girls you don't care for."

His friend grinned. "All rungs of society feed upon gossip, my child. The girls are nothing. It's their cousin who intrigues me. Lucien Fell."

Lucien Fell. Rumor coupled his name with those of the seedier actresses and money merchants. There was even talk about his connection to more dangerous figures in the London underworld. Stephen could not suppress a shudder. "What about him?"

"For myself, merely the fascination we all have for the truly disreputable. Beyond that… Let me say only that friends of a colleague of certain friends expressed interest. If, by chance, as you go about your social rounds, and hear aught about Friend Fell, let me know. One favor begets another, as the saying goes."

In the candlelight, with his eyes hooded like a cat's, Gilbert appeared more a stranger than a friend. *He has changed,* Stephen thought. His mouth had turned dry, and he wanted to call for a glass of water, but something in Gilbert's unblinking gaze made him think better. "Very well," he said. "I promise to do what I can."

Gilbert rewarded him with one of his old, affectionate smiles. "Dear Stephen, how astonished you look. Come, let us leave this miserable stuffy room. A walk should do us both good." He stood and held out his hand. "I've missed you, Stephen. I'm glad you decided to return."

It was odd, Stephen thought, how a long absence made all the familiar landscapes alien and strange. For the next two days, he spent his mornings paying calls—the social rounds Gilbert had alluded to. And just as dutifully, he had accepted dinner invitations from various influential men Lady Grey introduced him to at her soirée. But the whole business had an aspect of irreality about it, and he fully expected to blink and find himself transported back to his rooms in Paris.

His current surrounding did nothing to ease the impression. He had called upon his old advisor from University that afternoon, expecting to spend a quarter hour drinking strong tea and listening to a lecture on his morals. Instead, Doctor Adams had announced they would take an outing on this last fine day in autumn. Now Stephen found himself trudging through the leaf-blown gardens of the Crystal Palace Park. The palace itself glittered atop its hill, like a fantastical creature descended from the scudding clouds.

A sharp gust of wind spattered him with water from a nearby fountain. Stephen pulled his hat low over his face and leaned toward his companion to catch his last words.

"I said… I am surprised and pleased you called," Doctor Adams repeated. "I won't flatter myself that you want advice, so I won't give you any. My opinions, however, are another matter."

He leaned heavily upon Stephen's arm, using his cane to propel himself forward along. Stephen hurried to keep pace, wishing they had taken the sheltered passageway from the train station, instead of this windy winding path. "I ought to have written before," he began.

"There are many things you ought to have done. You did not. Forget them and concentrate on the future, Mister Eliot. Or have you forgotten all your lessons?"

Stephen smiled. "I seem to have, but now that I have you to remind me…"

Doctor Adams snorted. "Fools are those who depend upon others. Ah, speaking of fools…"

They had come to the so-called prehistoric swamp with its models of dinosaurs. Stephen squinted at the three Ichthyosaurus—massive crocodile-like creatures shown oozing from the waters. He was about to ask Doctor Adams his opinion on evolution, when he realized the old professor was not looking at the dinosaurs, but an enormous hot-air balloon, which even now was attempting an ascent, its basket filled with shrieking children.

"Fools," Doctor Adams repeated. "They'll have that balloon wrecked inside five minutes. The wind's all wrong."

"It's one of those new navigable balloons," Stephen offered.

"Doesn't make a damned bit of difference, as you well know."

The professor went on to lecture about wind currents and downdrafts. Stephen attended dutifully in spite of the chill and the lingering damp from the fountains. Once or twice, he tried (without success) to suggest they continue toward the palace itself. He had just succeeded in turning the old man back toward the path, when the sight of a familiar figure arrested his attention.

Eva Dubois.

She stood some distance away, swathed in a sensible dark-brown wrap, her head tilted back as she observed the balloon's uncertain ascent. Nearby was the sister—Lily, he remembered—who was engaged in close conversation with a short, stocky man with a swarthy complexion. The man leaned close to Lily Dubois, as she spoke earnestly in his ear.

Even as he observed them, the conversation ended, and Lily Dubois and her sister continued toward the palace. The unknown man stared after them a moment, then abruptly swung around and headed in the opposite direction. With a chill, Stephen recognized his face from countless newssheets—it was Lucien Fell.

"You're shivering," Doctor Adams said. "Shall we continue inside, then?"

"Yes, of course," Stephen said distractedly. He craned his head around, trying to see which direction Fell took, but the man had already vanished around a bend in the path, and so he gave himself over to following Doctor Adams toward the palace's grand entrance. They passed the great Sphinxes flanking the stairs and entered the central transept. It was warmer here, the grand space luminous with sunlight; the faint scent of orchids and other exotic flowers drifted through the air.

They spent hours visiting the palace's numerous exhibits, with Doctor Adams offering his observations on each one. By the time they completed a meticulous tour of the Technological Museum, then the basement with its collection of printing machines, Stephen had entirely lost his earlier sense of irreality. Now they were ascending the stairs to the ground floor. The newly installed inclined elevator rose to the second floor galleries; beyond it, the indoor gardens extended south. There was also a pavilion, where weary visitors might rest and take refreshments.

And there, sitting among the shabby and the fashionable, was Eva Dubois. She was alone this time, without even her elder sister for a companion. Her wrap had fallen from her shoulders, and she was scribbling furiously in a notebook, oblivious to the chattering crowds around her.

"Ah," breathed Doctor Adams. "It is Miss Dubois."

"You know her?" Stephen asked.

"I knew her grandfather. Let us pay our respects."

They threaded their way between the tables and chairs. As they approached the one where Eva Dubois sat, Stephen hung back, thinking he ought not to intrude upon her self-imposed isolation. Doctor Adams had no such qualms. "Miss Dubois," he called out, advancing toward her alone. "What a pleasure to encounter you here."

Eva Dubois glanced up and hastily closed her notebook. "Doctor Adams." Her voice was breathless. "You gave me such a fright."

"Hardly. You are merely being secretive, as always. I see you have not lost your old habits of writing in notebooks, just as you did when you were a child."

She smiled, but her cheeks took on an added flush of embarrassment. "Oh, not quite the same. I… I was just writing out a list for some errands. Lily and I have so much to accomplish before we leave the city tomorrow." As she spoke, she rose and drew her wrap around her shoulders. "And speaking of those errands, if you will excuse me…"

It was then her gaze encountered Stephen's. She paused in recognition. "Mister Eliot."

Stephen achieved an awkward bow. "Miss Dubois."

"You know each other?" Doctor Adams said.

"We met at Lady Grey's this past Monday," Eva said. Then to Stephen, "I had no idea you were acquainted with Doctor Adams."

"I—"

"Mister Eliot was a student of mine," Doctor Adams said. "I thought him quite promising at the time, and so naturally, he has wasted his talents abroad. But perhaps he might find inspiration closer to home." He nodded to Eva Dubois.

"Perhaps," she said dryly. She favored Stephen with a direct look, which seemed to identify and catalogue all his insufficiencies. Unsettled, he could not think how to reply.

Luckily, he was spared the necessity. "My dear," said Doctor Adams. "I just wanted to offer my condolences about your parents. If you and your sister need anything—anything at all—come to me at once. For your own sakes, as well as your grandfather's."

Her expression warmed and she offered Doctor Adams her hand. "Thank you. That is so very kind of you. But indeed we are quite well at the moment. So well, that Lily and I have planned a small gathering of old friends at our house this weekend. Very impromptu, I'm afraid, though we are sending out proper invitations today. We would be so pleased if you could attend."

With old-fashioned courtesy, Doctor Adams offered his regrets—unavoidable obligations, previous engagements, etc.— but perhaps Miss Dubois and her sister would come to dinner in the city next month. With equal courtesy, Eva Dubois explained they expected to take a long journey next month. "Though," she added, "there is a possibility we might have to delay our departure." She hesitated briefly, then turned to Stephen. "Mister Eliot, what about you? Do you also have other obligations this weekend? I spoke with my sister about you. She said she would be delighted to have you attend."

Taken by surprise, Stephen stammered something incomprehensible. Dimly, he heard Eva Dubois go on to mention the names of other guests—members of the Royal Society, well-regarded artists, friends of her grandfather and of Lady Grey. His parents would be pleased and horrified at the same time. He ought to refuse…

… if by chance, you hear ought about Friend Fell, let me know…

"Will your cousin be there?" he asked abruptly.

A brief silence ensued. "It is possible," she said slowly. "You mean my cousin Lawrence, do you not?"

Stephen recovered himself. "Yes. I meant your cousin Lawrence. But that was merely curiosity on my part. Of course, I would be delighted to attend your gathering."

"The generosity is all yours."

Her eyes narrowed with suppressed amusement. Again he had the impression of a sophistication beyond her years. *But she is a mere girl*, he thought, intrigued all over again. Before he could make a suitable riposte, however, Eva Dubois was repeating her excuses about errands and obligations to Doctor Adams. Another glance in his direction, a politely murmured good-bye, and she was hurrying toward the front entrance of the palace.

"You say Lucien Fell will be present?"

"So the girl implied."

"Ah."

A monosyllabic utterance that implied so much, Stephen thought. Satisfaction. Curiosity.

The written invitation to the Dubois household had arrived Thursday morning. Stephen had immediately sent a note to Gilbert Wardle, saying he would like to drop around in the evening. A silent manservant had ushered Stephen into a small parlor. After serving them port, he had departed and closed the doors. The room itself was far more richly appointed than Stephen had expected, even knowing about Gilbert's personal wealth—an enormous leather-covered Chesterfield, some very fine bronze figures, and several oil paintings of water lilies done in the modern style.

"Would you like to see the letter?" he asked.

Gilbert took the much-folded sheet and scanned it. "Hmmm... hopes to fulfill proper etiquette... begs your attendance...sister expressed a desire to continue....What a very odd creature. And her handwriting is more like a clerk's than a woman's. What is that about the sister?"

"Nothing," Stephen said hastily.

His friend tilted his head. "I would venture to say more than nothing, but never mind. We all have our secrets. Have you accepted?"

"I did but—"

"But you dislike the prospect of quarreling with your father. Such a weak excuse, my fair child. However, you are not entirely in the wrong. It's best if we avoid any unpleasantness. So, let me think. Let me think."

He leaned back and closed his eyes. Stephen sipped his port and scanned the newspapers spread over the table. The headlines were troubling. Entente with France. Menace of the German fleet. Trouble in Ireland. Rumors of further plots against the king. The world had tipped over from one century to the next. Even if he could transport himself at once to the Continent, he was not certain he could resume the carefree student life he'd known before.

"I know," Gilbert said, breaking into his reverie. "You shall tell your parents that an old friend from University days has invited you to his house in the countryside. Tell them we are traveling together in my carriage. Make up some excuse to leave your man behind."

"Won't that look suspicious?"

"Not if you drop hints that our dear friend has fallen on bad times, and that we are all roughing it in sympathy. Use your imagination."

Easier to say than do, Stephen thought. "And what about Lucien Fell?" he said. "Should I do anything? Say anything?"

"No. I want you to observe the man. Watch what he does. Note whom he talks to. If you can overhear what they say, do it, but whatever else, do not make a spectacle of yourself." Gilbert's face relaxed into a smile. "It's gossip, Stephen. One never knows what fruit the tree will bear. So we tend it, hoping for the best."

The next two days all went far more easily than Stephen had expected. His parents made no objections, and following Gilbert's advice, Stephen offered no explanations, though he felt a strong urge to. By late Friday afternoon, he was enclosed in his friend's carriage, riding through the glorious autumnal day. He ought to have experienced a sense of liberation once they passed the outer bounds of London, but he could only think how Eva and Gilbert both wished something from him, and it had nothing to do with friendship.

His first view of the Dubois estate did nothing to cure his uneasiness.

A ring of thick stone walls marked the edge of their property. Beyond the iron gates, a long paved driveway wound beneath oaks and chestnuts. Old money, Gilbert had said. And yet, there was a curious air of neglect about the place. Dead leaves smothered the grass. Here and there he noted bracken and weeds, the rank scent of wild things.

Another ten minutes brought the carriage to the front door. As Stephen disembarked, a dozen or more servants appeared to take care of his luggage. The house itself was a massive rambling structure—wings flung themselves out to either side, ornamented with porticoes and columns and a collection of buttresses. More signs of neglect met his eyes—patches of ivy grew over the walls, and moss made the stones slippery underfoot.

His rooms, at least, were clean and comfortable. Gas had not yet been laid here, but the candles were beeswax, the carpet thick, and the bedclothes freshly laundered and warmed. Stephen dressed with care and soon found his way back to drawing room, where the footman had politely informed him the guests would gather before dinner.

The first person he encountered was Lily Dubois, nearly unrecognizable in a flowing dinner gown of richly-figured Chine. "Mister Eliot. I'm so glad nothing prevented us from enjoying your company. Come, let me introduce you to the other guests."

She led him into the drawing room, which belied any signs of the neglect he'd noted elsewhere—fine crystal chandeliers, the polished dark wood floors and Oriental rugs scattered about. All signs of prosperity and taste. The centerpiece of the room was a massive stone fireplace, laid with a generous fire. He scanned the room, looking for Lucien Fell. No sign of that particular disreputable man. Indeed the company was most respectable. Among those gathered about the fireplace, he recognized Sir Benjamin Baker and William Huggins, both much-lauded members of the Royal Society. Not far away stood a celebrated author and his entourage. There were even a few women present, bright gossamer beings amongst the soberly dressed men in their black or grey dinner costumes.

Then, across the room, he sighted Eva Dubois, speaking with a stout, white-haired gentleman with a scientific air. He paused. She happened to glance in his direction. An uncharacteristic smile illuminated her face, one that produced conflicting impulses within Stephen.

The decision was taken away from him, when after murmuring something to the white-haired gentleman, she came forward. "Mister Eliot. I am so glad you came."

"Miss Dubois," he said, making a bow.

She held out her hands. He kissed them, thinking her manner had greatly changed in just two days. Far more cordial, almost intimate. She was not like other young gentlewomen he had met, even abroad; nor was she anything like the artist's models or professional courtesans he'd sometimes taken home. Eva leaned closer, speaking into his ear, her breath tickling his cheek. She was wearing perfume, a faint woody scent, very pleasing. The scent invaded his senses, causing him to lose the thread of conversation.

With some effort, he drew back, only to realize the butler had announced dinner. He heard Eva Dubois saying something about how the number of guests prevented her from sharing his company during the meal. "I'm so sorry," she murmured. "I had hoped to continue our conversation sooner, but there are other guests I must see to. Perhaps afterward…"

She vanished into the crowds. Stephen tried to draw a breath to clear his head, but the scent of her perfume clung to his hands and lips. In a daze, he allowed the servants to guide him to his place, between a scientist and a philosopher. Both were learned men, and Stephen did his best to engage in the debate, but he found it difficult to maintain his attention. He ate, vaguely aware of the fine dishes, and drank whenever the servants refilled his glass.

The dinner ended at last. Stephen rose at once, only to see Eva vanish through a small doorway. The number of guests had swelled, or so it seemed to his oppressed senses. He escaped into one of the smaller sitting rooms, where a few men—all strangers—had gathered to drink whiskey. He wandered past them, through a pair of glass doors and across a stone-paved patio, into the garden beyond.

Blessed darkness closed around him. He breathed in the cool clear air and felt the wine fumes dissipate. Gilbert and his schemes be damned, he ought to have refused this invitation.

Fell would never attend a gathering such as this one. The girl must have sensed his interest and used her cousin's name as a lure. But why? She was not the sort to fish for a liaison.

He walked on, pondering how to extract himself from the household without causing offense to either Gilbert or the Dubois girls. Gradually he became aware that he had left the house itself far behind, and that the surrounding gardens had turned into fields. He slowed, uncertain of the path. Just ahead he saw the gleam of water beneath a new moon. Then a movement in the shadows caught his eye—someone else had escaped from the house. He paused, thinking he would rather avoid conversation, when a familiar voice accosted him.

"Mister Eliot." Eva Dubois's voice carried the hint of suppressed laughter. "Are you running away?"

"No. I—I merely wished for some quiet."

She laughed and took his arm. "Then let us escape into the night."

Her warm hands encircled his, and she led him unresisting down the path. Eva Dubois wore a new perfume, he noticed—a much stronger, muskier scent that reminded him of orchids. Underneath it, the scent of the other perfume lingered, its woody notes combining with this new one to create a strangely intoxicating aroma, as though they had left England's tame gardens behind for some exotic jungle. Stephen shook his head to clear it, wondering where Eva was taking him. He glimpsed a wide field, beyond it a dark woodland, caught the warm rich fragrance of dying lilies. Clouds flitted over the moon's face, causing shadows to flicker over the leaves, and he thought about wild cats, hunting in the moonlit jungle.

"So tell me about your mathematical studies," she said. "Or have you given them over?"

"I… I haven't decided yet."

"Are you waiting for someone to *inspire* you, then?"

Vaguely, he remembered Doctor Adams using those same words. "You mean a wife?"

"Isn't that what it always means? No, I mean—Never mind what I mean. Here is what I wanted to show you."

They had come to a small building—quite far from the house, as Stephen discovered when he glanced around. Large crates and boxes obstructed the path around the building. The air smelled of crushed grass, as though many feet had trampled the fields. He turned toward the crates and boxes, curious, but Eva re-directed his attention back to the building, which he realized was an observatory. A quite fine structure, built along modern lines and with what looked like a splendid telescope protruding from a slit in its roof.

"My grandfather," Eva said, before he could ask. "He built it to confirm his theories about mathematics and the stars. My blessed father never saw a reason to dismantle it."

She unlatched the door and took him inside. There she guided him between more boxes and strange equipment, to the telescope. With an expert air, she adjusted the lenses and showed him how to gaze through the eyepiece to see the moon suddenly brought sharp and close. Jupiter and Mars were there, and beyond them the bright pinpoints of light across the gulf of night. All the while, she described her grandfather's exploration of the skies, which she had repeated and expanded upon. But as he listened, he realized she spoke of more than nebulae and star clusters and constellations. She spoke of other worlds, and how they might be inhabited, just as the Earth was.

"Other worlds?" Stephen asked, hardly able to keep the laughter from his voice.

She rounded on him. It was impossible to see her features in the gloom, but he could sense her anger, her passion. "Yes. Of course. We are hardly alone in the universe. Who knows when they might decide to visit us? Or we them?"

He hardly knew how to answer her.

"You think me bedazzled by a fantasy," she went on. "But remember, while you were traversing the Continent, free and unencumbered, I sat here alone and watched the stars. You cannot imagine how often I wished I could pluck myself from this house, this world, and go shooting outward—"

She stopped abruptly. "My apologies. I have embarrassed you, I see."

"No," Stephen said. "I understand."

"Do you?" She glanced up, eyes bright from tears.

"I do," he whispered.

There was a long moment, while neither of them moved. Then, Eva reached up and touched Stephen's cheek with her bare hand. The sense of her skin upon his was electric. A shiver went through him, and it took all his self-control not to kiss her.

Eva leaned close to him, her perfume flooding his senses. "Stephen," she said, and guided his hand to her breast.

His lips met hers. After that memory fragmented to individual sensations. The baring of skin. The discovery of blankets upon the floor. Before he was aware, Eva had raised her voluminous skirts, and he... he was plunging fast and deep into the warmth of her sex. Eva held him tight, urged him on in ways he had not experienced since certain nights spent with an Italian courtesan.

Memories blurred after that. He remembered little more than a final gasp, a moment where he was torn between violence and tenderness. Then, with his fingers gradually releasing his grip upon her hair, he drew back with a sigh.

Stephen came to himself in his own rooms. He lay, half-undressed, on top of the bedcovers. His body was damp. His

head was spinning—from the wine, no doubt. He had drunk far
too much at dinner. And afterward...

He bolted upright. The sudden movement brought a surge
of bile into his mouth. He clamped his lips shut and swallowed.
Wiped a hand over his face. His skin smellt of sweat and wine,
of Eva Dubois"'s perfume and the heady scent of their mutual
spendings. No dream. No doubt at all what had happened.

Remorse swept over him, followed swiftly by a flush of
remembered passion. He stumbled from bed and pulled on his
trousers and a shirt taken randomly from the clothespress. A
splash of cool water from the basin helped to clear his thoughts.
He had to find Eva. Apologize. She was merely flirting with
him, the way some naive girls did. But she was no serving girl,
to be bedded and forgotten. He had make restitution.

He lurched from his room into the darkened corridor. Pale
sunlight leaked through a window at the far end of the hallway.
It was dawn, or thereabouts.

"Sir, is something wrong?" The voice came from behind
him. Male. Deferential. A servant.

"Eva Dubois." Stephen's voice came out thick and garbled.
He swallowed and tried again. "Miss Eva Dubois. Do you know
if she has arisen yet?"

The servant seemed unsurprised by this request. "Miss
Dubois left word in case you should ask, sir. Come with me, if
you please."

They proceeded through more corridors, across an enclosed
courtyard, into a new wing of the mansion. Stacks of crates
lined the halls. Most were draped in canvas, but a few stood
open, with layers of cotton wadding torn aside to reveal glass
bottles, metallic cylinders, and other items Stephen could only
guess at. Sharp odors drifted through the air. He paused, trying
to identify them, but the servant was unlatching a pair of thick
double doors. He motioned for Stephen to go inside.

A long narrow room opened up before him. A very strange room, unlike any he had seen before outside certain buildings at University. On either side, he could make out worktables stacked neatly with more glassware, more strange equipment, and several devices that reminded him uncomfortably of the observatory. At the far end a light burned; a woman sat bent over a worktable, her attention entirely upon a glass beaker set over a tiny blue flame. Racks of vials crowded her desk, but he had the same impression of order and organization. Seemingly unaware of his presence, the woman selected a vial from a rack, measured out a liquid, and added it to the beaker. She observed the results a moment, frowned, and scribbled something into a journal book that lay open beside her.

Stephen coughed. Lily Dubois glanced up. With face illumined by the lamp and burner, she seemed even paler, older than before. "Mister Eliot. Good morning."

Stephen stopped halfway down the aisle. He licked his mouth and tasted the sourness upon his chapped lips. "Miss Dubois. I was—"

"—looking for Eva. Yes, I know."

"Then do you—"

"It would be presumption to say I know everything, but yes, I know the particulars. You need not worry, though I know you will."

The liquid in the beaker started to bubble. Lily's attention shifted abruptly to her experiment. She took up a glass rod and stirred the mixture. Stephen's attention was caught by the pale scars over her hands. Chemical burns. Of course.

"Mister Eliot."

Lily Dubois was observing him closely.

"You appear unwell," she said. "And the hour is far too early for most, I know. I suggest you retire to your rooms and try to sleep. All will be well. I assure you."

She turned her attention back to her chemicals—a clear dismissal. Stephen hesitated a moment, then silently retreated from that vast unnerving room. The same servant waited outside. With a deferential gesture, the man took Stephen by the arm and helped him back to his rooms.

"I am a touch unwell," Stephen murmured. "The air here does not agree with me. Please have someone pack my things and bring the carriage around. I must go back home."

He arrived at his parents' townhouse pale, but clean and neatly dressed. The same nameless, discreet servant had drawn Stephen's bath, laid out his clothes, and fetched a plain breakfast, all without any direction. Later, Stephen thought the man must have received instructions from Lily Dubois to make certain her guest was presentable before he fled. As he suffered through his mother's exclamations, and his father's grim silent looks, he was grateful for her forethought.

His manservant arrived at last, and led a sick and weary Stephen to his rooms, where he collapsed onto his own bed. His mother's physician arrived later, and pronounced him overtaxed. The diagnosis kept his parents and friends away. But within a day, Gilbert Wardle came to call, and Stephen knew he must face his friend's questions.

"You look horrible," Gilbert said lightly, as he settled into a chair beside Stephen's bed. "But not as horrible as the fish they served at our club last night."

Stephen shook his head and immediately regretted it. "Thank you for coming," he whispered. "But I'm afraid I must disappoint you."

Gilbert's eyes gleamed momentarily. "He was not there?"

"No. Nor did anyone mention his name."

"Interesting. He must have misled the girls. Did you happen to overhear anything of interest?"

"Nothing," Stephen said at once. "Nothing that I can remember."

His friend observed him silently for a moment. "I see. Well, perhaps it's for the best you did not stay the entire weekend." Then, in a lighter tone, he added, "Your parents were not pleased, of course. I confessed my part in the debauchery—nostalgia for our University days, sympathy for our friend, an ill-judged drinking contest, etc. However, they seem to recognize that young men must expend their wildness before settling into a respectable life. You'll find them stiff but forgiving when you rise from your bed."

Gilbert remained with him another quarter hour, confining his talk to commonplace subjects—the latest dinner gossip, rumors of the King's dalliances, *etc., etc.* Even as he took his leave, he made no more oblique references to the Dubois girls or to Stephen's sudden, inexplicable flight.

He knows, Stephen thought. *If not the particulars, then the larger shape of events.*

He sank back into his pillows and closed his eyes. He had spent a day pretending that the incident didn't matter. That Lily Dubois would take care of her sister, wiping out any need for him to act. *Ballocks,* he thought.

Head spinning, he forced himself to sit upright and called for paper and pens so he might write to Eva Dubois. He did not spare himself, he thought, reading over his words. No excuses. Only apologies for his brutish behavior and cowardice. It was necessarily an awkward incoherent effort, but perhaps she would understand.

She did not.

Or at least, she did not answer.

A second letter returned unopened. Then a third.

Two, three weeks passed. By this time, Stephen had learned through oblique questioning that the Dubois sisters remained at their country house. Lady Miriam Grey even sent him a teasing letter, asking what outrage he had offered her young friend, to frighten her away so thoroughly. Merely banter between friends, but Stephen found himself go cold as he read the words.

No more shirking. I did commit an outrage. I must make it right.

He waited until late afternoon, then took a cab to a district far away from fashionable Mayfair, where he hired a horse. By the early evening, he was riding down the wide gravel lane to the Dubois house. The lane was now thickly strewn with golden leaves, and his eye noted other signs of obvious disrepair. More weeds and fallen branches. The walls desperately needing mortar, and the driveway itself pocketed with holes. A cold misty twilight overspread the whole, adding to the gloom and sense of neglect.

In the courtyard, he dismounted. All the windows were dark, but lamplight showed underneath the main doors. He tied his horse to a rail and knocked. A cool breeze fingered his hair, carrying with it the scent of moldering leaves and something else he could not decipher. He shivered, and wished he had worn his winter overcoat.

The door jerked open. A thickset man filled the doorway, his features cast in shadows from the feeble chandelier behind him. He wore plain black clothes and heavy gloves. Not the butler Stephen remembered. A stranger, and definitely not the usual servant. "No one is at home," the man said, before Stephen asked.

"They are," Stephen said. "Miss Eva Dubois is at home. I know it."

"Miss Eva—"

"Never mind, Albert. I know the gentleman."

Lily Dubois motioned for the man to stand aside. She too wore plain dark clothing—men's clothing, he realized with a shock—trousers, a knitted jersey, and sturdy boots. Her hair was pulled back in a tight braid; a flush from the cold colored her cheeks, making her appear younger than before.

She returned his gaze with an amused smile, but he sensed an uneasiness. "Come inside," she said at last. "It seems we must talk at least once before it is all over."

She lit a candle and led him down a series of servant's corridors, toward the back of the house. Their footsteps echoed eerily, and the candle's flame cast unnerving shadows around them, emphasizing the emptiness of the house. Stephen nearly turned back more than once, but curiosity tugged at him, especially after he began to recognize the turnings as those leading him to the same laboratory where he last spoke with Lily Dubois.

"She's inside," Lily said, pointing to the familiar double doors. "I daresay she won't be entirely surprised."

Inside, he found the same familiar scene, but with a few important alterations. The strange equipment was gone, as were most of the books. And this time, it was Eva who sat at the worktable, scribbling in a notebook. Like her sister, she wore trousers and a warm knitted jersey.

Stephen strode forward. "Eva."

Eva straightened abruptly, eyes wide. "Stephen. You should not have come."

"I could not help it," he said. "I wrote—"

"I know," she said. "But, you see, there was no point in answering. Unless you agree, with my late father, that form and propriety outweigh the truth."

They studied each other a few long moments. She had changed, he thought, in any number of indefinable ways. Her mouth no longer had that tightly constrained look about it. Her eyes were bright—with anticipation? Excitement? Only now did he wonder what she did in her sister's laboratory. He glanced down and saw sheets of formulae, written thick upon the paper she held tensely before her. Hastily she turned the sheets over.

"You are confused," she said. "I'm sorry."

"Why are you sorry about now?" Lily Dubois said, as she rounded the worktable to stand beside her sister. "Still worried about the calculations?"

Eva shook her head. "No more than usual. They all still match our expectations." She managed a smile for Stephen. "You seem quite fagged out. Come. We shall have a last supper together."

It was the strangest, most unconventional meal he had ever participated in. No servants. Only a few platters of cold salted beef and stale bread, which Eva fetched herself from the pantry. Instead of wine, they drank well-water so cold it made Stephen's teeth ache. He could see now that Eva Dubois had seduced him, not the other way around, and that Lily Dubois had assisted by supplying those most unnatural perfumes. To what end, he could not tell. His only consolation was that Lily Dubois seemed as uncomfortable with his presence as he was with hers.

The meal ended. Eva Dubois nodded to her sister. "It's time."

"Long past time," Lily said. "He comes with us?"

"I see no other way," Eva replied. "Besides, he can assist with the work that comes after."

"Ah, you mean…"

"…exactly."

Without waiting for his reply—if there could be one to such a bizarre exchange—the sisters left the room. A moment's hesitation, he followed them. He hoped—expected—they would finally explain everything, but neither one spoke to him. They murmured to each other, their voices so low he could not catch their words, only the tone of barely suppressed excitement. Lily had taken up a candle to light the way through the empty corridors; when they came to a door leading outside, the same thickset stranger waited for them. He had a lit lantern, which he gave to Lily Dubois.

"Thank you, Albert," she said. "How are the preparations?"

"Nearly done," he said.

She nodded. "Very well. We'll go now."

Outside, the fog had dissipated, and stars speckled the clear night sky. With growing impatience, Stephen followed the two women along a wet overgrown path, around the observatory, and into a broad field. Torches illuminated the clearing; by their light, he counted at least a dozen men in work clothes moving about, loading boxes into what appeared to be an immense wooden basket. Ropes, attached to metal rings, rose into the air, to an enormous dark mass overhead. His heart gave a painful leap as he recognized what it was.

A balloon. They've manufactured a balloon.

"What are you doing?" he demanded.

"Escaping," Eva said calmly.

"Where—?""

"To the stars." She smiled at his incredulity. "Dear Stephen. I have been scouring the heavens a decade, my sister even longer. I am only surprised it took us this long to discover a species that monitors ours. And they do, you know. They were waiting for someone—anyone—to answer their call. So I did."

Visitors from other worlds, she had said, at his last visit.

Dimly, he realized she was babbling about radio signals from a nearby satellite and an alien ship waiting in the upper atmosphere. Impossible. Scientists would have discovered such a thing themselves. His protests died on his lips—it was clear Eva and her sister would not listen. Indeed, both were absorbed in examining a row of canisters lining the basket.

"Stephen," Eva said. "It is time to say good-bye. Thank you."

Lily, who was climbing into the basket, snorted. "Why thank-you?"

Eva sent her an inscrutable look. "Because it moves me to say so. Are we ready?"

"Of course. And you are a sentimental idiot."

Stephen's brain lurched forward. "You are leaving? To... to live with... monsters? But why? What if—?"

"If I were with child?" she said. "I am, most likely yours. As for why? I'm not certain I can explain it in words you would understand. Let me only say that I am weary of being invisible, Stephen. I want..." She drew a breath and lifted her gaze to the stars. "I want to find a world where I am truly myself—for good or bad, clever or indifferent—and not merely an inspiration for someone else's ideas. Or expectations." She smiled sadly. "I do not expect you to understand. Why should you?"

"How do you know? You have not even given me a chance."

Her expression did not change. Indeed she looked even sadder than before. "Dear Stephen. Even if you were not like the others, I could not live with you alone."

She reached for one of the levers. Stephen charged forward, intent on wrestling her away from the balloon, but stopped when Lily Dubois produced a small handgun. "You cannot stop us," she said. "Only we can stop ourselves."

Another gesture from the handgun told him to step back. Eva climbed into the balloon. She and her sister went through an incomprehensible series of checks. All clear, apparently, because Lily Dubois flung off the anchor ropes, while Eva ignited a burner. The ropes holding their craft drew taut. Lily flung back her head and grinned. Eva, however, was immersed in adjusting various valves. But then she too lifted her face to the stars. It was a look unlike anything he had seen before—delighted. Triumphant. He opened his mouth to call out when a hand clamped onto his arm.

"Hush," said Lucien Fell. "They know what they are doing."

"But—"

"But nothing. My cousins had paid me well to follow orders."

His lips pulled back from his teeth in a feral grin. Cold and shaken, Stephen watched as the balloon expanded to blot out the sky. There was a moment's pause, a hesitation where he thought they had miscalculated, then the balloon jerked and lifted free of the ground. Still Lucien Fell did not release him. His grip tightened as the balloon rose above the tree tops. Flames burst out, and the balloon shot higher. Just before the basket rose out of sight, Stephen glimpsed a wire mesh rising to cover the basket. It was not enough, he thought. Surely, they would die…

An answering burst of light came from higher above. The balloon soared upward. The sky went dark, only to reappear in a shower of stars.

"Come with me," Lucien Fell told him. "We have work to do."

… The stars were falling, thousands and millions, a great bright rain of fire. He blinked, and the brightness faded. Only a single pale halo of light remained, swinging up and down through the darkness. Lucien Fell, it was, swinging the lantern as he dragged Stephen through the dark cold Dubois mansion. On and on they marched, through the echoing hallways. Now they were in the kitchen, its tables shoved against one wall to make room for stacks of metal barrels. Lucien pried the lid off one—the acrid stink of chemicals rolled through the air. He nodded. She kept her promise. I'll keep mine. And you'll help.

With Lucien giving orders, they had spread the chemicals throughout the house, then over a fair part of the grounds as well, including the observatory. Lucien had lit a match and set it to the dry grass, which burst into flames—so swiftly it overtook them in their escape. The last Stephen remembered was falling to the ground, trying to beat away the flames, while all around him the bonfires of Guy Fawkes' Day blazed, and stars and embers fell from the sky...

He woke with a groan. Fire. He had to reach the road. Warn... someone about the conflagration, but he could not move his arms or legs. He struggled to fight free. Hands pressed against his chest, and a man's face hovered over him. He heard a familiar voice telling him not to be such a damned fool.

"Gilbert?" he whispered. His mouth felt cotton dry.

"Stephen." Unmistakable relief.

Stephen wanted to say more, but his tongue refused to work properly.

"No, don't try to talk too much," Gilbert went on. "I'm simply glad you woke up. The doctors... Well, between the terrible burns, and half the night spent lying in the cold wet fields, we nearly thought you wouldn't. Wake up that is." He bent closer to Stephen. "It's an excellent thing that someone noticed your disappearance that evening."

He followed me. No. An underling. A... spy.

"Lucien," Stephen croaked.

"Escaped," Gilbert said with obvious disgust. "At least, that is what we surmise from later events. But you..."

"Went... to find..."

"The Dubois girl. I know. Stephen, I'm very sorry to tell you that she and her sister did not survive the fire. You must take consolation that she surely died quickly. The fire spread so fast, so hot, as you know."

Ah, Gilbert. If only you knew all the truth.

Even in so much pain, he nearly laughed to think of his friend's expression if he heard about creatures from beyond the stars, or the marvelous scientific endeavors that allowed Lily and Eva Dubois to break free of the Earth's bonds, to sail free toward the stars, there to meet their otherworldly protectors.

Or were they protectors?

He had assumed that, of course, but now he was not so certain. Two girls—two women—sailing forth to join a very different civilization, and one of them bearing a child to carry on the human race. Were they refugees? Or conquerors?

But Gilbert was still speaking about Lucien Fell. How the man had obviously taken advantage of his cousins, using the grounds to store illegal explosive materials for his criminal activities. Lucien himself had escaped the inferno—they knew that from the later events—but clearly he had murdered his two cousins, whether by accident or cold-blooded intent.

"But enough of that villain. Stephen." Gilbert paused, suddenly diffident. "Stephen, I am sorry to have inveigled you into such a mess. I ought to have trusted you more. My superiors agree with me, and so I've come with an offer of a position. A sinecure," he added, with a touch of his old casual tone.

Stephen managed a smile. "Hardly a sinecure," he whispered.

Gilbert's mouth twitched. "Clever boy. Well, I won't press you for an answer now. There's time enough. We want you fully recovered and back in the arms of Society first. Speaking of which, Lady Grey has asked me to serve as her postman and give you this."

He handed Stephen an envelope, which Stephen took awkwardly in his bandaged hands. An invitation, clearly, judging from the expensive, scented paper and formal calligraphy. He tried to picture himself entering her fashionable townhouse, mingling with the other guests at one of her famous soirées, but could not. *Never again.* He closed his eyes and let the envelope fall onto his chest. Gilbert was saying something about that damned position again, then a murmured good-bye and a promise to visit him the next day. Stephen let him talk. For once, it was easy to pretend.

At last, the door clicked shut. Stephen breathed a sigh of relief. The reprieve was temporary, of course. Tomorrow would come more visits—from Gilbert, from his parents, and others. Possibly Doctor Adams. Most definitely Doctors Adams.

He sighed again. Thought about his so-called studies in mathematics. Doctor Adams had once called him promising. There were universities where he might take advanced courses, study in earnest this time. Ah, but that was impossible. He had used up all his chances in the past two years. Certainly his parents would not support him.

An ache welled up behind his eyes. Stephen raised his bandaged hand to rub his forehead; he encountered the forgotten envelope from Lady Grey, balanced between his body and the edge of the hospital bed. How odd that she would send him an invitation here, in a hospital. It was not like her to act so foolish.

No, never foolish.

Impatient now, and more than curious, he fumbled the envelope onto his chest and tore it open. Inside was stiff card—an invitation to one of her soirées. All very proper. But underneath the formal printed lines, she had written a single line in a swift, tiny script: *If you need help, come to me—M.*

Help. He wanted to laugh, then sob. Help, to climb to the stars? No, he was no brave adventurer like Eva Dubois. He merely wanted a second chance. Well, and it seemed that fate, or rather Lady Grey, would give him one.

Stephen drew a long shuddering breath and turned his head toward the window. Outside night had fallen, and cold bright stars illuminated the late November skies. Gazing at the milky constellations, he wished good fortune to the travelers.

Acknowledgments

My thanks to the many friends who have critiqued my stories with honesty and thoroughness, to my teachers at Viable Paradise and the Oregon Coast Writers Workshop who offered their insight, and to the editors who encouraged me. I owe a special debt to Sherwood, Lois, Greg, Steve, Fran, Liz, Jay, Mark, Nick, and Gardner.

Finally, my thanks and gratitude to my husband and son for giving me so much support over the years.

About the Author

Beth Bernobich fell into a fantasy world several years ago and discovered she liked it there just fine. Her short stories have appeared in Strange Horizons, Interzone, and Subterranean Press, among other places. Her first fantasy novel, *Passion Play*, is forthcoming from Tor Books in October 2010, and her first YA is forthcoming from Viking in Summer 2011. For more information, check out her website at www.beth-bernobich.com.

LaVergne, TN USA
30 July 2010
191525LV00002B/129/P

AUG 9 2010